BOMB SHELL

JANE HARVEY-BERRICK

Bombshell
Copyright © 2019 Jane Harvey-Berrick

Editing by Kirsten Olsen & Krista Webster

This ebook is licensed for your personal enjoyment only. It may not be re-sold or given away to other people. If you do, you are STEALING. I support my family through my writing. Pirate copies are illegal, and you've really spoiled my day.
Thank you for respecting the hard work of this author.

Jane Harvey-Berrick has asserted her right under the Copyright, Designs and Patents Act 1988 to be identified as the author of this work.
This book is a work of fiction. Names and characters are the product of the author's imagination and any resemblance to actual persons, living or dead, is entirely coincidental.
All rights reserved; no part of this publication may be reproduced or transmitted by any means, electronic, mechanical, photocopying or otherwise, without the prior permission of the publisher. All rights reserved.

Cover design by Sybil Wilson / Pop Kitty Design
Formatted by Cassy Roop / Pink Ink Design
Photographer: GG Gold / Models: Ellie Ruewell & Gergo Jonas

ISBN 978-1-912015-83-2
Harvey Berrick Publishing

DEDICATION

To the men and women who work to clear landmines in former war zones, all over the world.

BOOKS BY JANE HARVEY-BERRICK

Series Titles
* The EOD Series
Blood, bombs and heartbreak
Tick Tock (EOD series #1)
Bombshell (EOD series #2 – 1st March 2019)

*The Traveling Series
All the fun of the fair … and two worlds collide
The Traveling Man (Traveling series #1)
The Traveling Woman (Traveling series #2)
Roustabout (Traveling series #3)
Carnival (Traveling series #4)

*The Education Series
An epic love story spanning the years, through war zones and more…
The Education of Sebastian (Education series #1)
The Education of Caroline (Education series #2)
The Education of Sebastian & Caroline (combined edition, books 1 & 2)
Semper Fi: The Education of Caroline (Education series #3)

*The Rhythm Series
Blood, sweat, tears and dance
Slave to the Rhythm (Rhythm series #1)
Luka (Rhythm series #2)

The Justin Trainer series – on Radish
Guarding the Billionaire

With Stuart Reardon
*Undefeated
*Model Boyfriend

*Touch My Soul (novella – December 2018)

Gym Or Chocolate? (coming in 2019)

Standalone Titles

One Careful Owner

*Dangerous to Know & Love

*Lifers

At Your Beck & Call

Dazzled

Summer of Seventeen

The New Samurai

Exposure

The Dark Detective

Novellas

Playing in the Rain

*Behind the Walls

Audio Books

One Careful Owner

(narrated by Seth Clayton)

On the Stage

Later, After: Playscript

Later, After: DVD

Trailer

*These titles are published in languages other than English. Check my website for details.

A NOTE ABOUT THIS BOOK

Bombshell can be read a standalone story, because it deals with a new heroine in a different country with new situations.

But it is also the sequel to *Tick Tock*, so if you read that first, I think you'll have a better understanding of why James is the way he is, as well as Clay and Zada—two of my favourite supporting characters.

BOMB SHELL

JANE HARVEY-BERRICK

PROLOGUE

James

The first time I tried to kill myself, I failed.

Obviously.

The gun misfired. I kept pulling the trigger and nothing happened, just empty clicks and a cosmic frustration.

But next time, I'll do it right, no mistakes. I have it all planned out. There's a bottle of 25 year old Irish whiskey with my name on it, a handful of sleeping pills, and a plastic bag over my head. It will be a quiet end, peaceful. Which is ironic really, and nothing like the way I've lived my life.

So with everything in place, the last thing I want is to find a reason for living.

CHAPTER 1

James

THE PUB WAS DIM AND DINGY, with a lingering aroma of steak and kidney pie, and a carpet sticky from decades of spilt beer.

There weren't many old-school boozers like this one left in London. But if you knew some of the backstreets in the poorer areas, you could still find them.

I'd been haunting this place for a month now, and before that it had been a different dive, a different part of London—different places to sink into a drunken stupor, delaying the day when I'd make the decision to die. It was quiet here and no one bothered me. They didn't play music, there were no slot machines or pool tables, just a dartboard nailed to the wall. You had to bring your own darts, but I'd never seen anyone play.

During the day, older blokes propped up the bar, drinking inky-blank Stout and reading *Sporting Life* before deciding which bets to make on the horses or football. After work, a few younger people came in to drink imported lager, and then just before closing time, the real night life arrived, with shady characters doing deals in the dim alleyway outside.

I was content to sit and watch and drink, nursing my ninth or tenth whiskey of the day. Even that wasn't enough to fill the empty ache inside me or to numb the pain: whiskey was far less dangerous than women. Besides, my tolerance for alcohol was at the point where anaesthesia was hard to achieve. Even so, sleeping at night was something I hadn't been able to do for a while now. Passing out was the only option. The trick was to be sober enough to make it back to my flat, but not sober enough to remember anything about it. Perhaps one night I'd just drink myself into a coma and never wake up. A man can hope.

The door of *The Nag's Head* swung open again sending an icy blast through the pub, making the oldies grumble and scowl.

Out of habit, I glanced up with tired, bleary eyes. Then looked again.

The newcomer walked toward me, pulling off his beanie and unwrapping a long scarf from his neck.

"Hello, James. I'd ask how you're doing, but I can see for myself. You look like shit."

I was still sitting with my mouth open when Clay sat down opposite me, a small, sad smile on his face.

The last time I'd seen him, he'd been in a hospital bed waiting for his third or fourth operation because he'd lost his right leg in a blast injury. Eighteen months later, he looked fit and well, and was walking easily on a prosthetic.

Not that you could tell he didn't have both legs—I only knew because I'd been there when it had happened.

I shut my mind to the memory and lifted the glass of whiskey to my lips.

Clay's hand closed on my wrist.

"That's not the way, brother," he said gently. "It's not what she would have wanted. Seeing you like this, man, it would break her heart."

"Can't break her heart when she's already dead," I mumbled, then downed the whiskey in one gulp.

Clay didn't speak, he just watched me, his face solemn.

I had two questions tripping over themselves, but I couldn't summon up the energy to ask them. If he wanted to tell me how he'd found me and why he was here, well, he'd get to it eventually.

Besides, I suspected that I already knew the *how*: only our spook friend, Smith, would have the connections to find me when I really didn't want to be found.

So, that left the question of *why*.

I lifted my empty glass.

"Buy an old soldier a drink?" I smirked at him.

"Sure," he said easily, and went to stand at the bar.

It seemed to take him ages to get served, but when he returned, he was carrying two cups of coffee.

"I'm not much for strong liquor these days," he smiled, sipping down a mouthful of lukewarm gnats' piss, then shuddering.

The Nag's Head was a crappy pub and served crappy beer, but their coffee was even worse.

His response pulled a grin from me, something I hadn't done in a long while.

I didn't want coffee—I wanted to carry on drinking until I stopped having thoughts, but I looked up, meeting Clay's eyes.

"You've travelled all the way from Ohio to piss me off, so it must be serious. You need money, advice, or an alibi? Because I'm stony-broke, give shitty advice, and couldn't give an alibi to a nun."

He smiled and sipped his coffee, just shaking his head as his gaze took in my scruffy beard, dirty clothes and battered Army boots.

"How's the leg?" I muttered at last.

"You know, I wondered about that," he said thoughtfully. "Do you think they cremated it? Or maybe buried it? It seems weird that my leg might have had a funeral without me."

I gaped at him.

"Oh, you are listening. Great, just checking. Well, I tell you, brother, it's been a long road to reach this place." He looked around the pub, frowning. "Although I gotta tell ya, in my mind, our reunion was somewhere classier."

"Not romantic enough for you?" I asked through a mouthful of the dreadful coffee.

His dark eyes flashed with amusement.

"Now you mention it," he said cheerfully, "it's a shithole." Then his expression turned serious again. "Why are you here, James?"

My thoughts were still blurred around the edges, but I was pretty sure that was *my* line.

"I was going to ask you that."

He seemed to consider his answer, leaning back on his seat and studying me.

"I want to offer you a job."

I spat coffee on the table, then wiped my mouth with my sleeve.

"Your sense of humour hasn't improved, Clay."

He gave a thin smile.

"Oh, I don't know. Maybe the joke's on you, brother."

"Yeah, it definitely is," I growled. "Fucking cosmic joke, an interstellar joke. Yeah, the joke's on me alright."

He grimaced.

"I didn't mean it like that. Look, this is a genuine offer and I've come a lot of miles, so at least give me the courtesy of a genuine reply."

I choked down another mouthful of coffee as I scowled at him.

"Yeah? Who do you want me to kill?" and I snorted at my own joke.

He sighed.

"I've been offered a job working for the Halo Trust. You know what they do, right?"

He wanted to work for one of the biggest landmine clearance charities in the world? That was a sobering thought.

"Yeah, I know what they do. Clean up after the war's over: IEDs, landmines, large calibre ordnance, cluster munitions—all the debris of battles lost."

I remembered when I was a kid seeing Princess Diana on TV wearing body armour and a helmet as she walked down a road in Angola, 'DANGER' signs on either side of her, then spent hours talking to kids who'd lost limbs when they'd stepped on landmines.

I was eight years old then and I already knew that the world was a fucked up place.

Clay nodded.

"You got it. I'll be supervisor, running local logistics, but I need an EOD operator as the project manager to teach the locals how to search for and destroy the munitions left behind."

I stared at him as I shook my head.

"I'm not the man you need. You need someone who cares enough to get the job done right. You need someone who gives a shit, mate."

His gaze cooled although there was still a small smile on his face.

"A suicidal Ammo Tech? I would have thought this was the perfect job for you, James. Since you don't care if you live or die, why not do some good first?"

Do good.

The words echoed through my brain.

She'd wanted to *do good*. She-who-must-not-be-named.

I gulped down the filthy coffee and glared at Clay.

"I'll think about it."

He grinned broadly.

"Good enough, brother. Good enough."

CHAPTER 2

James

I LAY ON MY MATTRESS, EYES DRY and head aching. I hadn't slept, I'd just sobered up slowly during a long night of too many thoughts and all the painful memories stirred up by seeing Clay.

What was the point of anything? I hated what I was, who I'd become. And I hated that I didn't have the guts to finish it either. Each day when I woke, I thought today would be the day. But by the time I collapsed at night onto the filthy mattress in this shitty doss house, I'd lived another day. Not that anyone would call it living: I was existing.

Like I said, what was the point?

I reached for the bottle by the side of the mattress, but it was empty. I must have finished it during the night. I couldn't remember.

Rolling to my hands and knees, I clawed my way upright using the wall to support me, then staggered to the disgusting shared bathroom. It hadn't been cleaned in years, possibly decades, but I didn't care. It was a toss up which smelled worse: the bog, the scummy shower, or me.

My piss was the colour of rust which meant I was dehydrated. There was grim satisfaction in the thought that I was slowly killing myself with drink. Faster would be better.

A heavy pounding on the front door bruised my brain, but despite all the grey cells I'd been assassinating steadily over the last 15 months, I had a shrewd idea who was making all the racket, so I ignored it.

When the front door was flung open with sound of the wooden frame splintering, I sighed and shuffled back to my room to lie on my mattress, waiting for the inevitable.

I heard Clay's heavy footsteps clomping up the stairs, noting a slight unevenness to his gait. I closed my eyes, remembering again the moment I saw the explosion rip through him, the blood on my hands, my ears ringing. I could see the panic on her face, taste her fear, feel the futility boil inside me as time ran out, the inevitability of the seconds counting down—then flames and noise, the stench of burning, flying through the air and…

He kicked open two other doors before mine was slammed into the wall, sending chips of paint flaking from the ceiling, and my mind skittered and lurched back to the present.

"This place is a frickin' dump, James."

"Yeah, it suits me," I said tiredly, depressed that I hadn't been able to find another bottle of whiskey to sink into. "Well, you found me. What next?"

He didn't answer, but I heard him stomping around my room, so I cracked an eye, watching without interest as he tossed the few clothes I had into my old Army kitbag, emptying drawers and…

"Don't touch that!" I said sharply, sitting upright, suddenly very awake and very sober.

He paused, his hand hovering over a shoebox that I kept hidden at the back of the wardrobe.

"Make me stop," he said with a challenge in his voice.

Fury exploded inside me, piercing through the shield of numbness, and I launched myself at him. He stumbled, my weight knocking him backwards, but then he recovered his balance and put me down with one punch.

I lay on the floor winded, my jaw howling in agony as I felt my cheek start to swell.

"Aw, damn," said Clay, leaning over me to offer his hand.

I ignored his outstretched arm and scrambled to my knees, pulling the precious shoebox toward me as I hunched over it protectively. I didn't care about much, but no one touched that box.

I pulled off the lid, just to check, just to see, and stared down at the small square of folded silk. My fingers shook as I stroked it, taking the smallest solace from the feel of it, knowing it was safe.

"That hers?" Clay asked softly.

I nodded, my throat closing as I choked down emotion.

I touched the folded material once more before I replaced the lid, wiping angrily at my eyes.

Clay touched my shoulder.

"Come on, brother. Amira wouldn't have wanted this for you."

Hearing her name sent tremors racing through my battered body and broken mind. But Clay hadn't finished.

"She wouldn't want you living like this." He hesitated. "Look, Zada's in London with me and she'd really like to see you."

I shook my head. I wasn't in a position to see anyone, especially the woman who should have been my sister-in-law.

I glanced at Clay's hand resting on my shoulder and paused. He was wearing a platinum wedding ring.

"You and Zada?"

He smiled and nodded.

"You were invited to the wedding."

I hadn't known, hadn't checked my emails in months.

"Congratulations," I said dully. "She's a great girl. She's … great."

His eyes lit up.

"Yeah, she is. I'm a lucky bastard."

Then he picked up my kitbag and snatched my shoebox, tucking it under his arm.

"Hey!" I yelled, stumbling to my feet. "HEY!"

He was already out the door and halfway down the stairs when I came pounding after him. I tripped the last three stairs and landed on my hands and knees at the bottom, winded and pissed off.

"Give me my fucking box!" I yelled after him as Clay strode down the street.

"Come and get it!" he called over his shoulder.

Furious, I picked myself up and limped down the road after him, wheezing like an old and knackered sixty-a-day smoker.

After a few hundred yards when it became clear that I couldn't keep up with him, he took pity on me.

My head pounded and my whole body ached. Everyone else on the pavement was giving me a wide berth, avoiding the scary-looking homeless guy they saw.

When we hit the main road, Clay hailed a Black Cab, leaving the door open for me as he clambered in. The driver didn't look too happy about having me as a passenger, too, but Clay didn't give a shit, just throwing a hard stare until the man turned back to his steering wheel.

Hesitating, I held onto the door, out of breath and hurting, eyeing the shoebox on the seat next to Clay.

"Where are you going?"

"Do you care?"

I licked my cracked lips, then climbed in.

Feeling like shit, I tried to touch the box, but Clay moved it nearer towards him, a warning in his expression. So I slumped against the vinyl seat, closing my eyes. Clay didn't speak either, and I was nearly asleep by the time we arrived outside a large, budget hotel.

Clay paid the driver as I stood looking warily at the glass and concrete exterior. I didn't belong here with decent people. But Clay hustled me inside, stepping quickly past the frowning receptionist and into the lift.

Swiping his key card, we rose to the twelfth floor and Clay marched me along the corridor, opening the door to a small single room.

He tossed my kitbag on the bed, then carefully placed my shoebox next to it. I touched it quickly, avoiding Clay's eyes. Touching it helped.

"Get cleaned up," he said, then closed the door.

I sank down on the bed, too exhausted to hold onto my anger. I had two choices: pack up my shit and leave right now, knowing that Clay wouldn't come after me again. Or, I could stay.

I wanted to leave. The weight of Clay's hope was too heavy, his expectations too unmanageable, but I was tired of my own thoughts. Just so damn tired. And the bed was soft, the room clean and bright.

Then I noticed that there were two plastic carrier bags on the bed. I opened one gingerly and saw a pair of men's jeans, two shirts and several t-shirts. The other bag contained socks and underwear, a pack of disposable razors, other toiletries and a toothbrush.

I ran my tongue over my teeth, cringing at the furry gunkiness, and wondering how bad I smelled. I'd grown immune to it a long time ago, but something about the brightness of this hotel shamed me.

Pulling off my boots, I stepped into the tiny bathroom. Weakening further, I turned on the shower, marvelling at the hot water that came pouring out.

Making the decision to stay wasn't too hard after that. Bought for the price of a hot shower—I was a cheap date.

I stripped off all my clothes and stood under the water, and if tears mingled with that steady stream, no one would ever know.

When I finally climbed out, I cringed at the ring of grey scum that had settled at the bottom. Then with renewed energy, I filled the tub with water and poured in a healthy amount of shampoo, dumping all my dirty clothes and those from my kitbag in it. I couldn't remember the last time I'd done any laundry.

Or the last time I'd cared.

Wiping the steam from the mirror, I shaved off the bushy beard, then ran the razor over my scalp.

I looked gaunt, and even through the haze of steam, I saw the emptiness in my eyes. My body was too thin, and I could see my ribs well enough to count them. But from beneath the grime and hopelessness, I began to recognize myself.

I brushed my teeth four times, surprised to find pleasure in being clean.

When I turned to see how the laundry was doing, the bathwater was grey with accumulated filth. I scrubbed the clothes hard, and it took three lots of rinsing before the water ran clean. It was a huge effort to hang the dripping clothes over the shower rail, and by then I was completely knackered and collapsed onto the bathroom floor, out of breath and sweating alcohol.

My hands were shaking, too. This was the longest I'd been without a drink in months. Acknowledging that desperate craving ramped the need higher. I drank some tap water, but threw it up almost immediately.

My stomach hurt and my head felt like a road gang were drilling through it.

But Clay had thought of that, too, and I found a box of dry crackers and a packet of Ibuprofen in the goodies on my bed.

I swallowed four pills and managed to eat some crackers, as well.

I lay down on top of the bed, staring up at the ceiling that swirled and spun.

Going cold turkey was going to suck donkey balls.

Funny, it never occurred to me to go and find a drink.

If Clay thought I was worth saving, maybe I wasn't a lost cause. The question was: did I want to be saved?

It took three days for the alcohol to be purged from my body. Three days of shits, shakes and sweats, itching skin, racing heart and hallucinations that scared the crap out of me. I dreamed that I was back in our cabin in the woods, breathing in the scent of pine trees and our sweat in the humid summer. Those dreams were good until the ending, always the same ending, her blood on my hands and me screaming until I puked.

Clay came and went, bringing food that was left untouched, more Ibuprofen for the blistering headaches that made me think my brain was melting.

But on the fourth day, I woke up with a little more clarity, a trace more humanity. My head ached with a dull throb, but I was definitely feeling like my old self, which was not necessarily a good thing. Clarity brought back painful memories, and without the numbness to cope, I was a confused and anxious mess.

I couldn't explain why I kept going, kept trying to detox and get clean. I didn't understand my own motivation. Maybe because Clay wanted this; maybe because Zada was waiting to see me, and I knew I couldn't have let her see me as I was.

The hotel door opened and Clay walked in, a huge smile on his face.

"It walks, it talks, it's nearly human!"

"Fuck off," I grumbled without much heat.

"You're looking a whole lot better, brother. Think you can face some breakfast?"

I gave him a wry look.

"Not a full English, but maybe some dry toast and coffee."

He nodded.

"And Zada? Are you ready to see her?"

I sucked in a long breath, my jaw clamping.

"I want to see her," I said slowly. "But I'm dreading it, too. No offence."

He sighed.

"None taken. I get it. But she really wants to see you. You're important to her. She wants to feel this connection with you—for Amira's sake."

Searing pain throbbed inside my chest as Clay said her name. Grief and guilt, and the endless emptiness of knowing that she was dead—that I hadn't stopped her, hadn't saved her.

Clay rested his hand on my shoulder.

"Is it so bad that you can't even bear to hear her name?"

"It's just been a while," I murmured.

He hesitated, his lips pressed together.

"Do you want to talk about it?"

I shook my head, swallowing hard.

"James, brother … she cared about you, you know that, right? She wouldn't want *this* for you."

"I'll be fine. I just … I'll be fine."

He let me live with the lie and didn't comment further.

I showered and shaved as quickly as I could, given that my hands still shook slightly, and wore the new jeans and one of the shirts that Clay had bought for me. The only footwear was my old Army boots, but I cleaned them up as best I could and gave them a spit polish.

Clay laughed.

"Man, I haven't done that since Boot Camp. My old Drill Sergeant could spot a speck of dust from a thousand paces. He was a mean son of a gun."

I glanced up, amused.

"'Son of a gun'? Harsh language, Clay."

He laughed.

"Yep, I'm trying to swear off cussing along with drink. Living clean these days, buddy. You should try it."

There was a long pause and then I nodded.

"Maybe I will."

He held out his hand, pulling me up from the bed and into a tight hug.

"I've missed you, James. Promise you won't disappear on us again."

I tried to say something funny or stupid—tell him he was a damn pussy—but I couldn't do it. Sincerity gave his words power, and I felt them.

"I can't promise," I said, at last. "But I will try."

"Good enough for now," he said with a faint smile.

Then for the first time in four days, I left the hotel room.

Zada was waiting for us at a breakfast table. She looked exactly the same except she was wearing glasses while reading a newspaper.

And God, she looked so much like her sister, so much like Amira. The same beautiful dark eyes, the same caramel skin, the same slender hands. But it was the sight of her *hijab* that stopped me in my tracks.

It was the same.

It was the same colours, the same pattern, the same as the square of silk that I kept folded up in my shoebox.

I froze, mid-step.

"Ah, man," Clay said quietly. "I should have thought of that."

Zada's welcoming smile dropped and her hands flew to her headscarf.

"This? Oh James, I'm so sorry! I should have thought—my mother gave us one each. I wear it all the time to feel close to Amira, but I didn't think…"

My heart jolted painfully, but I bullied a weak smile onto my face.

"It's okay, it's fine … it's good to see you, Zada." I was lying. It hurt like hell. "And, um, congratulations. On the wedding."

Her eyes darted nervously to Clay, and he held her hand.

"Thank you," she whispered.

After the most awkward greeting ever, we sat down and even Clay seemed lost for words.

I could have kissed the waitress when she arrived with the menus.

Clay and Amira both ordered the full vegetarian breakfast.

"Only toast, please, and coffee."

The waitress left with our order and we all sat looking at each other. Zada's smile twisted.

"Did you know that Amira tried out to be a cheerleader once?"

I shook my head. There were so many things I didn't know.

Zada gave a hollow laugh.

"Dear Allah, what a disaster! She was such a klutz, you know? She knocked over a pyramid of six cheerleaders when her cartwheel went wonky. Complete high school fail. She never lived it down."

Her words caused a sharp stab of pain in my chest as I remembered Amira tripping in her *burqa*, and I'd picked her up, arranging her small body against mine. The pain of that memory was intense and unconsciously I rubbed the tattoo over my heart, my private memorial to her.

I looked up to see Clay and Zada watching me with concerned eyes.

"Maybe I shouldn't have said anything…" Zada began, her voice dropping to a whisper.

"No," I disagreed at once. "Tell me everything. I want to know."

And so she did—the good things, the sad things, the funny things—all those small moments that make up a life. All the moments that I hadn't been there for.

The pain of loss ripped me apart again. It should have been Amira telling me her high school stories, Amira making me laugh over her awkward attempt to be a cheerleader, but we never had the chance.

We never had the time.

And now, we never would.

It occurred to me that I'd never known Zada's Amira, the one who'd laughed openly. It hurt to think that I'd never known her light-hearted or free of the sadness that weighed her down. Our relationship had been forged in doubt and hardened in fire. Had we ever had a chance?

"She loved working in the ER," said Zada, her voice stronger now. "She loved the challenge, the adrenaline of never knowing what was going to happen, the rush."

She looked at me directly.

"That's something you both have … had … in common. Maybe that's why she … you know … volunteered in the first place. Maybe that's why she went to Syria." Her tone softened with uncertainty, questions in her voice. "Maybe she was addicted … to the intensity."

Was that true? Was that what we'd seen in each other?

We sat in silence, the coffee cooling in front of me.

It was Zada who spoke first. There was no preamble—she just dived in, saying what she'd clearly been waiting to say.

"I want you to take this job with Clay. I want you to keep him safe."

"Zada…" Clay began. "Let the man drink his coffee first."

"I'm sorry," she said, looking at me then back at him. "But it's been on my mind for weeks. You say James is the best, then no one else will do. I can't lose you, too, Clay. I love you."

His expression softened as he gazed at his wife, and I had to look away. Seeing their love so obvious, so easy, it ripped me open. I even glanced down at my chest, half-expecting to see blood oozing through my shirt.

But no, my worst wounds were on the inside.

Zada's words soaked through me and I found myself speaking firmly.

"I'll do it," I said. "I'll go with Clay. I'll keep him safe—or die trying."

Clay laughed uneasily.

"Hopefully, it won't come to that."

"Thank you," said Zada earnestly.

Then she leaned across the table and squeezed my hand. I nodded uncomfortably and slid my hand under the table.

There was a long, tension-filled pause. I swallowed and cleared my throat.

"So, what's the plan?"

Clay's expression cleared, and Zada leaned back in her seat.

"What do you know about Nagorno Karabakh?"

I searched through my memories but came up blank.

"Georgia?" I guessed. "Ukraine?"

It definitely sounded like somewhere in the former Soviet bloc.

"Close," replied Clay. "It's a disputed territory on the western side of Azerbaijan, mostly mountainous or forested areas: Russia to the north, Iran to the South. They've had nearly three decades of fighting since even before independence from the Soviet Union in 1991. The territory has been treated like a bone between a pack of dogs, with soldiers from Armenia, Azerbaijan, Georgia and Chechnya all joining in. Throw in some Kurd mercenaries and Mujahideen, and well, you can imagine."

"Jesus." I glanced at Zada. "Um, sorry."

"Yeah, I know," said Clay, ignoring my verbal stumble. "The Halo Trust has been working there on and off since 2000 de-mining tens of thousands of hectares, but Nagorno still has one of the highest per capita incidences of landmine and unexploded ordnance accidents in the world. James, a quarter of the victims are children."

His lips thinned as he quoted that statistic, and Zada was visibly upset.

I held back a sigh.

Clay was a good guy, a great guy, but he was also an idealist. And how he managed that after 11 years in the U.S. Marines, I'd never know. He thought he'd be flying out there to make the world a safer place, and maybe he would, but I knew ex-ATOs who had taken these non-governmental organisation jobs and found out that they were under-resourced with a fairly hazardous approach to health and safety. Hopefully, not this one.

Clay needed me more than he knew. And I didn't have anything better to do with my life.

I didn't have anything at all.

"When do we leave?"

CHAPTER 3

TWO MONTHS LATER...

Arabella

I leaned against the police sergeant's desk, my head spinning. God, I was drunk. I'd lost count of the glasses of champagne I'd knocked back.

"Name?"

"What?"

"What's your name, luv?"

"It's Harry," smirked my best friend Alastair, his eyes glassy as he lolled in the uncomfortable plastic seat next to me.

"It's not really Harry" I said, giving a confidential smile. "He's just being silly."

The policeman sighed, looking bored.

"Name?"

"Arabella Forsythe," I said, although it probably sounded more like 'Ar'bell Forzuth.'

I was smashed, totally bladdered. And there was no way I could manage my full name.

"The Right Honourable Lady Arabella Elizabeth Roecaster Forsythe," grinned Alastair, winking at me.

"Ah, yes. I always forget that bit," I smiled. "Such a mouthful."

Trust Alastair. He never could keep a secret.

The policeman rubbed his cheek tiredly.

"Welcome to Paddington nick, your ladyship. Empty the contents of your pockets into this."

And he slapped a plastic tray in front of me.

I sighed.

Oh well. At least he wouldn't find any coke on me because the last little baggie had disappeared up my nose several hours ago.

It wasn't the first time I'd been arrested. But it was such a bore waking up with a hangover in a police cell.

I shut my eyes at the thought of facing my father when he came to post bail in the morning. Not that I seriously expected him to come in person. He'd send one of his minions.

I giggled at the thought of a small yellow cartoon character turning up with my father's credit card. Giggling turned to snorting, and Alastair gave me a disgusted look when I belched loudly.

Still, an overnight stay courtesy of London's Metropolitan Police was preferable to dealing with my father. Infinitely preferable.

I SLEPT SURPRISINGLY well on the thin, lumpy, suspiciously-stained mattress. Although it was probably more like passing out than actual rest with an REM element. But waking up was just as ghastly as I'd expected. My head throbbed and my tongue tasted like the droppings from a parrot's cage. I didn't have a mirror, but if I did, I knew from experience that my makeup would be smeared, giving me a look that rivalled a Hackney hooker. My hair was flattened on one side and hanging limply, full of tangles on the other. I tried to comb it with my fingers, but the knots pulled at my scalp, sending a searing pain through my dehydrated body.

Thank God there was no mirror—I'd already suffered the indignity of peeing in the disgusting seatless lavatory.

My feet ached, and I realized that I'd worn my five-inch Jimmy Choos all night. I eased out of them with a wince, then sighed as my poor, swollen toes met the cool concrete floor. I wiggled them in pleasure. It really is the small things in life that count. I should know, because most people think I'm filthy rich.

Wealth means something different to a family like mine. It's simply to be accumulated so that you can pass it down to your heirs and secure the lineage. We've been in Debretts forever. Seriously, my family tree went back nine-hundred years, maybe more if anyone cared to look. Probably some Royal blood, too, if the wrong side of the bedsheets counts.

I was brought up in a castle, Roecaster Castle in Dorset, but I'm not rich. No, all the money and property passes down to the elder son, my brother Sinclair. It's always been that way. I don't think about it much, to be honest. I grew up knowing that's how it would be. And besides, if tradition said that everything was split amongst all the children equally, the castle and its grounds would have been long gone, sold to the National Trust to be another stately home for the public to visit.

Well, we did that, too. You know, let the great unwashed tour the castle and grounds on certain designated days throughout the year, sell them cream teas and a guidebook that I wrote in between my first and second years at university. But on the days when we were closed to the British public, the castle was my playground—I could get lost for hours wandering through the orchards and formal gardens, drifting ghostlike through the 124 rooms, not including the vast, dust-filled attics, or the chilly, dungeon-like cellars.

But rich, no. When I married—or if—I could expect to inherit no more than £50,000 and that was it. Not even enough to buy a one-bedroom ex-council flat in London.

It was irritating that I wouldn't get anything at all until I married some over-privileged Rupert.

No, I didn't have a fiancé named Rupert—it was just what my set called the Eton idiots who went to Sandhurst officer training because their family had been military since Nelson was a twinkle in his daddy's eye.

If you looked in the Oxford Dictionary, it would say something like this:

Rupert, A (noun). British Army slang for an Officer, especially one that is upper class, nice but dim, and utterly lacking in skill or sense.

Daddy planned to keep me dependent and tied to his apron strings until I married a man like that. It was positively feudal.

Nobody said what would happen if I decided not to marry—it was simply assumed that I would.

I rubbed my eyes then stared at my fingers, blackened from my eyeliner and the smoky-look that I'd been going for last night.

Wincing, I peeled off my false eyelashes and flicked them away with my fingers, just in time for the cell door to clang open.

"Time to go, Miss Forsythe," said the desk sergeant.

"Really? I was hoping for a cup of tea first, I'm parched."

He didn't seem to think I was amusing, so I jammed my poor, abused feet back into my torturous shoes and clip-clopped along the corridor past other cells with noisy inmates.

I wondered how much I'd have to brown-nose dear old dad to get out of my latest scrape? How many dreary charity balls would he make me go to as penance? It was a sobering thought.

My stomach roiled in protest when I saw the man himself standing waiting for me, and what little colour I had, fled from my cheeks.

"Arabella."

Those four syllables were imbued with disgust and disappointment. I'd heard the same tone from him a thousand times, so it was nothing new. I forced myself to remain slumped, fighting the urge to straighten my spine.

"Hello, Daddy!" I said with a saccharine smile.

It wasn't a smile that was returned.

"You've gone too far this time," he stated coldly. "Drunk and disorderly, urination in a public place."

It sounded a lot worse than it was, and I wondered idly what he was going to threaten me with this time: loss of allowance, servitude on the family estate, being arm-candy to one of his banking friends at some boring stockholder party.

He nodded at the police officers, thanking them briskly for their time and apologizing for my appalling behaviour. He also promised a chunky cheque to the National Association of Retired Police Officers.

And that was it. End of story. All crimes swept away under the carpet of birth, breeding, and a fat wallet.

He gripped me by the top of my arm as I was frog-marched out of the police station.

"I can walk," I snapped.

"Can you?" he asked icily. "It seems to me that even something as simple as walking is beyond your meagre capabilities, Arabella."

I grimaced. He'd told me I was stupid so many times, it was easy to believe him.

"I'm not a child," I muttered petulantly.

"No. You just insist on acting like a toddler having a tantrum instead. Well, I've had enough."

I tugged my arm free.

"So have I, Daddy!"

Stevens, the chauffeur, held open the car door for me.

"Thank you," I muttered as I slid into the expensive leather interior.

Dad didn't speak to me all the way home, a gloomy fifteen minutes where I was left to contemplate my many sins and ponder my punishment.

But as the Rolls Royce Silver Ghost slid smoothly to the porticoed entrance, he finally spoke.

"We'll talk about this later."

He didn't even look at me.

Well, that was going to be another fun conversation, one where he treated me like a child, and I promised it would never happen again.

But he hadn't finished.

"And Arabella, if you insist on dressing like a whore, try not to dress like a cheap one."

Shame burned in my chest, and I wrenched the door open before Stevens had even put the car in park. I kicked off my shoes in the opulent hallway of our London townhouse and ran up the stairs.

Nausea filled my stomach, and when I saw my reflection in the large mirror, I knew that my father was right. I looked cheap. Cheap and worn out and sad.

No, I wouldn't let him do this to me again. I was better than that.

I phoned Alastair to find out where he'd disappeared to last night.

"Did you get home, okay?" he yawned.

"No, I was kidnapped. But they were nice. They made me tea and recharged my phone. I think they're bringing me a bacon sandwich."

"Send one my way," he yawned again.

I rolled my eyes.

"Look, I need to talk to you because…"

"Oh God, it's not even ten o'clock. It's way too early! Call me later," and he hung up before I had a chance to speak.

Bloody typical.

I was tired of men cutting me off. I needed to find better friends.

I shuffled into my *en suite* bathroom and stripped off the hooker dress, shoving £1,200 worth of appliqued satin into the rubbish bin. I knew I'd never wear that dress again—I couldn't even bear to look at it.

The shower was my friend: gushing hot water soothed my sadness, and eased my aches and pains.

The hot water didn't run out. Daddy would never let that happen. Hot water was endless, along with the rooms in our houses and the money we spent on possessions. The only thing in short supply was affection. *Poor little rich girl.*

I wrapped myself in a thick bath towel, warmed by the heated towel rail, and stumbled into my room, squinting at the thin winter sunshine in the world beyond my window. I picked up the remote control, and the thick velvet curtains slid together soundlessly. Blessed darkness.

I'd only been asleep for a few minutes when a soft tapping on the door woke me.

I ignored it for as long as I could, but whoever was disturbing my beauty sleep wasn't going away.

"What?" I snarled, my voice muffled by my pillow.

The door opened and the light flipped on, causing me to groan.

"Your father wants to see you, Lady Arabella," said Mrs. Danvers.

Her name wasn't really Mrs. Danvers, but that's how I thought of her. She answered to 'Brown'. I think she had a first name, but even though she'd worked for my family for twelve years, I'd never heard anyone call her anything except 'Brown'.

Well, except for me. I also called her 'Chief Bitch'. She was so far up my father's arse, I was surprised she could see daylight.

"He's in his study."

"Yeah, whatever. Turn the light off when you go."

She went. Leaving the light on.

See? *Bitch.*

I wish I could say that I ignored my five minute warning and went back to sleep, but I didn't. I wish I could say that I wasn't afraid of my father, but I was.

His temper was legendary, and you did not want to be on the receiving end of that. My stomach clenched nervously.

Maybe throwing a party for two-hundred people in the Mayfair restaurant he owned, and running up a teensy little bar bill had pushed him over the edge. And getting caught peeing in the alley along with some of my male friends…

He wouldn't want that for his precious princess. *Hmm, my sarcastic voice sounded a lot like my normal voice.*

I dressed quickly. No one kept Sir Reginald Forsythe, Earl of Roecaster waiting. Especially not his younger child, his troublesome, tear-away daughter.

I slid into the study as silently as possible, trying to make myself blend in with the hand-printed wallpaper.

It didn't work. Even with his back to me, staring at a computer screen dribbling numbers, he knew I was there.

He swung around to face me, crossing one leg over his expensive wool-blend trousers. He scanned me leisurely, and I squirmed under his cool appraisal.

"Arabella."

"That's me!" I said brightly.

"You've always been a disappointment."

Wow, straight for the jugular.

"Exposing this family to public ridicule."

As he was factually correct, I kept my mouth shut.

"Thank God your mother died before you could disappoint her, too."

I cringed, feeling the slice of his surgical repugnance.

"You've failed in everything you've ever attempted: school, university, even finishing school, although how you managed to be sent down from that still astonishes me."

"If only you'd let me get a job, Daddy…" I began bravely.

"I'm talking!" he roared, his face turning purple. "You don't bloody talk when I'm talking! When I stop talking, that's when you talk!"

"Sorry, Daddy."

"At least God has given you a modicum of beauty, because He hasn't given you brains."

Lashed by his words, I was silent.

"Tomorrow morning, I'm leaving on a business trip. You're coming with me as you're obviously not capable of being left without constant supervision. I've told Brown to pack for you. The car leaves at five. In the morning."

He turned back to his desk and I was dismissed.

I knew from bitter experience that there was no use arguing with him. I had no idea where he went on his business trips, but my father had his manicured fingers in many pies. It could be Shanghai or New York, Sydney or Vanuatu.

But as it turned out, it wasn't any of those places.

CHAPTER 4

Arabella

Freezing rain pelted me as I scuttled down the steps of the small aeroplane, catching a glimpse of snow-capped mountains in the distance. Hunching my shoulders, I headed for shelter in the nearby arrivals building.

It was our third airport of the day, and I had only the haziest notion of where we were. No one had spoken to me except the flight attendants, and there was only so much nasty in-flight tea and coffee one could drink without regrets.

For the last nine days, I'd followed my father to boring business meetings in far-flung corners of the world: Namibia, Chile, Siberia, Kazakhstan and now here. He was buying up coalfields at a time when other businesses were turning to Green energy. It was his belief that with the Chinese opening a new coal-powered station each week, their demand for fossil fuels would soon outstrip their own national production. And when that happened, he'd be ready to supply.

Not that Daddy Dearest ever spoke to me directly, he just introduced me to the people he was doing business with, showing appropriate fatherly affection before dismissing me to a bland hotel room. He'd also taken away my credit cards, so shopping trips were out of the question.

I was bored out of my brain, but didn't have a means of escape. Instead, I watched a lot of terrible subtitled TV, or swam in the tiny pools, or even worked-out listlessly in the tired hotel gyms. Dad made sure that I didn't have a chance to drink anything stronger than coffee, or sometimes a single glass of wine on the rare occasions I was invited to dine with him, all carefully supervised, of course. Because I couldn't be trusted. I was a disappointment, and I wished I could feel indifferent.

It was a subtle punishment: proximity to a parent without any of the love that I might have hoped for. 'Hope' and 'my father' weren't words that I'd united in a sentence since I was seven.

Today, we'd flown into Armenia, a country that I'd vaguely heard of (but couldn't find on a map), although I'd learned that there were untapped coal seams within the forests just across the border into Azerbaijan (which I'd had to learn to spell), and just the teensy problem of the countryside being littered with landmines from a previous war.

Daddy Dearest was here to donate to a charity that cleared war-torn countries of landmines. And it was all tax deductible.

What a coincidence that there were coalmines to plunder, too.

Although I wasn't completely sure where 'here' was since we'd landed at a large airport—somewhere I couldn't read the name of because the writing system was unfamiliar. It didn't look like anything I'd ever seen before. It made me feel very small, very insignificant.

Then we'd driven another six hours, edging along a steely blue lake before heading ever upwards through the mountains, past a long-forgotten monastery, winding along hazardous hairpin bends that had me closing my eyes, a torturous journey, painful in its silence, until the scenery widened into patches of farmland and we arrived at our destination, half quaint Alpine-style buildings, half ugly Soviet grey concrete monoliths.

Our driver, a silent, Slavic type with ruthless eyes, drove us to a modern hotel, all glass and chrome, but tiny in comparison to other more cosmopolitan hotels in other world cities, and with just 33 rooms.

My luggage and I were escorted to a large, modern suite with a double bed, but I was somewhat disconcerted to see that the towels had been cunningly twisted into the shape of swans, with rose petals scattered across the crisp sheets.

My escort appeared very proud of the swans, so I smiled politely and left a couple of dollar bills on the coffee table for him. Over the last week, I'd learned that hotel staff always preferred American dollars to the local currency.

I sat on the bed, and the two swans collapsed, the romantic gesture crumbling, which seemed fitting. Nevertheless, I pulled out my phone to call Alastair. The bastard hadn't returned a single text since I'd been away, but I was so bored and lonely, I was willing to overlook his inadequacies and give him another chance. He was supposed to be my best friend.

He finally answered after the first three times I dialled his number had gone to voicemail.

"Bloody hell, Harry," he grumbled, "are you stalking me?"

"Don't be a bigger arse than you have to be, Alastair," I sighed. "I'm stuck in the middle of nowhere with no one to talk to except Dad's shady business associates."

"Well, I don't know what you expect me to do about it," he complained. "I'm not supposed to talk to you, and besides," he hissed, lowering his voice, "I'm entertaining a rather nice little tart that I've just met and you're cramping my style."

My head spun with so many pieces of new information.

Alastair and I had known each other forever although we'd never been official. Neither had we wanted to be, but we'd been each other's plus-ones at all the weddings this season and he wasn't bad in bed. I'd assumed … I wasn't sure what I'd assumed.

"What do you mean, you're not allowed to talk to me?"

He sighed theatrically.

"Harry, darling, your dear papa paid my bar bill at Claridge's and Annabel's, and bunged me a couple of grand to go and shag someone else. Apparently, I'm leading you astray and you're too thick to know it. Didn't he tell you?"

I swallowed the insult along with the pain.

"You're such a bastard, Alastair."

"I know. That's why you love me. Now be a good girl and bugger off—I'm trying to get my leg over."

He cut me off, leaving me staring at my silent phone.

I was twenty-six years old and my own father was paying my friends to stay away from me.

I didn't think I could sink any lower.

Dinner that evening was a gloomy affair. I'd dressed nicely, although my Alexander McQueen gown was totally wasted, apart from curt introductions, no one talked to me except to inquire how I found the soup (in a bowl garnished with a mint leaf), how I found the *Dolma* (on my plate, minced), would I try the local *Pakhlava* pastry saturated with syrup (probably not—one must watch one's figure, and try not to throw up at the dinner table). Thank God I hadn't tried the *Ayran*, a frothing beer-mug full of cold yoghurt-beverage mixed with salt.

I smiled dutifully and stared longingly at the bottles of wine the men drank, but Dad had told them I didn't drink, so that was that.

I excelled at small talk—every girl of my class and education did, but the only way I could punish my father was to remain as incommunicative as possible without actually being rude. It was the only morsel of control I had in my life. If he treated me as a child, I'd behave like a petulant one.

I still didn't understand why he'd brought me on this trip. If he wanted to curb my drinking, just send me to rehab in Primrose Hill. At least I'd be with friends.

Dad hadn't told me anything about his ongoing plans, so I had no idea how long I'd be away for, or where we might be going next. But during dinner, I managed to glean a few snippets, such as we'd be heading into the mountains the following day and that there was still snow on the higher ground.

I understood now why Mrs. Danvers had packed my ski gear, although the silly cow had forgotten my ski boots so now I'd have to buy a new pair—I certainly wasn't going to rent any. God knows what sort of sweaty feet used rented boots—it was one of the reasons I refused to go ten-pin bowling. Shudder.

It galled me that the housekeeper knew more of Dad's plans than I did. I bet she'd enjoyed that knowledge of her power over me.

I'd never heard of a ski resort in Azerbaijan, but I suppose the former Communists had to ski somewhere other than Klosters.

I loved being on the slopes with freshly fallen snow, and the mountain air sharp and clean. Off piste was my favourite type of skiing.

Maybe this trip was looking up after all.

So the next morning, I dressed in coral pink salopettes with matching jacket, and sashayed down to the car.

"Good morning, Ivan!" I trilled to the surly Slav.

His name wasn't Ivan but it seemed to irritate him, so I said it every time I saw him.

My mood took a dive when Dad appeared.

He glanced at my outfit then climbed into the car without a word and we started another long, silent drive.

The scenery began to close in, the hillsides thickly covered with towering fir trees that shut out the light. I saw piles of dirty snow at the sides of the road and glimpses of brilliant white on the distant peaks, until finally, we approached an ugly straggle of prison-like huts.

With a sinking sensation, I knew that skiing was not going to be on the schedule for today.

Barbed wire circled the huts, making it look like a Siberian stalag. The only things missing were the machine guns.

A tall black guy wearing jeans, heavy boots and a thick jacket came striding across the muddy forecourt outside the desolate concrete block buildings. He had the look of someone ex-military and walked towards us, extending his hand to my father.

Rather incongruously, an acid yellow lollipop was sticking out of his jacket pocket.

"It's a pleasure to meet you, sir. Your generous donation will enable us to continue our work for many months to come."

Now I understood. This must be the base for one of those landmine demining places, whatever they were called. Although this was a lot more squalid and grey than the videos I'd seen of Princess Diana wearing body armour in bright African sunshine.

As Dad soaked up the words, spoken with an American accent, I longed to tell this man that my father's donation wasn't selfless or altruistic—it was a down payment to the Azerbaijan government, an unspoken agreement that my father would be in pole position to exploit the coal beneath our feet.

"And this must be Miss Arabella Forsythe," said the man with a friendly smile. "We're honoured that you're here—we certainly need all the volunteers we can get. I'm Clay Williams, Head of Operations."

I smiled politely, wondering if this American was getting me confused with someone else.

"My daughter is a true humanitarian," Dad replied with a reptilian smile.

His words were perplexing, and we shook hands in silence. It was also the first time that one of my father's business associates had known my name in advance. An uneasy sensation trickled through me, a sense of dread that I couldn't identify.

"The accommodation is limited," said Clay, his smile more wry now. "But the welcome is warm. I'm sorry my wife isn't here to welcome you. She's in the village, helping out at the health centre. You'll see her later. Let me take your bags."

Panic flashed through me.

"Dad? Are we staying here?"

Clay's smile slipped entirely, his questioning gaze flipping between us. But Dad spoke first.

"Yes, Arabella, you are staying here. Mr. Williams requested volunteers and I volunteered *you*. You'll make yourself useful and work under him for the next three months."

"Three months!" I shrieked. "No way! I won't do it!"

My father grabbed my arm and dragged me out of earshot.

"Did you think that your punishment would be gadding about, accompanying me to a few business meetings? Do you think that makes up for the £37,000 restaurant bill you ran up? The tradesmen's bills all over London? The shame you've brought on our family? Do you think I'll put up with bailing you out of the drunk tank again? No! It's enough, Arabella. You will volunteer here, where no one knows you or cares about you. You *will* do this. You will *not* embarrass the family ever again. Do you hear me? *Do you hear me?*" he hissed, shaking me until my teeth rattled.

"Daddy, please! I promise…"

"Your promises mean nothing," he said coldly, dropping my arm abruptly.

His temper switched from fire to ice in seconds, a skill he used to throw his opponent off balance. It always worked on me.

I swallowed hard and stared at him.

"Why do you hate me so much?"

His lip rose in a sneer.

"Don't be melodramatic, Arabella. It's beneath you. Rehab hasn't worked—maybe this will."

He turned away and stalked back to the car where my Louis Vuitton luggage was already being piled in the mud.

"Williams," he said to the man who'd greeted us, "I'll expect your weekly reports on clearance progress."

Clay's warm expression had disappeared.

"And on your daughter, sir?"

Dad stared back, dismissing him with a shake of his head.

"Only if she fucks up."

Then he drove away.

CHAPTER 5

Arabella

I WILL NOT CRY. *I WILL NOT CRY.*
And I didn't. I'd had years of appearing indifferent to my father's volcanic rages, but it was humiliating to have it witnessed by this stranger.

Clay shouted something at two women who were standing around watching, unaffected, as sloe-eyed children played around them.

Glancing up at me briefly, they picked up my luggage and carried it towards one of the concrete blocks.

Clay grimaced and shoved his hands in his pockets.

"So, I'm guessing it wasn't your idea to volunteer here?"

"What makes you think that?" I said bitterly. "I'm *delighted* to be here. Positively ecstatic."

He sighed.

"Look, I know this isn't ideal, but we really could use your help. Resources are limited and every pair of hands makes the job safer and faster." When I didn't answer, he nodded his head in silence. "Let's get you settled in."

I trailed after him, my £900 Fusalp salopettes already heavy with the thick clods of mud that clung wetly. My feet dragged, as heavy as my heart.

How the hell was I going to stand being stuck here for three months?

But there was worse to come.

The room Clay showed me to was more like a cell than any cells I'd ever been in. There was a narrow cot-bed pushed up against the wall, with iron-grey blankets piled on top; a line of nails across one wall were decorated with forlorn plastic coat-hangers. And that was it.

"I know it doesn't look much," Clay announced with admirable restraint, "but we thought you'd be more comfortable with your own room. The other women live in the bunkhouse."

"So, this is like the presidential suite?" I said, forcing away the tremble in my voice with an overly bright tone that bordered on hysteria.

Clay smiled, his white even teeth glinting in the twilight.

"I never thought of it like that, but from now on I sure will," he laughed. "There's a bathroom at the end of the hall, but don't expect too much from the showers—the water never gets really hot." He shrugged apologetically. "Look, I know you don't want to be here, but you might surprise yourself."

Gratitude clogged my throat.

"Thank you," I muttered, humbled by the kindness of this stranger.

"Great!" he said, clapping his hands, relief obvious in his voice. "Dinner is in thirty minutes. You've just got time to get unpacked. You'll meet Zada and Turul then."

I gave him a questioning look that he understood immediately.

"Zada is my wife—she's a trained paediatric nurse, so she volunteers at the clinic in the village, but like I said, she'll be back soon. Turul is our local fixer and he's the only one here right now who speaks passable English. But tomorrow you'll meet my friend James—he's the EOD operator here—our bomb disposal expert—and we have Yadigar, the interpreter. They're pulling an overnighter at a remote location tonight, but they'll be back in 24 hours," and he smiled. "They'll be looking forward to getting back to all this luxury."

A startled laugh leapt out of me and Clay's smile widened.

"See you later, Miss Arabella."

"You can call me Harry," I said.

"Harry? Really?"

"It's what my friends call me," I said, suddenly shy.

"See you later, Harry."

After Clay left, I sat on the lumpy mattress, festering with hurt and anger. I couldn't believe that Dad had done this to me. Rationally, I knew that I'd brought it on myself, but wasn't the punishment supposed to fit the crime? All I'd ever wanted was to be allowed to get a job and live my own life.

I suppose I should have been careful what I wished for.

Sighing, I began to unpack my bags, but realized quickly that my designer clothes were badly out of place here.

Hot tears burned the back of my eyes, but I would *not* surrender to this. If my father thought this would break me, he was probably right, but I would try, try, try to prove him wrong.

I pulled my phone out of my pocket, but as I'd suspected, there was no signal.

I had nothing, I had no one. I was no one.

I WALLOWED IN misery for twenty minutes. I thought that was fair enough, but after that, I started to grow bored. I changed out of my designer boots with the slippery soles, and rummaged through my case until I found an old pair of Uggs that Mrs. Danvers had tossed in. They'd soon be as muddy and disgusting as anything, but ballet flats that looked divine on Kensington High Street were not going to cut it here.

Digging further, I found a cricket sweater that I'd pinched from my brother and pulled that on under my ski jacket, then ventured out into my new life.

Even though the hour wasn't late, the sun was already setting and the air cracked with cold, the scent of wood smoke hanging in the stillness. I smelled the latrines before I saw them. I couldn't grace them with the word 'bathrooms' as Clay had done. They were gross and basic and freezing. I peed quickly and rinsed my hands in water so cold, I was sure it must have been snow minutes earlier.

A woman with a colourful headscarf and caramel skin approached me, her smile careful.

"You must be Harry. I'm Zada, Clay's wife. I came to tell you that dinner is ready."

Like Clay, she had an American accent, but where he was warm, she was wary, and I sensed that I would have to earn her trust.

"Thanks, I'm starving. I could eat a horse." And then I wondered if they ate horses in Azerbaijan. I had no idea. "Well, maybe not an actual horse…"

"Vegetable stew and meat stew," she said. "We make a lot of stews, it's the easiest thing to do for thirty people and one small kitchen. And the local *Tandir* flat bread." She shrugged. "You'll get used to it."

"How long have you been here?" I asked, more out of politeness than real interest.

"Nearly nine weeks now."

"And how long do you think you'll be here?"

"The bosses told Clay three to four months, but James thinks it could take six across both locations."

She shrugged as if it didn't matter.

That was okay, I didn't care. I'd only asked for the sake of something to say, and we descended into silence again.

The dining hall was a long concrete hut that formed the spine of the little community. Long trestle tables with benches lined the room, and the air was filled with a spicy scent of cooking.

Twenty women and as several small children were already lining up in front of steaming vats of the stew that Zada had mentioned, and my stomach growled hungrily.

"We help ourselves," said Zada, throwing me a challenging look as if I was expecting to be served on a silver platter.

I smiled tightly and lined up with the other women. I wondered where Clay was and why this seemed to be a community of women and no men.

I was relieved when I saw him enter the room, his large personality making the place seem less gloomy.

"Hey, baby," he said, planting a kiss on Zada's lips, his affection far louder than his quiet words. "You found Harry, that's good," and he grinned at me as if we'd pledged ourselves to be best friends forever. "How'd it go today?" he asked, turning to his wife.

Her lips thinned.

"Better, I think. But it's hard—they have so little."

Clay glanced at me, his face shining with pride.

"I told you that Zada's a paediatric nurse—well, she's volunteering at the local health centre and also running a class in school twice a week teaching the kids English. Is that something you'd be interested in helping with?"

I restrained a shudder.

"Not really within my skill set," I said honestly.

To me, children had the charm of serial killers.

"What *is* your skill set?" asked Zada crisply.

"Oh, I'm rubbish at everything," I laughed. "Can't boil water without burning it."

"We'll figure something out," said Clay kindly.

"What sort of jobs have you done before?" Zada persisted.

Shame infused my reply.

"I've never worked," I said, but I spoke airily.

Never let them see your pain.

She exchanged a look with Clay. I didn't need a degree in communications to work out what she thought of me.

"Maybe I could help in the office?" I offered tentatively, wondering if they had an office.

Clay grinned.

"Now you're talking! Paperwork is my least favourite thing, and James is worse at it than I am." He smiled at me. "Ever seen the movie *The Hurt Locker?*"

"Oh wow, yes, I have! That was incredible!"

"Well, what we do is nothing like that. That's just Hollywood blowing smoke—literally. What we do is slow and careful, dangerous at times, and then there's a ton of paperwork that comes after. To make the land safe again, we need to keep accurate records of *exactly* which areas are mined and which have been cleared. Mess that up, and it's another child killed, a friend whose lost a foot or both legs." His friendly smile faded and his dark eyes turned hard. "Paperwork is a pain, but it's a necessary pain."

I wondered what on earth I'd just volunteered for.

We reached the front of the queue and were handed a plastic bowl and a hunk of hard bread.

"The stew on the left is meat, probably goat," said Clay. "The one on the right is vegetables."

"You're vegetarian?"

"No, just getting tired of an all-meat diet, even though it's halal."

"Oh," I said stupidly. "Right. Are you Muslim?"

"Zada and I are Sunnis," he said, lowering his voice slightly. "Armenia is a broadly Christian country, as is Nagorno, but our team was recruited in Azerbaijan—they're mostly Shia Muslims—we're respectful to all faiths."

I blinked, trying to remember anything I knew about the different branches of Islam, but coming up blank.

"I don't think Arabella understands the difference," Zada said.

Her voice was polite, but her sharp eyes told a different story.

Obviously, I knew that there'd been fighting in Afghanistan and Syria recently, but I hadn't paid attention to the politics. I'd never worried about it before, but Zada's scathing comment left me feeling ignorant and inadequate.

 Oh well. I was used to that.

Following their lead, I opted for the vegetarian stew rather than the doubtful-looking meat of indeterminate origin. But it was surprisingly tasty and I made quick work of it, mopping up what was left with bread.

"Hungry?" asked Clay, lifting one eyebrow.

I laughed lightly.

"I skipped breakfast and we didn't stop for lunch."

"People don't skip meals here," said Zada.

I wasn't sure what to say to that, so I stayed silent. I definitely had the impression that she didn't like me. I was used to that—other women rarely did. But here, I'd be reliant on her, as one of the few people who spoke English.

We were joined by a giant of a man who carried two bowls of stew, although they looked like teacups in his beefy hands. I was mesmerized by his enormous moustache, the ends curling like a pantomime villain.

"Is this the English princess?" he asked in a heavy accent, a twinkle softening his eyes.

"Nope, 'fraid not," I answered. "And now Meghan Markle has taken Prince Harry off the market, I never will be."

He laughed a huge belly laugh, and even Zada cracked a smile.

This was Turul, the fixer, which probably meant he knew who needed to be bribed. Yes, I'd actually listened at some of Dad's meetings.

"What language do the locals speak?" I asked, not bothering to hide my ignorance.

There was no point pretending I knew anything. At least here, I could wallow in stupidity without being yelled at by my father.

"Most speak Armenian or Azeri," explained Turul. "English is beginning to be taught in some schools now, but few speak it. None as well as I."

His voice was stern but proud as he said that. I could order a glass of champagne in French and German, but not much more. Once again, I felt inadequate.

It was clear that Clay and Zada were making efforts to learn, and over dinner, they had an impromptu lesson with Turul.

Hello was *Barev*, and *Goodbye* was *Hajoghutyun*. *Enjoy your meal* was *Bari akh.orzh.ak*.

I tried to pick up a few words but I was tired, and depression was weighing on me again.

How would I manage three months in this strange place without an anchor?

CHAPTER 6

James

My team was exhausted but we had another half-mile of tough terrain to navigate before we reached our transport; maybe another painstaking hour of searching for mines, as well. It wasn't work that could be rushed.

It had been a hard slog all day, sometimes working our way through knee-deep snowdrifts which slowed us down even more. But now, with the light fading and conditions worsening by the minute, the threat increased incrementally.

It was Ohana and Maral's turn to use the Vallons, the metal detectors that would tell us if a mine was buried on the narrow track. I had been keeping a close eye on both of them, making sure that their sweeps were intersecting arcs and that they were covering all the ground. But an hour ago, Ohana had slowed down even more, holding up the team who followed, so I'd taken over, swinging the Vallon in a wide arc across the path, working parallel to Maral.

It was boring, tiring work, listening in the headphones for the telltale beeping—exhausting to concentrate for so long.

If you stepped on a mine, you'd lose a limb as minimum collateral damage. It wasn't like in the films where the heroic bomb disposal officer replaced a man's weight with a large rock.

There were two ways of disarming it safely: blow it up with a small charge; or the second, more dangerous method, was by putting a pin on the safety hole of the trigger, then removing the detonator manually—then you had a harmless mine that could be easily transported.

Slushy piles of snow tugged at our boots, and it wasn't easy to keep parallel because of the saplings that sprung up around us, or the boulders that tried to trip us, but it was important to work in tandem, because if the arcs didn't intersect, that could be the point where a mine had been planted. And then someone, one of my team, could tread on it and be crippled in a spray of blood and bone.

I never wanted to see that again.

I knew that I'd never ease the guilt when I thought back to that day in Times Square where all our lives had changed forever. The day I'd found Amira gagged and handcuffed with a suicide vest strapped to her body. The day I'd held her life in my hands and begged a God I didn't believe in to save us all.

We'd survived, although Clay had lost a leg.

But he never complained, even when his prosthetic was painful, or when the cold or altitude affected the blood supply to his stump. He had Zada to look after him and he didn't need a moody bastard like me bugging him.

The teams here loved Clay, and his addiction to teeth-rotting sweets and candy. Hell, everyone who'd ever met him loved the crazy wanker. Even me. And I hated just about everyone. But to balance things out, no one here liked me, but they respected that I was good at my job. And that was enough. Each day I had to believe that we were saving lives.

At the same time, I couldn't help wondering why the hell anyone would bother to lay mines in such a Godforsaken part of the world, but then again, God had forsaken me long ago, just like here. It didn't make me special.

I'd definitely shaken up the health and safety protocols since I'd been here, rewriting the manual, so to speak. I wasn't losing anyone else, not on my watch.

But changing the status quo through brute force didn't breed many friends.

Sweep.

Identify.

Expose.

Extract.

That was the mantra that I tried to drill into my team.

My Vallon beeped, and I held up my hand so that everyone stopped. Silence crept through the forest and I listened intently to the beeping in my headphones.

Working in snow made it much harder. Not only did it mask the landscape, but the Vallons were less reliable with a couple of feet of snow between them and the mines; much harder to get a ground signal.

It meant more work had to be done by hand.

We needed a Gauss, a metal detector that could work at greater depths. It was on the wish list that I'd given to Clay. We needed it, but we didn't have it. One of many things that would have made the job safer.

Instead, I lay on my belly and dug through the foot of snow with a plastic trowel. A metal one could potentially arm a device.

Lying in the snow was fucking freezing, the icy cold and wet seeping through my clothes, but it was safer this way. Explosive forces go upwards, so being at ground level was the way we worked; and using just my left hand, so that if the device was triggered, I'd only lose one hand.

When I was training, I used to think about the way those rules had been designed, the people who'd learned lessons the hard way, the deadly way.

Carefully, I scraped at the snow with my left hand as my fingers began to go numb, until I found a round, bowl-shaped object, and gave a satisfied grunt. It was an old Russian MON-100, one of several that we'd found on this trip.

It was an anti-personnel mine, which meant it was designed to wound or kill by fragmentation and had 2Kg of explosives in it. Big bugger.

It was also a directional type of mine, so it should never be approached from the front, always from the rear or side.

Ohana handed me a slim rod with a red flag attached, a warning to stay clear until we could come back and deal with the nasty bastard. Not only that, but the flags were a way of seeing if there was a pattern to the way the mines were positioned.

At least I didn't have to risk my life neutralizing it today; later, we'd blow it to kingdom come. But not today.

Maral was about to step forward when my sixth sense told me something wasn't right.

"Wait!" I yelled.

Maral gave a little gasp and froze on the spot, hardly daring to breathe, her eyes darting around.

I inched toward her, covering the ground with the Vallon.

There was another device here. I knew it, I just couldn't find it.

I switched to a smaller handheld metal detector. I wished we had the version I'd used in the Army, a Hoodlum, but the Americans had donated us Garmins, so I used what I was given.

Time ticked past and I ignored the restless grumbles behind me from the rest of the team who were tired and cold, and believed that I was the only thing between them and a warm bus back to barracks. Maybe I was wrong.

No, I was never wrong—not about this.

I'd spent my adult life listening to my gut instincts.

Slowly, I raised my eyes, searching the foliage around us.

And then I spotted it, in the trees—a det cord link rising upwards directly above Maral's head ... and another anti-personnel mine. One more step and she'd have been killed along with at least three people following behind her.

I pointed, putting my finger to my lips. Her face paled as she tilted her head upwards and muttered something that could have been a prayer.

Shaking, she sank into a crouch, then scuttled sideways on her hands and knees until she was out of the danger zone.

Slow tears of shock from the near miss leaked from her eyes but I didn't have time for that. I held my hand out for another red flag, then looped it around a small branch so it hung near the device, but not close enough to touch it, even if the wind picked up.

Normally, I'd neutralize these UXOs on the spot—who doesn't like fireworks? But I needed to pass on the skills to others so they could carry on the work when I was gone. For that, I needed good light and a place where I could do show-and-tell in safety—never during a Task.

Breathing a sigh of relief, we circled past the small pennants, trudging on, eyes gritty with tiredness as dusk descended.

"James-*syr*," said Yadigar the terp, slapping my shoulder. "The bus is just over that rise, below the tree-line. We'll be drinking *Xirdalan* and sleeping in our beds tonight." He paused, lowering his voice. "Maybe Maral will show you her thanks later in bed," and he wiggled his thick eyebrows like a cheap, music hall villain.

He'd done this before, trying to hook me up with one of the women from the team which was annoying and unprofessional. But there was no use trying to explain that to him. I'd begun to wonder if he received money for pimping on the side. It was a theory I hadn't tested yet, but if I came across any evidence...

I just shook my head, my expression stony.

I had no intention of drinking, and hadn't touched any alcohol since the night Clay had found me in the *Nag's Head* over two months ago. Besides, *Xirdalan*, the local beer, was a light lager the colour and taste of piss. But it was cheap and therefore popular.

Yad knew that I stayed away from it and stuck to *chai*, the sweet black tea everyone drank, but there were times when I still longed for the numbing relief of alcohol. Yad was sure that I'd give in one day. I was sure he was right.

We were all looking forward to being back at the compound tonight. Exacting work and sleeping rough weren't an ideal combination, especially in sub-zero temperatures, so the thought of tepid showers and our own beds was something we were all ready for.

Even so, being back at base also meant being around Zada. I still had mixed feelings about that. It was getting easier. Never easy, but easier.

I was mostly over the shock of how much she looked and sounded like Amira, but at least their personalities were totally different: Amira had been fiery and emotional; Zada was slower to anger, more likely to think before acting.

Each evening, over dinner, she talked and I listened. Gradually, she told me all the things about Amira that I hadn't known before: what she was like as a child, what she was like at high school and as a nurse, how she was before their brother Karam's death, when the person that she'd been had died with her grief.

I'd known Amira in fear and definitely intensity. Would that have translated into a relationship in ordinary life?

I smiled wryly—there was nothing ordinary about my life.

I pushed the thought away, swinging the Vallon across the remaining yards that led to the bus, and unclipping the battery pack with a sigh.

Another mission completed. Mines located: 23. Deaths/injuries: 0.

Released from concentration, the team became vocal, laughing and talking among themselves, leaving me to my thoughts as I settled into a seat near the front of the bus and they crowded into the back.

"A good day, James-*syr*," said Yadigar as he passed me to join the others.

"Yep, a win for the good guys," I agreed.

He smiled broadly at this.

"I am good guy!"

It was a five-hour drive along hairpin bends and thousand-foot drops to HQ but we were used to this. We'd already cleared large areas of the roadsides, tracks and pathways around the compound, so now we had to travel farther afield. Clay thought that we had another two weeks' work before we'd be forced to move the base. And that meant that not all of the team would travel with us. Mostly, they were women with families who did this difficult and dangerous work because it paid well, compared to poorly paid positions in the declining oil industry, which was the only alternative employment.

A few would travel with us, prepared not to see their families during the next four months because this was the only way they could earn the money to feed them. But when we moved, we'd have to recruit at least four new members, maybe more, and that meant losing precious time to train them.

Time wasn't precious to me, of course, but with a finite budget to get the work done, Clay was on a time crunch. The Halo Trust was a charity, but much of their funding came from the UN who never had enough to go around, and businesses who were only generous because it got the land cleared of mines and UXOs at a cut price. I despised the people who skimped on resources, who gave us five people when we needed ten, who thought that local people were expendable, because they were cheap—women who cleared landmines for a living were very cheap. Yeah, very expendable.

Bastards.

I let my eyes drift closed, falling into an uneasy sleep with violent dreams.

I jerked awake when I heard screaming, wondering if we were under attack, and Yadigar shook my shoulder so roughly, I nearly fell off the bench seat of the bus.

"What the fuck?" I snarled, turning to him angrily.

His face was carefully neutral, hiding his real feelings, his disdain.

"You were screaming, James-*syr*. Very bad. You scare the women."

I rubbed the sleep from my eyes and dropped my gaze to my boots so I wouldn't have to see the scorn in his expression.

"Ah, fuck. Sorry, Yad," I mumbled.

"You okay? You want beer? I have some?"

I gave him a furious look and he retreated hastily back to his seat.

He knew the rules—no alcohol on a Task. It was too risky. If I reported him to Clay, he'd be off the team instantly. But we'd scoured the area for competent English speakers and they were hard to find. You couldn't make-do when people's lives depended on it.

I rubbed my face again and glanced around, curious eyes flitting away as soon as they met mine. It was one of the reasons people stayed away from—because I scared the fuck out of them.

Better not fall asleep again. It was why I had a room to myself at the compound.

As we approached the motley collection of ugly buildings that I currently called home, a wave of tiredness came over me. It was always the same at the end of an op, the relief of surviving another one, the letting go of all the awareness, all the tension of responsibility to not get anyone killed.

But before I could do anything else, I had to report to Clay and decide what to do about Yad.

I dragged my weary arse toward the prefab building that was the Trust's office, and stopped.

Why do we want what we can't have?

That was my first thought when the woman walked into the prefab hut ahead of me.

My second thought was, *what the fuck is she doing in a flea-infested shithole like this?*

I was in the armpit of the world, one of the most dangerous and corrupt territories to come out of the ex-Soviet Union, and she was wearing a luminous pink ski suit, with blonde hair tumbling over her shoulders.

Am I hallucinating? Have I finally gone completely crazy?

But if not, what the hell was she doing in the middle of landmine country, with Russia to the north, Iran to the south, and hell on earth all around?

I knew what I was doing here.

Penance. I was doing penance.

But this woman?

My head started to swivel when I saw her, and if I'd been a cartoon character, my tongue would have been drooling on my mud-caked boots.

She was stunning. No other word for it. A real bombshell. Tiny waist, nice tits, rounded hips, and long, long legs. Her hair was waist-length, curling in silky blonde waves. It seemed unreal against the backdrop of mud and grey.

But when she turned and her eyes caught me looking at her, there was no light of triumph, no recognition that she was God's gift to man. Instead, the dark blue irises were emotionless. Her gaze flicked up and down my tatty, dirt-stained clothes without interest, her expression of weary resignation and an untouchable, impenetrable isolation.

There was something old in her eyes, something that said she'd seen enough, even though she couldn't have been more than twenty-five. For the first time in a long while, I wanted to understand, wanted to know what she'd seen, what she'd experienced—and that was a scary thought. I didn't like being scared and I didn't like feeling guilty—it made me angry. I should stay the hell away from her.

But I got it, I did. She was the kind of woman that men fought over. She probably started wars. She was a goddam Helen of Troy.

And you know what happened to the Trojans…

CHAPTER 7

Arabella

My instinct was to take a step backwards, but instead I held my ground and stared straight ahead, meeting the stranger's angry gaze.

With his shaved head and blazing eyes, he looked dangerous, as if volcanic violence was coiled inside him waiting to be released.

But after a few seconds, his eyes iced over, and I couldn't hold his intense glare any longer, so I let my gaze drop to the rest of him. There was a streak of mud across his forehead and his clothes were filthy but functional. Then my eyes widened as they came to rest on the gun strapped to his hip.

The only guns I'd been around were shotguns when we had a pheasant shoot on the family estate—not handguns. Not squat, black, deadly-looking pistols.

Who was this man?

Was he one of the mercenaries that Clay had warned me about? One of those men with allegiances to no one except the highest bidder?

Or was he a bandit, one of many who haunted these mountains, preying on the weak and unprotected for food, clothes or weapons.

I swallowed uneasily and could have cried with relief when I saw Clay striding across the muddy compound towards me.

"Yo, James!" he called out, waving a bright green lollipop. "You're back earlier than I expected. How'd it go? I just saw Yad. He says you saved Maral's life today. Nice work, brother."

Brother?

I stared in surprise. Clay's skin was dark, almost ebony, but this man had an unhealthy pallor, his skin chalky with dark circles under his eyes, almost disguising the good genes that had blessed him with a strong, handsome face, if somewhat unsettling eyes of pale blue.

Of course! He'd called him 'James'—I'd just been too flustered to take it in. This was Clay's co-worker, the only English speaker in the camp that I hadn't encountered so far.

"Did you meet Harry yet?" Clay continued.

The man swung his pale blue gaze to Clay.

"Who?"

Clay laughed, tilting his head back, his eyes creasing with amusement.

"Yeah, sorry about that. I'd better do the introductions right. Arabella, this is my friend and co-worker James Spears, our EOD operator and Project Manager. James, this is Arabella Forsythe, our new volunteer, also known as Harry."

The man's fierce gaze swung back to me but didn't soften. If anything, his gaze hardened.

"Her? She won't last five minutes."

How rude!

Irritated, I was also surprised by his English accent—I'd expected him to be American like Clay and Zada. If pushed, I'd say he was working class, probably Home Counties. That Estuary accent was everywhere these days. Not that I cared two hoots, but I knew that as soon as I opened my mouth I'd confirm everything he already thought about me just from seeing me in my coral-pink salopettes.

'It is impossible for an Englishman to open his mouth without making some other Englishman hate or despise him.' George Bernard Shaw put that line in his play *Pygmalion* over a hundred years ago, but it still held true today. I wondered if it was the same in America. Perhaps.

Not that I despised James for his accent or upbringing, but I was pretty sure from his surly demeanour that he wouldn't return the favour.

"Dude, can you stop being an asshole for a whole minute and say hello to the lady?" Clay frowned. "She's travelled a long way to work with us."

Grudgingly, the man studied me slowly, then held out a dirty hand, the nails black with grime, his expression challenging.

I shook his hand gingerly, forcing myself not to reach for a tissue.

"Delighted to make your acquaintance, Mr. Spears," I trilled, my cut-glass accent ensuring that I would meet his low expectations.

"Likewise, Ms. Forsythe," he said.

His voice was flat and unemotional, yet somehow still imbued with sarcasm.

Clay smiled, his eyes darting between us.

"Go make your report, James. Show Harry where we file the electronic copy and the hard copy. She's going to be helping us organize the office a little better. May as well start now. Then both of you come on in to supper. Stew again—yum yum yum!"

He slapped James on the shoulder, then we both watched silently as Clay strode away sucking on his lollipop, calling greetings to a group of dishevelled women who must have been with James out on Task, as I'd learned it was called.

They looked as tired and dirty as him. I couldn't begin to imagine what their work was like. I had a lot to learn.

Without speaking, James turned on his heel and I tiptoed after him, picking my way through the mud, back to the office where I'd just come from. He stopped at a standpipe that had a bucket next to it, and proceeded to wash his hands in the freezing water, breaking the ice first.

It made me shiver just looking at him.

"Are you going to watch me clean under my fingernails?" he asked without looking up.

I jumped, surprised that he'd addressed me directly.

"Yes, it's fascinating," I chirped, determined to slay him with smiles.

He grunted, wiped his hands on his muddy trousers then opened the office door. I was surprised and pleased when he held it open for me.

"Thank you, James."

He didn't respond, but I hadn't expected him to.

In the office, he shrugged off his heavy coat and tugged off the muddy scarf that he'd been wearing.

His hair was shaved to almost nothing—more than military short, only a millimetre of hair covered his head like a pelt. Not many men could have carried off the look without seeming like a thug, but to my irritation, he was just handsome.

I sat quietly, gazing around the dusty office while he typed up his report with two fingers. There was a huge map on the wall covered in coloured pins. I looked closer and realized that it was a map of landmines in the area—some cleared, some still to make safe. A shiver ran through me and my eyes flicked to James.

He might be rough around the edges, but he saved lives. And me? For all my polish, for all my expensive education, I was useless. There was no point to me.

Sighing, I turned to the filing cabinets. This morning, Clay had shown me where the personnel records were kept, but it was a confusing mess because some were in English and others were in Armenian. At least I think that was the language. Clay said some of the locals also spoke Azeri. Either way, to me it was an impenetrable mass of squiggles.

I realized that James was no longer typing, so I spun my secretarial chair around to look at him.

His lips were pressed together in a thin line as if my mere presence annoyed him.

"Finished?" I asked brightly.

"This report gets emailed to head office and copied to the local government liaison, then saved into the day log here," and he pointed at a folder on the screen helpfully entitled 'Day Log'. "You print off a hard copy and file it."

I watched carefully as the ancient printer whirled and whined, then finally spat out two sheets of paper.

James clipped them together, pushed the document into the cardboard folder and slapped it onto his desk.

He scowled again and each word he spoke sounded like it had been yanked out of him.

"The power fails here regularly. There's a backup generator, but we can't always get the oil to run it, so it's crucial that each time you create or alter a document, you save it to this flashdrive," and he pointed at a shallow dish containing a plastic USB stick. "There's an automatic backup onto tape, but we don't want to rely on that." He shrugged. "Old technology."

"Why don't you send it to the iCloud?" I asked, trying to be helpful.

"Mountains."

"Pardon?"

I could almost hear him grinding his teeth in irritation at my confusion.

"We're surrounded by mountains. There's no WiFi, no phone signal, only a Sat-phone for emergency comms."

"Oh," I said stupidly, "but you were sending emails?"

He breathed in deeply then out slowly, and I cringed, recognizing the signs of someone struggling to hold onto their temper.

"They're in the Outbox right now. When Clay gets the chance, he takes the laptop down to the village, logs into the UNMAS database and NDMAA, and sends the comms in a batch."

"Right, got it. Um, UNMAS? And the other one?"

He closed his eyes, his nostrils flaring slightly, but when he spoke he was civil and composed.

"United Nations Mine Action Service and NATO Defense Manpower Audit Authority. We get some funding from the UN, so part of the job is to report back to them. This report," and he waved the Day Log folder at me, "it says the number and type of mines that we found per 100 metres, the depth we found them at, how we neutralized them, and whether or not it was a nuisance minefield."

I blinked at him.

"This is probably a stupid question, but aren't all minefields a nuisance?"

He glanced up at the ceiling as if searching for divine patience. When he finally spoke, it was slowly and clearly.

"A 'nuisance' minefield means that the mines are spaced irregularly— it makes it harder to find them—and significantly more dangerous."

"Oh, that makes sense," I said awkwardly.

He ignored my comment, and I wondered if I was supposed to be taking notes.

"UNMAS reports to the Inter-Agency Coordination Group on Mine Action," he continued. "They need to know which areas we've identified and which we've cleared."

"Okay, another stupid question: why don't the governments pay for the mines to be cleared?"

"You'd think, wouldn't you? Politics, cost," he sneered. "Four-fifths of all landmine clearance around the world is done by Halo or Mines Advisory Group, and they're both British charities. We have the expertise."

He stood up from the desk so suddenly, I scooted back in my wheeled chair and crashed into the filing cabinets.

He shot me a look of contempt and strode from the room.

That just pissed me off.

I leapt up, rubbing my head where it had bounced against the metal drawers, and raced after him, slipping and sliding the mud.

"Wait!" I yelled, but he ignored me. "Just wait one bloody minute, will you?!"

He spun on his heel, his face taut with anger.

"What?"

I slid to a halt, breathing hard.

"I think we got off on the wrong foot," I offered breathlessly. "Somehow, I seem to have annoyed you, but since all I've done is say 'hello' and, you know, breathe, I'm at a loss as to why that might be. Perhaps you could enlighten me?"

I crossed my arms over my chest and glared at him.

For a second, he seemed taken aback, a flicker of surprise in those glacial eyes. Then he shrugged.

"I'm not treating you differently to anyone else," he said grudgingly.

"So you're just rude and miserable with everyone?"

He cocked his head on one side, considering my question. Then he nodded curtly.

"Yeah."

He turned and walked away.

Unbelievable!

CHAPTER 8

James

That woman was annoying. Her questions were keeping me from showering, eating and sleeping—my three current objectives. I'd only closed my eyes for four hours in the last 48, and I was pretty sure I hadn't slept then either.

I wasn't lying when I said I treated everyone the same. Clay put up with my bastard behaviour because he felt sorry for me and I was good at my job; Zada, because she felt sorry for me, because she understood.

She'd endured an incredible amount of loss in her life already—her brother and then her sister. I sometimes wondered if she put with me for Amira's sake, because I'd loved her sister and she knew that. We shared the same loss—we understood.

All the others just ignored it, ignored me, and I was fine with that. I wasn't here to make friends—I was here to keep Clay away from the dangerous shit and train the teams that followed, to keep them as safe as possible. I was expendable.

This woman looked more like a socialite than a humanitarian aid worker, and yet she'd been the only person who'd called me on my shit—and within the first thirty minutes of meeting me, too. Pretty impressive. But, like I said, annoying.

I unlocked my room and grabbed clean clothes, then realized too late that I'd trailed mud over the peeling lino. Swearing under my breath, I walked back to the standpipe to clean my boots then trudged back to the men's shower block, finally managing to wash off the sweat and dirt of the last few days, wishing the water was hot and plentiful, when the reality was tepid with a two-minute limit for each person.

My mind replayed the day's work. That near-miss with Maral had been closer than I liked. I couldn't seem to make the team realize that threat-triage was not just linear. You had to search upwards, you had to look down, you had to do 360° search. Maybe today would make them aware, at last. I definitely needed to set up more training, but we were always short of time and manpower.

Shivering in the cold, concrete cubicle, I dressed quickly and tossed my dirty clothes into the empty washing machine. I had 38 minutes for the washing to complete a cycle. I had to be back by then or my kit would mysteriously disappear. I knew it was my co-workers, but I wasn't sure if it was dislike or poverty that drove them to steal. Probably both. But I couldn't afford to lose another set of clothes. So I had 38 minutes to eat dinner, then hang up the wet laundry in my room and lock the door before the blissful oblivion of sleep. Or not.

I couldn't remember the last time I'd slept a solid six hours without the aid of alcohol.

Dinner was the same stew as always, but this time there were three people sitting at our table when I arrived. I didn't know why that surprised me—where else would the new woman sit?

I helped myself to a bowl of stew and slid into an empty seat without speaking. Zada said once that I ate my food like I was angry with it. Whatever that meant.

I stiffened immediately when she stood up and hugged me.

"That's from Maral," she said, her dark eyes glistening with emotion. "She has five children. She says thank you for saving her life."

I patted Zada's shoulder awkwardly, thankful when she pulled away. Across the room, Maral nodded gravely then stood up and began to clap. The women on her table copied her and soon the whole room was noisy with applause and Yad yelling.

I hated it. I hated their acknowledgement, their idealization of what I contributed. I was doing my job. No one was hurt. That was enough. This was … too much.

I buried my head in my food and ignored them all, relieved when the noise died away. I was on edge, waiting for the new woman to ask what I'd done, but she didn't. Instead, she turned to Clay and Zada.

"Will it stay this cold for long?" she asked.

Yes, be British and talk about the weather.

Grateful for the change of subject, I began to relax, concentrating on shovelling stew and flatbread into my mouth as quickly as possible. I was ravenous, as if the empty days and endless months could be filled with food. They couldn't. They couldn't be filled with anything, only obliterated with alcohol.

But now I'd stopped drinking, my strength was coming back, that much I knew, and the deafening cry to kill myself with whiskey was a little quieter now, a little less demanding.

"The mountains stay cold all year around," Clay answered. "And the Task teams will be heading further into them over the next couple of weeks. After that, in the Spring, we'll be covering land that's more agricultural further onto the open plains, so it'll be temperate, mild and foggy—like a British summer, right, James?"

I grunted, not wanting to be drawn into the conversation.

"I'll miss working in the health centre and teaching English at the school," sighed Zada. "But maybe I can find something to do at our next base."

"You will, babe," Clay said affectionately, placing a kiss on the top of her headscarf. "You always do."

I scraped the last piece of bread around my bowl then pushed away from my chair and left the room, feeling the eyes of the new woman burning into my back, her unasked questions hovering in the silence.

My washing had another twelve minutes, so I squatted on the floor, unseeing as my clothes whirled around in front of me. I was tired, so tired, but something had changed in me today. I could feel it, I just wasn't sure what it was. Like something had woken up, something I hadn't known was still alive inside me. I was too tired to work it out, so I watched the clothes spin faster, hypnotizing, my life on the final cycle.

Clay had told me that he'd stay with the Trust for a couple more years at least, but he and Zada were trying for a baby and when that happened, he'd send her back to the U.S.

The guy needed his head seeing to if he thought she'd go without him. I didn't know anything about relationships, but even I could tell him that being apart wasn't going to work for them. They'd stay together, no matter what. The reminder that Amira hadn't stayed was a bitter taste in my mouth, seasoned with sadness and silence.

I hadn't really known Zada before, except as Amira's little sister. I didn't know anything about what she'd been like, her hopes or dreams. I did know that she was thriving out here, loving the challenge of her work, trying to organize medical aid where it was needed, and teaching in the school. I couldn't imagine her going back to the States alone. But maybe having a kid would change all that. That's what you did when you loved someone more than yourself—you put them first. At least, that's what I'd been told.

The washing machine beeped at me, and I pulled out an armful of damp clothes that cooled quickly in the frigid air, then walked back to my room, footsteps dragging with tiredness.

Tomorrow was another day.

Unfortunately.

CHAPTER 9

Arabella

I followed James's sudden departure with astonished eyes.

"Is he always so…"

"Sad?" Zada finished.

I'd actually wanted to say 'rude' but had been searching for a more diplomatic alternative. What Zada said surprised me: I wasn't getting sad vibes from him. Resentment, yes. Bitterness, definitely. Rage, hell yeah.

Even though I should have known better than to ask, my curiosity was piqued.

"Why's he sad?" I asked.

Zada sighed, meeting my curious gaze.

"It's a long story," she said.

"It's James's story, babe," Clay added, glancing across at his wife.

"It's our story, too," she chided gently.

"Yeah, you're right," he agreed with a long sigh, wistfulness in his expression as he stared at the door James had just passed through.

"I don't mean to pry," I lied.

"The short answer is that James was in love with my sister," Zada said quietly. "Her name was Amira. She was an ER nurse. She's why I decided to go into nursing. She was seven years older than me and I always looked up to her." She paused, her eyes glassy with tears. "She met James when they were working together but…" Zada blinked hard, taking a deep breath as Clay held her hand. "Amira died 18 months ago and ever since then James has been…" She searched for a word, then gave a small shrug. "Broken."

Clay leaned towards me, his eyes full of emotion.

"I know he comes across as an asshole, but the man's been through a lot. I'm hoping that being out here, working, helping, that he can … I don't know … find himself again." He looked at his wife, and his eyes were full of love. "Amira wouldn't have wanted this … emptiness … for him."

They shared a moment, and once again, I felt like an outsider.

"So, if you could just cut him some slack," Clay finished. "Plus, my brother is good at his job. He saved my life."

My eyebrows flew upwards.

"He did? Really?"

"Yeah, really."

Clay rolled up his trouser leg to reveal a prosthetic limb.

"I've got this as a souvenir, but without him, I would have been killed."

I was utterly taken aback.

"I had no idea! You walk really well."

I felt my cheeks redden. Was that the wrong thing to say?

Clay didn't seem offended; he simply nodded.

"Yeah, well, I had to learn again, but this gal here," and he smiled at his wife, "this woman pushed me hard, making me keep trying when I felt like giving up. You're a total drill sergeant, babe."

"And don't you forget it," she said, raising her eyebrows. Then her smile died. "So when James is being rude—like just now—ignore it. We do. He's a good man, you'll see."

I was already re-evaluating my opinion of him. I couldn't imagine what it was like to lose the love of your life, to have her ripped away from you. But I envied him a tiny bit, too. I'd never been in love. And I'd never been loved. Well, perhaps my mother had loved me, I was just too young to remember it. I liked to think she had.

I wanted to ask about Zada's sister, but I sensed that this wasn't the time, with their emotions already raw.

"How did James save that woman Maral today?"

It wasn't the question I really wanted to ask.

"He stopped her from walking into a landmine," Clay answered. "The way Yad, tells it, everyone was tired and wanting to push on to get back to the bus, but James has this sixth sense and he *knew*, he just knew there was something else out there. So he did a fingertip search of the area and found this MON-100 hanging in a darn tree. Another footstep forward, and Maral would have walked right into it." Clay's expression was serious. "If she had, it would have killed her and half the team, as well as injuring the others. James saved a lot of lives today. He's *that* good at his job."

I listened to the story open-mouthed. It was so unimaginable, being that close to death on a daily basis.

"Oh my God! That's … wow, I don't know what to say! I really don't! Does … is … does that happen all the time?"

Clay shook his head.

"Thankfully, no. But it's always a possibility. That's why the work is so stressful. We train the teams as much as we can, given the timeframe, but James's training can't be equalled. He was in the British Army for 11 years; he trained for seven years to be a high threat bomb disposal operator."

"You may as well tell her everything," said Zada quietly.

Clay sighed and nodded.

"Did you hear about the Times Square bomb two years ago?"

I scoured my memory, vaguely remembering something about a

bomb in Times Square that had gone off, but could have been much worse.

"Yes, it's a little hazy, but I remember seeing something on the TV news," I said hesitantly. "A woman had been kidnapped and put in a suicide vest. That's right, isn't it? Two off-duty soldiers rescued her. One of them got hurt, I think?"

"Pretty much, yeah." Clay gave a sardonic smile as Zada reached out and held his hand. "The woman was Zada's sister, Amira, and the two off-duty soldiers were me and James. He was the one in the bomb suit." He shrugged. "He saved all our lives that day."

My brain struggled to process what Clay had said, and when it finally did, I felt humbled just to sit in the same dining room with these people. Next time I saw James, it would definitely be with fresh eyes. I felt ashamed of how judgmental I'd been.

"I'm so sorry!"

My words were inadequate, but that was all I could think of to say.

People judged me all the time as a vapid blonde bimbo—of course, in that particular case, they weren't wrong. Not that I was completely thick, whatever dear old Dad said. And the only reason I hadn't received my Communications degree was to do with the little problem of having told the University Chancellor that he was a dickless wonder after drinking two bottles of Taittinger's, but I *swear* I felt his hand on my arse and not the edge of the table like he claimed. Still, being sent down a week before graduation didn't win me any Brownie points. Story of my life.

God, that all seemed so trivial compared with what I'd found in this forgotten corner of the world. I didn't even know why this land was mined—some distant war that I'd never heard of, but why or when, who or how, I had no idea. The best thing I could do was keep my mouth shut and make myself useful.

But what if Dad didn't come back for me? I shivered at the thought. No, no need to panic—Clay and Zada would help me, I was sure of that. Maybe James, too. That's what he did, wasn't it? Helped people?

I just wished I could turn off the need for people to like me. It got me into so much trouble, time and time again. I'd do pretty much anything if it meant that I earned people's smiles or laughs. Pathetic, I know. And I didn't need psychoanalysis to explain why—I had abandonment issues and Daddy issues by the bucket-load.

Anger flooded through me as it did every time I thought about Dad dumping me here. He'd meant it to punish me. Well, wouldn't it be a kick in the pants if it was the thing that *made* me? If I went home stronger?

Maybe James was a miserable bastard, but he had good reason, and yet he was still here helping people. I was going to take a leaf out of his book. I'd drown my sorrows and selfish triviality in helping others. At least I could try.

That night, curled up in my uncomfortable bed in my concrete cell of a room, I promised myself that I'd do better, that I'd *be* better.

Waking up the next day to the reality of cold showers, concrete floors, and dollops of 'hearty' stew for breakfast hadn't become any easier, but a new determination to take it on the chin made me get my backside out of bed, queue for the lavatory, queue for the shower, smile agreeably at the other women who were obviously talking about me, and make myself useful.

I didn't see Clay or James at breakfast. I already knew that Zada had left early to catch a ride down the mountain to the village with Turul, which left me alone at breakfast with the only other person who spoke English, the big bear of a man they called 'Yad'.

"Ah, the English princess!" he said with a wide grin. "Turul has told me about you."

I squinted at him, wondering if that was sarcasm or just a friendly greeting. I decided to give him the benefit of the doubt and sat opposite him with my bowl of stew, staring down at it unenthusiastically.

It was slightly off-putting to see him spoon enormous portions into his cavernous mouth with bad teeth, pieces of meat and carrots caught by his untrimmed beard.

But that wasn't why I didn't like him—there was something wild in his eyes, something dark and sly, and I didn't like the way his gaze undressed me. Physically, he was very much like Turul, the local. But Yad had a careless cruelty that reminded me of my father.

I pushed the bowl towards him and stood up.

"Hey, where you go, English princess?"

"I don't seem to have much of an appetite, but be my guest and finish it off."

"I would like to be your guest," he said with a leer, flicking his tongue between two fingers in an obscene gesture. "Any time, Ice Princess!"

Refusing to respond, I marched straight to the office, determined never to be alone with him if I could possibly help it.

At the office, I turned on the paraffin heater the way Clay had shown me, then rinsed out the coffee pot at the standpipe where James had washed his hands. My gel nails were standing up to the abuse well, but my hands were purple with cold. Who'd have thought I'd be pining for rubber washing-up gloves?

I hurried inside to make some of the foul coffee that Clay drank all day long. Maybe the bitterness offset the amount of sugar from the sweets and candy he ate continuously. I shuddered at the cost of his dental insurance.

He entered the office with James, their heads bent together in conversation, Clay's dark skin and bright smile contrasting with James's pale skin and dead expression.

"Tell me what you need, brother. You got enough det cord? Enough fuzes?"

"Always need more high explosives, det cord, plain dets and safety fuze. American pull igniters. Then electric dets and shrikes, if you can get them. And can you get another ceramic knife and a pair of ceramic scissors? And we need that bloody Gauss yesterday."

Clay sucked his teeth.

"Shrikes? Oh yeah, electrical blasters, right? I'll do my best. Got some contacts that I can ask for the Gauss. Official channels are slow," and he sighed.

"We need it now."

"But ya know, we're not badly resourced compared to some deminer ops."

James's lips tightened.

"Stop pissing in my cup and calling it tea."

Clay laughed out loud.

"Okay, okay! I'll get it. Somehow." Then he looked up and saw me. "Hey, Harry, how's it going?"

"Tickety-book, thanks, Clay. Hello, James."

He nodded, meeting my eyes with a flash of pale blue, before glancing away.

Clay smiled.

"James is going to give you a list of the things he needs when he goes to do dems, okay?"

"Sure. Um, what's dems?"

"Do you know anything about what we do here?" James growled.

"A little," I said, lifting my chin. "Clay has filled me in."

The two men exchanged a glance.

"There are three main methods used for humanitarian demining on land—which one you use depends on the type of mines, terrain, and local resources," James explained, spitting the words out like bullets. "In wide open land, we'd use mechanical clearance—armoured vehicles fitted with flails so the mines would be safely detonated. Trained detection dogs are also used, but here, we use manual detection using metal detectors."

I blinked at the influx of information, and Clay patted my arm reassuringly.

"You'll get used to the jargon. Demolition of UXOs or mines— that's unexploded ordnance."

To me, 'demolition' meant blowing up an office block so it tumbled down in a cloud of dust, but somehow I didn't think that was what Clay meant. James caught the uncertainty in my expression.

"I'm going to blow up all the mines we found on our last Task," he said. "It's the quickest and safest way to get rid of them. When we find small arms ordnance, we gather it together and transport it to a safe location to run a dems."

"Is that dangerous?" I asked.

"There's always danger," Clay nodded. "But James will ensure that it's done safely."

James's eyes flared suddenly.

"It's never *safe*," he snarled, his eyes narrowed. "Never."

Clay lay a hand on his shoulder.

"I know, brother. But it is a lot safer if *you* take care of it than leaving it lying around, or even handing over the main charges to the local government officials and seeing them get stolen and re-used in other devices."

James dropped his eyes, the sudden ignition of his anger already dying away. I wasn't quite sure what had caused it. Understanding him was a minefield of its own.

He left the office after that, striding away across the mud.

Clay sighed and shook his head.

"Don't mind him."

I smiled blandly and hid my thoughts.

"No problem. It's fine."

CHAPTER 10

James

The sky was heavy and threatening, shutting out the moonlight utterly. The locals were forecasting heavy snowfalls over the next few days. Time was not on our side.

It was four hours before dawn—or the middle of the night as far as Yad was concerned when I shook him awake and dragged him out of his blankets that stank of beer, cigarettes and cheap perfume. He'd better be bloody sober by the time he was needed.

I knelt on the concrete floor, facing East, head touching the ground. I couldn't say for sure why I did it—to honour Amira? Not for God or Allah, because I didn't believe in either of them. Not anymore.

I stood up and strode to the minibus.

"Everyone got their full PPE kit?" I snapped out impatiently, waiting for Yad to stumble through the translation for personal protection equipment. "Body armour vests, helmets, visors, boots, tools, food and water?"

They all nodded sleepily, yawning widely, then filed onto the minibus.

I'd chosen five of my most competent team members to come on this Task with me. By the time we reached the mined area up in the mountain, we'd have about six hours of indifferent daylight to neutralize all of the 44 mines we'd found during the last ascent.

I climbed into the minibus with the driver Clay had hired, a miserable looking bad tempered bastard, who cursed in Azeri and Armenian. The five women of the team were sitting at the back, chatting quietly before falling asleep. Yad sprawled across two seats and belched loudly.

When the bus settled into silence, all I could hear was the asthmatic drone of the engine as it churned up the steep mountainsides, the noise becoming part of the background.

My mind whirled chaotically until I forced myself to focus on the Task ahead and the problems we were likely to encounter.

Given the choice, I'd have sniped most of the mines rather than moving them. Not always everyone's choice but for me it was in the armoury of responses—and I'd enjoy the shooting. But MON-100 anti-personnel mines had 2Kg of explosives in each of them, and were usually mounted above ground as a shrapnel mine. The blast radius was wide and we'd been told that locals hunted in the woods, so that option was out.

The plan was to collect the mines, take them to a more secure location—a fairly deep depression in the ground that I'd already identified—then blow in stacks from a command wire.

If possible, I initiated each explosion at the same time of day so the locals wouldn't be scared shitless by a dirty great bang.

The process would be to identify the means of initiation, take control of the firing point a safe distance from the mine, twist the wires together to ensure I had electrical safety of the detonation. The Russian demolition dets had a screw thread on them, so usually I just unscrewed them.

As we trundled through the grey landscape, my mind drifted, as it often did, and Amira's face swam before my eyes.

She'd chosen to go to Syria without me, despite the way I'd begged her like a dog, and she'd died there. I'd loved her and I'd hated her but I couldn't let her go. I saw her in my mind all the time, I heard her voice, and I saw over and over again the moment she'd died in my arms. And in every dream and every nightmare, I could never ever save her, no matter how hard I tried—she always died.

The world was a darker place without her.

Clay's new volunteer, Arabella, was her polar opposite: vain, shallow, privileged. I'd known a lot of women like her—before I knew better, before I'd had better. She was such a stereotype—the golden girl who shopped at Harrods and only worried about her next manicure. She wore candy pink clothes and half-inch long nails. She wore false eyelashes while we were up to our knees in mud, and she smiled too much.

I thought she'd have been on the first plane home within 24 hours, but I had to admit that she'd surprised us.

I frowned, irritated that I'd been thinking about her at all.

Dawn filtered grudgingly through the minibus's dirty windows, and we ground to a halt at our mountain base camp. From here, we were hiking.

I zipped up my coat and pulled a beanie over my head, then slung my day pack over my shoulders, hitching up the fifty pounds of equipment with practised ease.

My breath steamed in the frigid air, and the team mumbled and stamped their feet.

"We know what we've got to do today," I said slowly, waiting for Yad to translate. "We're dealing 99% with ground-placed mines, so if we're lucky, there will just be a det-cord link between two mines. But if we aren't lucky, we have to expect some sort of trap switch, which will mean excavating the mine. It's possible that two or even three could be stacked on top of each other, so be extra careful."

I stared at each of them, hoping like hell they'd understood.

Military booby trap switches were usually easy to pin, which was why I let my local team do them.

But mines could be initiated by a number of fuzes, so the threat would come from VP13 seismic controller or even tripwires. And then it would be up to me.

I ran through the process, seeing it all in my mind.

We'd already marked out the safe path through the woods, so we hiked upwards, climbing steadily into the mountains as Yad gasped for breath at the back. After 20 minutes, we stopped and put on the body armour and helmets—the first red flag was just yards ahead of us.

Time to go to work.

Fazila and Gunay went first, locating and neutralizing the mines, then Ohana and Yad carried them down the mountain to our designated dems pit, while Maral and Hamida went for the next pair.

I kept an eye on all of them at each stage, but especially when they took out the fuze. Sometimes it was rusted, so I added some muscle to the process of unscrewing the damn things.

Even though the temperature was hovering just below freezing, we worked up a sweat: up and down the mountain to the dems pit, climbing higher and scrambling further with each red flag.

By the time we came to the pair of mines that had nearly killed Maral, the team needed a breather and it was time for me to earn my keep.

My gut told me that there was more to this mine than I'd seen so far—and I'd saved this nasty bastard for myself.

After I'd taken this charity job, I'd been surprised to find that the contractor world was worse resourced than the military: something I hadn't expected. Where I might have commented on being sent to war by the British Army in what amounted to an unarmoured bread van, with body armour held together by duct-tape, with half an EOD robot that worked half of the time, low ammo and no radio, it was still better organised than the NGO world.

I had the impression that Clay didn't believe me when I'd told him that, but then again, the Americans always had the best quality kit and resources—that's why my muckers had spent half our deployment thinking of ways to nick it—aka 'borrow' it with no intention of returning.

I'd been paid £35,000 a year to neutralize IEDs in a number of countries—less than the salary earned by a London Tube driver.

The pay here was a few grand more, but the likes of Maral and Ohana earned just £12,000 annually for their work. They said that was good wages.

Clay had been working his arse off to get the teams here better equipped.

I pulled off my daypack, then made sure I had all my tools where I could easily reach them. The two red flags hung limply, and even the soft sounds of the forest fell silent.

I crawled forwards on my belly, my plastic trowel and a long thin stick, my own personal weapons of mine destruction.

Carefully, I scraped the snow and dirt from the first mine, a big fat fucker anti-personnel mine. I exposed one side carefully, cursing when I found a 200gm block of TNT sandwiched between two anti-lift mechanisms with the mine sitting on top.

I held my torch between my teeth, blinking when I caught the glint of something thin and silvery.

Damn it! A trip wire. So what the fuck was it attached to?

Easing forward, I saw that the trip wire was attached to a tilt mast, with another bloody great MON-100 set into the muddy bank. And surrounding the whole friggin' mess were three smaller PMAs, anti-personnel mines—not forgetting the tricky fucker wedged in the tree.

Someone had done a very thorough job to make sure no one came through and lived to tell the tale.

Six mines, all linked, and any one of them could kill me: at best, I'd lose my hand, maybe my sight.

Civilians and soldiers outside the trade, they ask me how I do it. You don't feel in moments like that. You do whatever instinct tells you.

You survive by switching off the part that feels, by shutting down emotions. If I started to think about how very dead I could be, I couldn't complete the mission. Instead, it was a Chess game—my logic and my skill against the bomb maker's plan to destroy, and each time I made a move, I had to be sure it was the right one. Being wrong was not an option.

I lay on my stomach in the snow and frozen mud, my body slowly going numb as I grappled with the bombs. I worked methodically, solving each puzzle one at a time.

Identify.

Expose.

Extract.

Lift here, cut there, drill here: analyze, neutralize, move on.

But the cold was creeping through me and I began to lose feeling in my fingers—not a good sign; plus, the light was fading as twilight edged closer. I swore, needing something to go right. I couldn't leave this set of mines half-finished; I needed to keep going.

I yelled at Yad to bring me more light, but it was Maral who stood over me holding her flashlight—Maral who had five children.

Sweating, enduring, fighting the pain in my shoulders and neck, keeping focus, staying one step ahead of the bomb maker…

Scrape, expose, analyse, neturalize.

Over and over again—each mine a new problem. My body felt detached from me, cold taking its toll. Every few minutes I had to stop and blow on my fingers, rub them together to keep the blood flowing. It was slowing me down and so fucking frustrating.

When I removed the final det from the bomb propped in the tree, I was so exhausted that I fell to my knees then collapsed, lying face down in the mud. Maral shook my shoulder gently.

"James-*syr*," she said, her voice worried. "Okay, James-*syr*?"

I rolled over, staring up at the dark branches hanging over me and her worried face haunted in the light of her torch.

"Yeah, okay," I replied hoarsely. "Okay."

She gave me a half-smile as I sat up and examined the six neutralized devices lying next to me.

I stretched and groaned as my muscles tried to function. Maral smiled with relief and held out her hand to help me up. I moved like an old man, but there was still one further job to do.

Even as I'd been working on that last device, another part of my brain had been worrying about another problem, chewing on it like a dog with a bone.

I relied on my instinct, I had to, but it had been sharpened and honed by training. So what was it about this track through the forest? Why mine *this* path? It was steep and remote, so what was special about it?

I studied the area around me carefully, peering through the gloom. But with the poor light and thin beam from the torch, there wasn't much to see.

Almost ready to give up, I finally noticed that there was another trail, maybe an animal trail, but so close to the booby-trapped area, which could mean…

I followed the overgrown path, ignoring Yad's shouts of annoyance as I moved further into the forest, ignoring everyone, until I seemed to come to a dead-end, a high escarpment soaring in front of me with no way through or around. But the path had to lead somewhere…

And then I saw it, a narrow opening in the rock. I held the small torch in my mouth, turning sideways to fit through the crack to get inside, but it was worth the effort.

As my torch illuminated the cave, I could see boxes and boxes of ammunition that had been stored in the cave—a weapons' dump from the decades old conflict.

Or maybe not.

I looked closer—some of the crates were old and rotting, but others looked much newer.

Yad pushed his bulk in beside me, swearing in his own language at what I'd found.

"James-*syr*! You are magnificent!"

I grunted. I was glad I'd found it, but it just meant more work when my team had already performed miracles.

"We'll carry this crap down the mountain and destory it with the other devices that we've found."

Yad's expression crumpled.

"But James-*syr*, we could sell this! It's valuable! Bullets are expensive, even on the Black Market, I know this."

He backtracked hastily when he saw my frown.

"My cousin is Chief of Police. He tells me this. We could sell the bullets to them—very safe." He took one look at my face and changed his tactics again. "And the money could go to the charity. Save lots of children. Very fair!"

"Yad, this weapons' dump probably belongs to Black Marketeers—they'll be very unhappy if you try to sell it—even if it's to the police … especially to the police. They'll hunt you down. And secondly, the crap that's been lying here for seventeen, eighteen, maybe nineteen years? Some of the munitions could have decayed in that time, so it's not safe. We're going to do a burns instead and get rid of this shit."

His expression became ugly.

"No! We tell police! They'll be very happy."

I took a step back from him and rested my hand on the Smith & Wesson M&P 9 at my hip.

"This is my call, Yad, and I'm saying all this is going to be demolished. So get this shit down the hill. Now."

His eyes narrowed.

"If a man pulls a gun, he should be prepared to shoot."

"Not a problem, Yad. Not a problem. Now back the fuck away."

For a moment, he looked enraged and I thought he was going to charge at me, but then his shoulders sagged in defeat and he turned away muttering to himself.

We carried the final neutralized MON-100 mines down the mountain, the PMAs, and the boxes of munitions, Yad still warbling on about their value. I tried to keep him in eyesight the entire time because I didn't trust the bastard, but there was too much to do and too little time, and several times he disappeared from view. My spidey senses were on high alert.

Our muscles strained under the weight we carried, awkward as well as dangerous, and our head torches cast blobs of light in the darkness, following our well-trodden path, until we reached the dems pit.

I watched as the devices and boxes of bullets were placed alongside the Russian anti-personnel mines, then planned where to put the command wires.

I automatically counted the mines as I worked, but something didn't add up.

"Wait!" I shouted, turning my accusing gaze on my team. "There are only 44 MON-100 mines here. With the extra one I found today, there should be 45, so one's missing. Yad, what the fuck?"

He stared at me with calculated blankness.

"Don't know, James-*syr*."

He translated quickly and the team stared back at me, exhausted and empty-eyed as they muttered amongst themselves.

"Jesus, have we missed one?" I asked. "Check your log books. How many have each of you cleared today?"

Grumbling and obviously unhappy, the five women pulled out their logbooks. I couldn't understand their writing, but the number of marks in the *mines cleared* column was easy to read. I checked three times: 45 MON-100 mines found and carried down the hill, including the new devices and UXO that I'd found today.

But now, one mine was missing.

My suspicious gaze fell on Yad. He was the one who'd been absent when I'd called for light earlier, the one who'd argued about selling the munitions on the Black Market, but I also knew that I'd get nowhere accusing him now. Besides, I hadn't missed his boastful connection to the local Chief of Police.

And it was possible that one of the women had miscounted, but I didn't think so. They were my most trusted workers, on this Task for a reason.

Swearing uselessly, I finished laying the command wires then pulled everyone back from the perimeter, checked the position of my team twice, before detonating over 80Kg of high explosives, bullets exploding wildly, as if the Gunfight at the OK Corral was being re-enacted.

The blast would have been heard over four miles away.

We drove back to the base camp in darkness, my mind full of suspicion, the worm of mistrust burrowing through my brain.

CHAPTER 11

Arabella

Snow fell in thick swirls, covering the buildings in a blanket that softened the ugly concrete, making it almost pretty. It was the end of my second week in Nagorno Karabakh and we were snowed in for the third day running.

I'd already tidied up the office and whipped the filing into shape, but with no Tasks running, there wasn't much for me to do. But I did have a question for Clay.

He stared at me in shock.

"You want to do what?!"

I'd woken up early, anxious to make the most of the day and my determination to do good, to make a difference. So I'd decided that I needed to see what the Task teams did—I wanted to see James at work.

"You can't go on a Task," said Clay flatly. "It's too dangerous."

I stared at him mulishly.

"You send the women from the teams out—how is it different for them?"

"They're trained," he said patiently. "They've been doing this for months now."

"Then train me!"

"It's James who does the training," he said gently, "and he doesn't have time to teach you. Taking you out with him as an observer would slow them all down and potentially make things more dangerous."

"Oh," I said, deflating. "I don't want to make things harder—I just want to understand."

He smiled at me sympathetically.

"I know what you mean, I get it. It's tough being the one left behind, right? But you can help me a lot in the office, Harry. There's always a ton of paperwork and it might seem meaningless compared to what the Task teams are doing, but it's not. It gets everyone where they need to be with the equipment to keep them safe as they do their jobs." He paused then sighed. "If you really want to know what James does, I'll send you out with a Task team when we move bases in a couple of weeks. We'll be moving down to the flatlands where the risks are different—mountain terrain is too dangerous for you. But yeah, when we move on, you can go and observe." He paused, eyeing me warily. "But that does *not* mean you'll be doing anything other than paperwork!"

"Really?" I said, scared and excited at the same time.

"Yup. If that's what you want."

I wasn't sure it was, but it would be incredible to find out.

"Yes, please! Not that I don't enjoy spending time with you, Clay."

He laughed.

"Yeah, right. All that sexy paperwork—can't beat it. But you've had enough of office work—I guess you want to see the grass roots, what it's really all about."

"Well, yes. And James is kind of hot, too," I teased.

Clay's forehead crinkled.

"Are you crushing on my buddy?"

"No, just appreciating the scenery."

He couldn't stop himself grinning.

"Yeah, okay, you got me. Even I know that he's a good looking bastard."

"Do *you* have a crush on your buddy?"

"I'm a happily married man," he grinned. "So it's strictly a bromance with James."

BUT LATER THAT afternoon, Clay came up with a new plan for our third snow-day.

"The weather is too bad for the teams to go out, as you know, so I'm going down to the village school with James and Zada to talk to them about mine safety. We've de-mined all the areas we know about up here in the mountains, but there's always a chance of something being missed. This has been a very heavily mined area, so we need to teach the kids how to be safety conscious. Would you like to come?"

"Oh, a field trip! Yes, please. That would be fantastic. I'm going stir crazy up here."

I winced and smiled at him apologetically.

"Eesh, that came out worse than I meant. It's not *that* bad…"

My words petered out as I realized that I was only digging myself in deeper.

"It's okay," he laughed. "I get what you're saying. Yep, field trip in 20 minutes. Meet us at the minibus."

I hurried back to my tiny cell, slipping and sliding on the compacted ice. I wasn't keen on children—understatement—but the chance to escape our little grey fortress for a few hours was not to be missed.

I changed out of my coral snowsuit and into jeans and a thick sweater with a fleece over the top. Not my most alluring look, but at least it was warm.

Zada was also wearing jeans, but looser and less booty-hugging than mine, and her colourful silk headscarf was in place, as always.

Clay hadn't changed and wore his ever-present smile, watching, always watching as James strode to the minibus, avoiding eye-contact, as usual.

We didn't have an interpreter with us since one of the nurses at the health centre spoke good enough English to translate, Zada said, and was coming to the school to help us this afternoon.

On the drive down the mountain, Clay explained a few facts to me.

"A landmine costs between three and ten dollars, but a hundred times that to remove it. That's why so many are left behind after conflicts. No army, no government ever budgets for their removal when they lay them: they should, but they don't. Landmines inhibit refugees from returning home and prevent land being used for the country's economic regrowth in agriculture or minerals mining or whatever." His face was grim. "So the mines are left, which means that almost 10,000 children are injured by landmines every year. They go out to play with their friends and…"

He left the sentence unfinished.

"Adults are affected, too, of course, about 16,000 every year across 64 different countries around the world."

"How many landmines are we talking about?" I asked cautiously, trying to be sensitive to the appalling situation, unsure if I had the right words.

"Seventy or eighty million," Zada answered, her face tight with emotion. "Although that's really just an estimate."

I swallowed. That was a far higher figure than I would have ever guessed. James and Clay would have enough work to last ten lifetimes.

Clay sighed.

"Three years ago, a number of countries signed up to the Maputo +5 Declaration, pledging to try and make the world landmine-free by 2025. But that will take money and political will. The world is kind of short on both."

A shiver ran through me at the thought.

"Um, this is probably a stupid question," I said, biting my lip, "but why don't you just drive a tank through a minefield and blow up everything like that? I mean, I see why you can't do that in the forest, but, well, it just seems safer," I finished lamely.

Clay nodded.

"There are devices similar to that which are used sometimes, but none has 100% reliability. You still need a human element. Unfortunately. And there's a difference between a minefield which has been laid by professionals, and a 'mined area'. Those are rarely mapped and we have to rely on local knowledge to locate the target area."

"What about sniffer dogs?" I asked.

"Yes, canine units can be used to good effect."

I thought about the fat and lazy Labradors that I'd had as a child, and then the lean and hungry hounds used on the local Hunt.

"Dogs can detect vapours emitted by mines and UXO under difficult conditions and cover large areas faster than standard manual searching methods or where metal-detecting technologies fall short, but creating a man-dog team can take up to six months." He tugged at his short beard. "Most of the methods for mine detection are pretty much unchanged since the Second World War, but new methods are desperately needed. And something that had 100% reliability—that would be awesome news. I've read about all sorts of voodoo where they use bees, even rodents, both able to detect mines using scent. They're even developing bacteria that glows a fluorescent colour when it comes into contact with small amounts of explosive vapour in the soil above the landmines. That would be seriously amazing if it aids the ability to clear large areas with 100% certainty." He paused. "There are 10 million landmines in Afghanistan alone." He sighed. "Not sure any of that would work in the Falklands Isles, for example, because of vapours emitted by the peat cycle. That's probably a bridge too far right now."

James spoke for the first time.

"Humans are quicker to train. Lives are cheap."

I fell silent, beaten by the economics of the whole horrible business. I despised my father, but at least his business interests had led him here, to this lonely place, with the intention of ridding them of landmines for good, and I couldn't despise that. I understood that his sort of investment was welcome here, no matter the shaky ethics behind it.

"MRE—mine risk education—that's something I want to develop out here," said Clay. "And James is just the man for the job. Taught me everything I know," and he grinned widely.

"Do you like working with children?" I asked James curiously.

Clay laughed loudly.

"Have you *met* James? The dude doesn't like working with anyone."

"Fuck off," James muttered, but I suspected his gruff words hid a smile.

"Just remember," said Clay cheerfully, "If the world didn't suck, we'd all fall off."

"Remind me why I married you," sighed Zada. "Oh right, for your sense of humour."

"Yeah, babe. Caught you on an off day," he grinned.

The village school was a low, white building, almost hidden as it blended into the snowy roads surrounding it. But a closer examination showed that it had probably been built in the seventies and hadn't been modernized since. I'd always wondered why schools were some of the ugliest public buildings you could find—hardly starting one off with the right motivation on a miserable Monday morning.

Zada led us inside where we were met by an older woman in a nurse's uniform. Her name was Madina and she was our interpreter for the afternoon. I was glad Yad wasn't with us.

She shook hands with Clay and hugged Zada warmly. But it was her greeting of James that surprised me the most, almost running towards him, kissing both cheeks, and pumping his arm with both hands as she spoke in heavily-accented English.

News of how he'd saved Maral had spread.

"Thank you, thank you, thank you!" She panted, wiping tears from her cheeks. "Maral is the wife of my third son. She is a good girl, a good mother."

She hugged him again, and I watched with amusement as his cheeks turned pink and he tried to edge away from her enthusiasm, but she was a dauntless woman, pursuing him until he was pressed up against a wall as she pinched his cheeks, then his waist and told him he was too skinny and that he should come for dinner. She told him that heroes needed their strength.

She was right. James was a hero in dirty jeans—it was his disguise. His superpower was incredible bravery.

He was saved by the head teacher, a large, rawboned woman, severely dressed in navy-blue with flat, functional shoes. She reminded me of my old headmistress, and I quavered under her cool, hard stare, smiling guiltily as if she'd found me spraying graffiti in the teachers' lavatories. Which totally wasn't me and something I'd never condone.

We were ushered into a large hall where it seemed half the school were sitting on the worn linoleum. The children had an air of excitement that came with any break to the tedious routine of institutionalized learning.

It was fascinating to see Clay in action. He charmed and amused his audience, then rolled up his trouser leg and showed them his prosthetic.

"And this, boys and girls, is what happens when you play with landmines. My friend James, here, is going to tell you what to look out for and who to tell if you find something. And if you find a one-legged hitchhiker, don't tell him to hop in your car."

There was a confused silence.

"Huh, I don't think that translated so well. James, buddy, over to you."

James shook his head at Clay's antics, then took centre stage.

To my surprise, he made eye contact with as many of the children as he could.

He'd brought with him a range of devices that had been made safe, and explained how they'd be hidden but what signs to look for.

"It's a good idea to keep to animal tracks if you're going through the forest. If deer have been there before you, it's more likely to be safe."

He waited for Madina to translate, and I saw many of the children nodding at the wisdom of what he was saying.

"If you see wires sticking out of the ground or pieces of waxed paper that bombs often come wrapped in, walk back the way you came and then tell your teacher or a police officer. Don't ignore it—your best friend might be thanking you because you didn't keep it to yourself," and he glanced at Clay.

He invited the children to come up and see the different devices in detail and talk about how they worked. With this audience, doing his job, he was at ease. I even saw him almost smile several times.

As he knelt down to show some of the younger children what they must never, ever touch, one little boy leaned against him, patting his shoulder, and a young girl touched his non-existent hair, then giggled.

Madina smiled.

"She asks if you're very old because you have no hair."

"Yes," James deadpanned. "Very old. Ancient."

The children laughed, then the little girl pointed at me.

Madina raised her eyebrows and smiled.

"She wants to know if the lady is your girlfriend?"

James frowned and shook his head.

"No," I said quickly. "Just friends."

The little girl didn't seem to like that answer and pouted at both of us, saying something else which Madina didn't translate.

"What did she say?" I asked.

Madina sighed, an amused look on her face.

"She says that you're pretty like a princess, so you'd make a good girlfriend. She likes your hair. It's long and blonde so she wanted to know if you're Elsa and can turn the world to ice."

I laughed, only slightly embarrassed; more entertained, really. And I was well aware that my nickname at the compound was 'Ice Princess'.

I glanced at James who was watching me impassively, obviously not thrilled with the idea that these kids might assume I was his girlfriend. I felt an unrestrained desire to tease him.

Loosening my hair from its long plait, I let it hang down untamed, a wild mass of waist-length curls. Men loved my boobs, my hair and my booty, in that order. Enough of them had told me that to know it was true. Personality came a loooong way down the list. If at all.

The little girl stroked my hair with her grimy fingers, and I tried not to cringe. Several of her friends joined in, until I had half-a-dozen under-sevens crawling all over me. I kept a smile plastered on my face like a pro.

And then Clay finished off the afternoon by challenging some of the older children to a hopping race, yanking off his prosthetic and handing it to Zada to hold.

He won, and the children cheered.

James hadn't spoken to me once.

SNOW CONTINUED TO fall overnight, and the next day all the roads were impassable. Zada couldn't get down to the village, so she and Clay had retreated to their room after breakfast, presumably to practise baby-making.

She'd warmed up to me once she'd seen how much I'd helped Clay in the office, although I didn't think she was going to invite me over to paint our nails together anytime soon.

But I didn't want to sit with the other women either, or Turul and Yad, all of whom were drinking the nasty local beer and singing folk songs. Champagne and cocaine was more my style: one put me to sleep, the other kept me awake to party some more. The good old days.

The women here still eyed me with suspicion, and in turn, I didn't like the way Yad looked at me, or the sneer in his voice when he called me 'princess'. I particularly disliked the subtle insinuation that he could have any woman here and that he'd be doing me a favour if I was on his list. Yuk.

But solitude didn't suit me any better than boredom; I much preferred to be *doing*. Time to think made me depressed. And it was soooo long before I could go home. Counting down the days until I could leave didn't even begin to explain how I felt, but being busy helped pass the hours and minutes and seconds.

I sat in the office chair, spinning in circles as I stared up at the ceiling. I worked out that 12 spins made me dizzy, and 23 took me to the point of nausea.

I know, pathetic. I always managed to find a way to make myself feel bad—it was a gift.

I'd already done all my laundry, trudging through the knee-high snow and getting a good workout from the effort. I couldn't use my phone for anything, was bored of all the songs I'd downloaded, didn't have a TV to watch or even a book to read, so I decided to take a short nap until lunchtime but as I was passing the men's accommodation block, I noticed that there was a light shining through the dirt on James's window. I wondered what he was doing in there all by himself. I was desperate for something to alleviate the boredom and longed for conversation with another Brit, even if he generally seemed to stare right through me.

Most men were simple beings, but James was a puzzle I hadn't solved.

I entered the small building and tiptoed down the peeling linoleum that lined the narrow hallway, and tapped lightly on his door.

There was no answer, so I pushed the door open. I liked my own privacy, so I had no right to invade his, but curiosity overcame manners.

"Oh!"

James was sitting on the bed, his long legs stretched out and crossed at the ankle, a scowl on his face. A thick book rested on his knees. Clearly, I'd interrupted him reading.

"Sorry, I didn't think you were here."

I gazed around the bare room: ugly floral curtains and a wooden chair were the only decorations. His room was so tidy, it wasn't obvious that anyone lived here. It seemed more than military precision—the neatness was either obsessive or some sign that he didn't even want to exist. Or maybe, when your life is chaos, maybe that one small piece of control matters.

Gosh, I'd never thought that my Psychology 101 class would come in useful. [*Insert sarcasm*]

"But you came in anyway."

James's voice was flat and unemotional, just as always, but I could hear the annoyance by his tone.

"I know, it's rude," I sighed, sitting uninvited on the end of his bed so that he had to move his feet. "But I'm so bored! Everything in the office is up-to-date; I've reorganized the personnel files and read *all* the manuals and reports. I don't want to drink that horrible beer they're all enjoying; Yad gives me the creeps; and Clay and Zada are enjoying some quality time." I gave him a weak smile. "So here I am! Lucky you!"

He stared at me for a moment, then his gaze returned to his book.

"I'm busy."

"Don't be such a grouch," I said, scratching my hair and eyeing him warily.

I hated not being able to shampoo and condition it every day. Here, I had to make do with every three days. Most of the time, I wore it in a long plait down my back to keep it out of the way.

James was still frowning at me. So I stared back. I'd already worked out that his bark was worse than his bite. At least I hoped it was.

"Whatcha reading?"

When he didn't reply, I grabbed the book from him and read out a sentence.

"Do they not see the birds controlled in the atmosphere of the sky? None holds them up except Allah. Indeed in that are signs for a people who believe."

Puzzled, I turned to the book's cover.

"You're reading the *Qu'ran*? Why? Did you borrow it from Zada?"

He plucked the book from my hands as I gazed at him in surprise. I was sure he would have been reading a thriller, something like Andy McNabb.

"No," he said shortly. "It's mine."

Realization hit me.

"Oh, because of Zada's sister, right? You and her."

My words were careless and thoughtless, so I shouldn't have been surprised when sudden fury darkened his eyes, and his whole body tensed as if he was about to leap up.

"Sorry, I'm sorry," I whispered nervously, edging away from him. "I didn't mean to upset you."

"You haven't."

"Oh, but…" I waved to the book in his hand. "Why are you reading that?"

"It's a book."

"But isn't it … anti-Christian?"

"What?" he said, his lips curling in a sneer. "Like all Muslims are terrorists who support Daesh, and all black people play basketball?"

"I'm not a racist, Mr. Spears," I said stiffly, shocked by his vicious words.

"No, just ignorant and uninformed."

He raised his hand, and I honestly thought he was going to hit me, and I couldn't help jerking out of reach. But then his hand dropped back to the rough blanket he was sitting on.

"You've got lice," he said.

I blinked at him, thoroughly confused and a little afraid.

"You've got lice," he said again. "In your hair."

Then he reached over my shoulder and held my braid in front of me. My eyes widened as I saw little black specks running up and down.

Horrified, I leapt up and screamed.

"Get them off me! Get them off!"

I whirled around, feeling like I was under attack, panic overtaking me.

"Get them off! Get them off!" I shrieked, flapping my hands uselessly then tearing at my scalp.

James stood up quickly, his boots thudding onto the torn lino. When he drew a knife from his pocket, I screamed again. He yanked my plait with his left hand and with a fast slashing motion, severed it in one smooth movement.

Stunned, I stared helplessly as he grabbed my arm and hustled me out of his room and out of the building, not even pausing as he tossed my long braid into the snow like a piece of rubbish. Tears of shock and loss burned my eyes as he dragged me across the snowy courtyard and then pushed me into the kitchen.

Without a word, he slammed a hand between my shoulder blades, forcing me to bend over the sink.

I squeaked as he poured something cold over what was left of my hair. A strong smell of vinegar filled the room, and I watched open-mouthed as he sprinkled salt liberally over my head.

Then he pushed me into a chair, contemplating me carefully as I gasped in heaving breaths.

"W-what?" I stammered. "What did you do to me?"

He cocked his head on one side.

"You told me to get the lice off. So I did. No more lice."

I blinked up at him, thoroughly humiliated, but I wouldn't let him see me cry.

With trembling hands, I touched the blunt ends of my hair. No longer waist-length, it barely reached my shoulders and was dripping with vinegar.

"Vinegar dissolves the exoskeletons of the nits," he explained as tremors ran through me. "And salt kills the adult lice. Leave it on until it dries, then run a narrow-tooth comb through it. After that, you can wash it out." He turned to leave then paused. "Did you share a towel with someone?"

"No!" I spat out, horrified.

"Then you probably caught nits from the schoolkids yesterday."

James saw the dawning awareness on my face because he nodded.

"Wash all your bedding, all your clothes and towels. And don't share anything: not a brush or comb. Don't share hats or scarves, and don't share towels."

Then he strode away without looking back.

Only when I was sure he'd gone did I allow myself a few tears of anger and frustration. I stank of vinegar and my beautiful hair, my crowning glory, was gone.

Feeling sick and shaky, I headed back to my room, pulling sheets and blankets from the bed, determined to wash everything … and grabbed a comb.

I stuffed all four washing machines in the laundry room with my bedding and entire suitcase of clothes. Everything was recently washed already, but I couldn't risk that those little bastard bugs hadn't already re-infected my clothing. It all had to be washed again: even the dryclean-only dresses and silk blouses, praying that the water would be hot enough to kill, neutralize and destroy the lice and nits. And then I realized my mistake as I stood naked and shivering. I had nothing to wear—literally nothing. I could have cried with frustration at my continued stupidity.

I had no choice but to stand here freezing until the washing cycles had finished, even if that meant wearing something wet after. What choice was there? God, I'd end up with pneumonia or hypothermia or both.

I knew that Zada would lend me something, even if she was

smaller than me, but I had no way of letting her know that I needed her. Maybe she'd miss me at lunchtime and come to find me. Maybe one of the other women would come here and help. But what if it was Turul, or worse still, Yad? The gravity of my situation began to dawn on me and I shivered with fear as well as cold.

I gasped as I heard a knock on the door.

"It's James. I've brought you some clothes."

"I … I'm naked," I whispered.

"I thought you might be."

The door opened and he thrust an arm through the gap, handing over a thick jumper, olive green Army trousers and a pair of flip-flops.

"Get dressed," he ordered.

The jumper reached mid-thigh but the trousers only just fit over my hips, although they were big at the waist. The flip-flops were huge, like a pair of flippers on my feet. I'd thought that James was giving me Zada's clothes—clearly these were his.

"I'm coming in," he announced.

He pushed open the door, staring at me with a stern expression, his eyes drifting over my absurd outfit.

"What's your problem with Yad?"

That wasn't what I expected him to say. I shrugged half-heartedly.

"It's nothing really. I just don't like the way he watches me or the things he says. He hasn't really done anything," I admitted. "He gives me the creeps. Sorry."

James frowned.

"Don't be sorry. Go with your instinct—it's probably right."

"Oh!"

Again, not what I'd expected him to say.

I was still shivering, my bare feet turning blue and my hands shaking with cold. I'd never felt so low, so useless, so pointless, but then James took my comb from my trembling fingers, and started running it through my hair from the scalp to the tips, pausing occasionally to rinse off gunk.

Despite the freezing conditions, my cheeks flared with the heat of embarrassment. He stood with his chest pressed to my shoulder as he combed my hair thoroughly—presumably removing the lice and nits. God, that was disgusting! But he smelled lovely and his body was warm. It was the most comfort I'd felt in a long time.

When he'd finished, he washed the comb and poured bleach over it before handing it back to me.

"The laundry cycle finishes in 12 more minutes," he said. "You've got time to go and wash your hair." Then he pointed to the plastic bag he'd brought in with him. "There are more clean clothes in there—because now you'll need to wash the ones you're wearing."

I hugged my arms around myself as he left the room.

"Thank you," I called after him. "For everything."

He paused but didn't turn back, so I might have imagined him murmuring, "Sorry about your hair."

CHAPTER 12

James

THANK FUCK THE SNOW had cleared at last.

I'd been crawling out of my skin for the last five days—too awake, too aware, too many thoughts, memories and regrets swirling through my head. I didn't know what was worse—remembering or trying to forget.

These mountains, this land, they didn't count the minutes and hours, the days or years. I wanted to be like that—just to exist, just to be, not to think, not to dream. No emotions. No memories.

The last Task before we were snowed in had been a nightmare, and Yad made it clear every day that I hadn't won any popularity contests with him. Instead of being ultra-friendly like he used to be, he stared at me with barely restrained hostility. I couldn't give a flying fuck about that, but I did need to get up the mountain and check to see if a device had been left behind; and Yad wasn't a man I wanted to watch my back.

I really hoped that human error was the reason we'd been one landmine short when I'd done the dems. When I'd told Clay, he was hopeful that was the case, because if I didn't find it, it was incompetence at best, but at worst, it could mean that we had one of the team selling explosives to radicals or separatists or plain ole criminals. I needed to trust my team to watch my back, to watch each other's. But if someone was making a few extra bucks on the Black Market…?

I'd re-read all the log books one by one and couldn't see any obvious errors, but I wouldn't know for sure until I'd gone back and checked that all the logged mines had been removed.

Yad was definitely in my sights. Sure, he'd been friendly enough up until now and adequately competent at his job, but had he been too friendly? Too eager to help? Until he'd been absent on the last Task and Maral had stepped in. When I asked him, he said he'd been taking a leak.

I didn't trust him and I'd long suspected that his cover story of learning his English from pop songs was a bunch of bullshit, although I knew it wasn't impossible. But he had that air of being ex-military, whatever he said. I'd even began to suspect that he was former KGB. Or possibly still FSB. Yad was the obvious choice to have removed one of the mines, but in truth, it could have been any of them. Clay agreed that as soon as we had comms, he'd ask Smith, our friendly spook, to investigate.

It was interesting that Arabella had picked up on some negative vibes—she definitely didn't trust Yad. There was a lot more going on under her glossy surface than I'd given her credit for.

I hoped she wasn't too upset about her hair—it really had seemed like the best solution at the time, although maybe a little extreme. But really, I was doing her a favour. Not that she'd see it like that.

I had to wait until mid-morning before the roads were passable, then I took the team who'd been with me on the last Task back up the mountain for the third time. We swept every nook and cranny with the Vallons for hours and went over all the old ground but found nothing.

I retraced our steps to every spot where a landmine had been removed—the same number that had been logged—we hadn't missed one, we hadn't miscounted.

Which left only one conclusion: there was someone on the team I couldn't trust, and that in turn left three possibilities: the mine had been stashed far away from where we were sweeping; it had already been retrieved by a third party; or the mine had been hidden on the minibus and taken back to camp.

Yad hadn't been away from the team long enough for scenario one, but two and three were feasible. I didn't like any of the answers that I came up with. And anyway, it might not have been Yad.

Clay wasn't happy either when I told him the next day after an overnight drive back to base.

"I don't like it, bro. I don't like not being able to trust my team. Are you sure?"

He gave me a significant look. I hadn't always trusted Amira either, and I'd been wrong about her.

"I'm sure, Clay. Somewhere, two kilos of high explosives is missing. Any one of the team could have taken it while I was neutralizing that booby-trapped device."

He tugged on his scruffy beard and leaned back in his chair.

"Okay, here's what we do: I've already put out some feelers about Yad—but it'll take time to get answers—so I'm going to bring forward the move. We're heading down the mountains tomorrow."

THE NEXT DAY, we shifted operations HQ to a new location further west, close to the border with Armenia. Technically, we were still within Nagorno, but the land was disputed, and on the journey, I saw several signs for minefields. Technically, we were on a battle area clearance mission, expecting to find a mixture of explosive remnants of war, such as unexploded shells and bullets, as well as landmines. Mechanical clearance—using a damned great remote-controlled mine-roller with flails—wasn't an option because we were too close to an important road. Besides, those weren't as reliable as the human version of mine clearance. So the job was down to my team.

Our new barracks were thirteen kilometres from the minefield, in an abandoned school. Bunk beds had been installed in the old classrooms, and the school hall was our Mess.

We spent the first day sorting out our personal gear and ensuring that the equipment was securely stored in one of the school's outbuildings.

I didn't trust the locks that were already there which looked ancient and rusty, and there was always the possibility that other people still had a key.

It took me four hours to install new locks and secure everything to my satisfaction, then I dragged my weary arse into the Mess.

Most of the teams had already eaten, so it was just Clay and Arabella sitting together sipping the sweet local tea.

"James, my man, how's it going? All good?"

"Yep," I said, slumping down onto the wooden bench. "Tighter than a duck's arse."

I glanced across to see Arabella smiling into her mug.

"Good, now get some food inside you," ordered Clay.

Wearily, I turned away to glance across at the serving table, where a pan of stew sat, covered with a plastic lid, and slowly cooling as the grease formed itself into fatty lumps. I'd eaten worse.

"Stay there, I'll get it for you," said Arabella, pressing her hand onto my shoulder.

I was surprised, but for once I didn't argue. Not sure why. I wanted to argue. I wanted to tell her not to be so damned nice. It was irritating.

Clay smiled at me and winked.

"Fuck off," I muttered.

"Didn't say a word," he grinned, his defence as thin as toilet paper.

Arabella placed the plate of stew in front of me together with two thick slices of dark bread.

She was silent as I began to eat, then revealed the reason for the niceness. People always want something from you.

"I'd love to come and observe tomorrow's Task," she began.

"No," I said automatically.

"I think it would be a really useful part of my training…"

I glared up at her.

"What part of 'no' didn't you understand? The 'N' or the 'O'?"

"You're being a dick," Clay said bluntly. "Harry's keen to learn and I've already told her she can go, provided she does exactly what you say and stays at a safe distance at all times."

I started to protest.

"James, shut up and listen, brother. Harry's dad is funding this op, but all he's interested in is clearing the land as quickly as possible. It'll help *all* of us if Harry can explain to him the reason why it's not always going to be fast, the issues that hold us up. She'll be useful."

Arabella threw him a grateful smile.

"Bullshit," I said coldly. "Either of us can explain the challenges, the reality of the situation."

"Yes, but neither of us is 5'5", cute as a button, and *related* to the dude," Clay said, raising his eyebrows. "We need a Gauss, you said so yourself. Preferably two or three."

"What's a Gauss?" Arabella asked, avoiding my angry stare.

"It's a metal detector that can work at greater depths." Clay shrugged. "There's a lot of equipment on our wish list."

Arabella stared back at me.

"I'll see what I can do."

She stood up.

"What time should I be at the minibus tomorrow morning, James?"

The stare-off lasted three seconds before I decided I couldn't be bothered to fight her on this.

"Oh-five-thirty."

She nodded.

"Thank you. Goodnight, Clay. Goodnight, James."

"Night, Harry!" Clay called after her, then looked at me. "Why are you such a dick to her? She's a nice person."

I didn't even bother to look at him as I continued shovelling stew into my mouth.

"One: she doesn't belong here. Two: it's *dangerous*. Three: she doesn't belong here."

Clay grinned at me then held up three fingers.

"One: she's done a great job in the office, especially with all those pesky reports that you hate with a fiery passion. Two: she has great contacts through her old man, contacts that are going to help us get the equipment we need and potentially save lives. And three," he raised his middle finger, the universal sign of giving me the bird, "and three, seeing her get under your skin is better entertainment than a month's worth of Netflix."

"Fuck you, Clay," I growled, slamming my spoon onto the plate and splattering us both with stew. "This isn't a fucking game! Every day, there's a chance that someone is going to get hurt on a Task. Maral nearly died. It was just sheer bloody luck that you weren't writing a condolence letter to her family. Taking Arabella on a Task, even as an observer, is taking stupid chances. And as for her dad helping us, didn't you tell me he acts like he hates her? Hell, she didn't even know that she was coming here or that he'd leave her here alone for three months. *She doesn't belong here!*"

Clay's expression had grown serious.

"I hear you, brother," he said calmly. "Now hear me. Harry has worked her socks off for us, whether she expected to be here or not. She's smart and thoughtful, and she's improved our comms with Head Office. They friggin' love the PR pieces that she writes for them and says they've placed stories in all the major British news sites, as well as with Reuters."

He caught my surprised glance.

"You didn't know that, huh? I'd say that there's quite a lot about Harry that you don't know." He stood and stretched his arms. "But best of all, brother, when you talk about her, you actually sound like you care about something for a change, so she stays." His eyes burned into me. "She's going on Task with you tomorrow—look after her."

CHAPTER 13

Arabella

I DIDN'T GIVE JAMES A CHANCE to leave me behind. I'd heard him arguing with Clay the night before: I'd heard every word, but as far as I was concerned, I was going on a Task with the team and nothing was going to stop me.

I arrived at the minibus twenty minutes before James had told me to be there. I wasn't surprised to see him already loading equipment into the back.

To my surprise, he met my eyes and spoke to me directly.

"Arabella, this is dangerous work. You should stay with Clay and Zada. Seriously."

I was taken aback by the apprehension in his voice, but I was determined, too.

"I appreciate your concern, and I really don't want to add to your burden. I promise I'll do exactly as I'm told—I won't put a finger out of place. I'll do what you say, when you say it, and I won't argue. James, please," I said, softening my voice, "I really think I can be of use to you, to the Halo Trust. I may seem like a vacuous bimbo to you, but

I don't rely completely on my father for connections." He grimaced. "I won't be here forever, but let me do some good while I'm here. Let me understand. I want to understand what you do."

His expression grew chilly.

"You can't. Unless you've been me, unless you've seen what I've seen, you can never understand."

"I can try!"

He pushed his handsome face closer to mine, rage and pain darkening his ice-blue eyes.

"Unless you can consider the gross horror of seeing a dismembered body, you're not even close."

I shuddered and tried to move away from him, but he pinned me to the minibus, the cold metal biting into my clothes.

"I've been close," he said, his voice harsh. "I'm trained to think like a terrorist. Have you ever thought about that? The person making an IED only has to be lucky once. I have to be lucky all the time. I have to think how *they* think. So why would I think for one second that someone like you could possibly understand?"

I stared at him, shocked and without words. I'd begun to think of him as a man utterly devoid of emotions, but he wasn't. With his words, he'd shown me the pain and horror and darkness inside him.

But it didn't scare me. Instead, I pitied him.

And I wanted to help.

He turned away, back to his work of loading up the minibus.

I watched in silence.

Eventually, Clay arrived with Yad and the de-miners who were going on Task with James today.

I gave them a thin smile, still shaken by my run-in with a dangerous man.

Clay handed me a helmet with my name painted in white across the top and a body armour vest that was far heavier than it looked, so I nearly dropped it.

"It has blast plates in the chest," he said, looking at me seriously, "and these gloves are made of Kevlar. Wear them at all times."

"I will, I promise."

He nodded and handed me a thick pair of leather boots.

"These are too big for you, so wear them with a couple of spare pairs of socks. They're tough old Army boots. They're the best protection for your feet."

"That's so nice of you," I said seriously, taking the spare socks and heavy boots.

He gave me a warm smile.

"They're not mine. They're James's. He wanted me to give them to you. You can thank him later."

My mouth dropped open. Would I *ever* understand that man?

The other women were curious but friendly as I joined them on the minibus. Yad, on the other hand, leered at me with undisguised enthusiasm.

"English princess, I think you miss me!"

"Not enough," I said under my breath, then louder. "Oh, I'm sorry, Yad—is 'Arabella' too difficult a name for you to remember?"

I smiled so sweetly that he wasn't sure if he was being insulted or not. Instead, he grunted and sat back in his seat.

I moved up the minibus and sat down next to James. He didn't seem happy to see me, let alone have me sit next to him for the short journey.

"Can you tell me about how you assess a site where you suspect there are mines? What do you look for?"

For a moment, I thought he was going to tell me to bugger off, but he didn't.

I pulled out a small notebook and looked at him expectantly.

"It depends on the kind of site you're looking at. In the UK, there would probably be a desktop risk assessment, doing all the research on the area from existing records: conflict history of the site and surrounding area, historical and archived material from the public domain, local research including select interviews with local inhabitants where appropriate, or looking at old newspaper reports. That's especially true of areas that were heavily bombed during the Second World War, for example. I'd also look at military historic records, as well as any available historical aerial photography. From that, I'd assess the likely nature of UXO contamination, weapon features and bomb penetration depth. Then I'd make a risk assessment based on risk minimization measures." He gave me a sideways look. "That's assuming that time isn't a factor."

"And when it is? When you have to hurry?"

"Send in a robot so you can see as much as possible beforehand."

"And if you can't send in a robot?"

"Trust the team at your back and know what the fuck you're doing."

He sounded like he was running out of patience with me, but I was intrigued.

"How did you get into this … line of work? I mean, I know you were in the Army…"

He stared out the window, his eyes following the flat fields, mountains towering ominously in the distance.

"It took me seven years to become a high threat operator. That's a lot of training courses, a lot of studying. It's very physical, but a mental job, too. You have to be able to focus for long periods of time."

"Will I see that today?" I asked tentatively.

"Yes, to a certain extent. We'll have a team of five searchers who'll lead with the Vallons, the metal detectors. They'll flag the areas that need manual investigation. Both jobs need a high level of focus. It's too dangerous to take shortcuts."

I looked around at the women on the minibus—it was hard to truly understand the danger of the job they were about to do. I felt my breakfast try to climb back up my throat and swallowed hard.

"My job is to make sure everyone keeps their focus and that every safety protocol is met," James continued, watching me carefully. "It's my job to bring everyone home."

We only had a short journey to the minefield, and it was easy to spot with large signs depicting a red triangle with white writing in the local script that I couldn't read, as well as the word 'DANGER' written in broad letters above a skull and crossbones. That was *very* clear, and a shiver ran through me.

Two police cars had cordoned off the area at either end of the road next to the minefield to stop any traffic passing through.

James stepped out of the minibus with Yad, shaking hands with the police officers and pointing to the minefield, asking a few questions and showing them the area on a map.

The other women didn't seem interested in the discussions, instead chatting to each other and yawning as if they were about to go to shopping in the supermarket, but when James signalled them, they all climbed out and started to don the heavy protective clothing with which they'd all been issued.

James approached me, his face shuttered.

"Wear your PPE clothing at all times," he said. "If you're not sure where to stand that's safe, fucking find me. If I'm busy, Maral will show you. If she's busy, wait in the minibus."

As Maral heard her name, she looked up and smiled at James, throwing me a quizzical glance.

He gestured at the pile of body armour next to me and she caught the hint, helping me on with everything.

And it was really heavy! The chest piece alone weighed me down, and combined with the enormous boots that I'd been given to wear, I could barely move. Then Maral placed the helmet on my head, lowering the visor.

It was like being a deep sea diver. Immediately, the sounds around me became muffled, and my peripheral vision was severely reduced. I could only look straight ahead.

She pulled the heavy gloves onto my hands, then nodded, pleased with her work.

I plodded behind her as she donned her own protective clothing.

She also picked up a number of digging tools that she settled into a thick leather workbelt, then unpacked one of the Vallon metal detectors from its case, checked the battery, handed it to one of the other women and lined up with the searchers.

I stood well back, feeling the sweat build up on my body, despite the chilly air and piles of slushy snow that still clung to the more shady spots.

My back started to ache with a dull throb and my shoulders were bowing under the weight of the body armour. My hair was sweaty and sticky, and my breath fogged up my visor.

Nevertheless, the women in the team worked slowly and steadily, the searchers leading the way, Vallons in hand: swing, listen, concentrate, repeat; swing, listen, concentrate, repeat.

Then Dilara found something.

I found myself holding my breath as she paused, swung the Vallon, listening to the sounds. She nodded to herself and raised her hand. James was with her immediately, listening to the tell-tale bleeps through the earphones and confirming that she had indeed found something that was giving a positive reading. She placed a jaunty red flag in the ground and carefully moved on.

Maral was following, having the equally dangerous job of removing the landmine from the ground.

Taking a long, thin wooden stick, she pushed it into the soft, muddy ground cautiously, prodding carefully all around where the signal had come from.

Then she used secateurs to trim back the tough grasses and shrubs, so she could reach the landmine more easily. I'd been told that she had to be careful not to get too close in case the device was magnetized. It was a horrifying thought.

I watched, appalled and fascinated as she cleared the scrubby plants, then slowly scraped the earth away using a flat trowel, until the landmine was exposed.

At that point, she signalled to James, and he was back again, kneeling in the dirt next to her, pointing out something.

He pulled a handyman tool out of his belt and proceeded to loosen a screw on the top of the device. He paused briefly, clearly telling Maral to move back.

I wanted to close my eyes, but I couldn't. Although his visor and body armour was in place, his hands were bare, the smooth tanned skin clearly visible.

Bile rose in my throat and my hands flew to my mouth, trying not to be sick. Time ticked by slowly as he remained kneeling next to the ugly device, Maral's eyes fixed on his broad back.

When he stood up slowly and gave a thumbs up, a happy little cheer erupted from me. Well, more like a squeak than a cheer. No one else reacted except Maral, who gave me a curious look.

Out of the corner of my eye, I saw Yad watching him, squatting in the dirt like a discontented toad. Hatred sparked in his dark eyes, and a shiver of dislike forced me to stiffen my spine so he wouldn't see, wouldn't suspect that he scared me.

The hours dragged by, more dirt, more landmines, more dangerous back-breaking work.

When one of the women found something, they left the ominous red flags behind them.

Then the de-miners moved in. Bending, kneeling, sometimes lying prone to scrape soil away from scary-looking devices, carefully lifting them from the ground; while James seemed to be everywhere: supervising, encouraging, instructing, occasionally taking over a particularly difficult job.

I watched, heartsick, as James lay in the dirt, his face just inches from a device that was proving trickier than the others, a device that could kill him, as close as he was.

"That one's booby-trapped," said Yad, sounding bored. "It's designed to kill anyone trying to lift it from the ground."

I hadn't realized he'd walked up behind me and I stiffened immediately. He leaned closer, his garlic breath penetrating even through my visor.

"You have to be broken in the head to do it!" and he laughed loudly.

I walked away, even as a part of me agreed with him.

For three hours, the women continued their slow march across the minefield, and I stood in awkward awe of the work they did.

I felt incredible relief each time they took a break, stopping to drink flasks of hot, sweet tea, then rest again over their lunch break, always cheerful, always glad to relax away from the intensity of their work.

I removed my helmet but found that my own appetite had vanished.

They sat in the cool sun, legs out-stretched, joking about something, flashing quick shy smiles at James.

I could see the hero-worship on their faces and the attraction in their eyes; but none of them were brave enough to approach him.

He sat apart from the others, studying the distant mountains, lost in thought. But clearly he was more aware of his surroundings than he was letting on, because when Yad stood up, I saw James following him with his eyes.

Yad unzipped his trousers, pulled out his penis and peed in full view of the women, a golden stream steaming in the cool air. They looked disgusted but unsurprised. One of the women said something that made the others laugh, and I got the impression that they disliked him as much as I did.

When Yad walked back toward the minibus, tucking himself in, he smiled smugly when he caught me watching him.

"You want a closer look, Ice Princess?" he asked, grabbing his crotch.

"I don't have a microscope with me," I said, moving closer to the other women.

His eyes hardened and he spat in my general direction.

James shouted something in the local language and everyone fell silent. The two men eyed each other, until finally, Yad swore and slunk away to sit inside the minibus.

The tension lessened slightly but we could all see feel the violence in the air.

James took a final sour look at Yad, then stormed up to me and hissed in my ear.

"Don't wander out of my sight, understand? Not even to take a bathroom break."

I nodded quickly.

"I won't, I promise."

Frowning, he stamped away, shouting at the women to follow him.

I walked behind, tiptoeing through the dirt, feeling scared and ridiculous.

At the end of the day, James and the team had a collection of 23 ugly anti-tank mines. Ugly metal discs glinting dully in the failing light, squat and deadly.

Cold had settled into my bones that was nothing to do with the falling temperature.

How could he do this, day in, day out, knowing that each day could be his last? I understood the women's rationale better—this was a well-paid job for them in an economically depressed country. What they earned in these months of work could change their lives and those of their families for years ahead.

But why did James do it? What was his motivation? It seemed impossible to understand.

I watched from a distance as James carefully arranged the landmines in a depression in the ground, then laid a wire from them and prepared to detonate.

We all had to lie down on the other side of the road, and not look up.

The explosion shook the ground, and I almost wet myself as dust bloomed in the sky and clods of soil rained down.

I sat up slowly, pulling off my dirt-encrusted helmet with shaking hands.

Maral looked over and reached out to squeeze my arm reassuringly. "Okay?" she asked.

I nodded and gave her a weak smile.

I could only imagine how much worse it was when the explosion wasn't controlled.

James walked back toward us, his clothes covered with mud, and exhaustion etched on his face. He glanced at me.

"Now we go back to HQ and report on the area we covered, the type and number of devices we found and how we disposed of them. About an hour of paperwork."

I winced in sympathy. I'd nagged him about the paperwork almost every time he'd come back from a Task. It was obvious he loathed it, but for the first time I understood that it was a mountain to climb after a day like this.

Without asking his permission, I sat next to him again on the minibus for the short ride back to our base.

"That was … I can't even being to explain how intense today has been. The work you guys do … it's insane."

He closed his eyes and leaned his head back.

"Yep, been called that before."

"Well, not insane," I backtracked hurriedly, "but crazy. I mean, those are bombs! They could explode at any moment, and you just walk up to them." I took a breath as he opened one eye and squinted at me with bemusement on his face. "You can be such an arsehole, James, but you're a very brave one."

And for the first time, he gave me a genuine smile.

"Thanks. I think."

We didn't speak for the rest of the journey, but it was a comfortable silence.

That evening, with pent up adrenaline from the emotional rollercoaster of the day surging through me, unable to relax, unwilling to force my company on the other women who were drinking with Turul and Yad, I prowled the compound. And when that didn't help, and Clay and Zada had already retired for the night, I went to look for James.

He was the wrong man at the wrong time, but I was drawn to him. Underneath that scary, bad-tempered exterior, that aura of danger, he was a kind and thoughtful man. I'd seen him with his co-workers and I'd seen him with those schoolkids, so patient, so calm. And I'd experienced his odd brand of kindness firsthand.

I fingered my chin-length, scraggy hair with a wry smile. I'd asked him to get rid of the lice and he'd done it instantly. I could have been angry with him about that, but somehow I wasn't.

I found him on his cot-bed reading, but this time he was smoking, as well. I didn't know he was a smoker, never seen him with a cigarette before, although Yad and Turul smoked like chimneys.

James was wearing sweatpants, but his chest and feet were bare. I saw for the first time that he had a tattoo on his left pec, directly above his heart. It had been designed to look like claw marks from some huge creature. How strange—he didn't strike me as the whimsical type.

My gaze skittered across his body, drinking it in, as if at any second he'd grab a shirt and cut off my view.

I stared, my eyes growing wide at the sight of his bare arms and chest on the right side of his body. More in horror than appreciation. There were pale gashes carved into the tanned skin, around his rib cage and along his right forearm.

"Shrapnel," he said without looking at me.

I swallowed hard, the reality of his life sinking in.

But other than those scars, he looked strong and fit, although perhaps a little thin, a little pale. Except for his face, neck and hands which were tanned a golden brown. Maybe the deeper scars were on the inside.

I was surprised to see that he was wearing British Army dog tags. I knew he'd been in the Army but he definitely wasn't anymore. Odd. I wondered why he still wore them. Habit, perhaps? Or maybe just practical. I knew that the tags recorded blood type, name and serial number, as well as religious affiliation.

He took another drag on his cigarette and the fragrant scent caught in my throat. My eyes widened.

"Is that grass?"

He nodded slowly, his eyes never leaving his book.

"Is that … safe? I mean, for you. Um, I don't mean smoking in bed, although that's not safe either," I warbled on, "but for your work?"

He answered without looking up.

"We're not doing a Task tomorrow. The local Chief of Police has requested a meeting, and Clay can't say no. Political crap. The boss gave me the day off."

"The rest of the team are having beers in the Mess," I mentioned hesitantly.

"Not interested."

"Oh, well, that's fine. I just thought … whatever."

He continued to ignore me, but I was bored and lonely and on edge. If he wanted me to leave, he'd have to throw me out.

He still hadn't met my gaze, but I was used to that now. I sat on the side of his bed, staring longingly at the joint, wishing he'd offer it to me. In the end, I gave up waiting.

"Can I have some?"

He paused, turned the page, then took the blunt from his lips and passed it to me without comment, without even looking. I took a hit, feeling the sweet smoke sink into my lungs. It had been a while since I'd had grass, but the analgesic effect was immediate. My sore, tired muscles began to loosen, and the breath that I felt I'd been holding all day, finally left my lungs.

"Today was intense," I said, taking another hit before passing it back to him.

"It's either this or whiskey if I want to feel numb," said James, surprising me by speaking, "and I've given up whiskey."

The bleak honesty of his words saddened me.

I stared at his eyes as they worked their way steadily down the page of his book, those icy blue eyes that tilted cat-like, as I searched for the emotion he hid so well.

"Do you want to feel numb?"

"Yep."

His answer was brief, but I'd expected that.

"Me, too," I sighed plucking the joint from his fingers for a second time. "Can I ask you something? Why do you do it? The landmines, the bombs. I don't understand."

He shrugged, still not looking at me.

"I'm good at it."

I waited for more, but that was all he gave me.

"I'm sure you're good at lots of things."

"Then you'd be wrong."

It didn't take a genius to work out that I wasn't going to get any better answers tonight.

I turned the cover of his book face up.

"The *Qu'ran*. Again. Why are you reading that? You never really explained."

He pulled the book from my hands and stared at me for the first time.

"Maybe I'm a Muslim."

I blinked and raised my eyebrows.

"Are you?"

He hesitated, weighing up whether or not he was going to answer me. But then he surprised me again by speaking.

"I was planning to…" His words hung in the air, heavy and oppressive. "Now I'm not anything."

I glanced at his chest again.

"But … your dog tags say 'Church of England'…"

He didn't answer, just continued to stare.

"Oh!" I stuttered as realization hit me. "I see. You would have converted for her? Zada's sister."

His gaze lowered.

"Amira."

He said her name with such sadness and longing, it sounded like the loneliest word in the whole world.

"Yeah, I was going to convert to Islam," he continued. "I was having lessons … but like I said, I'm not anything now."

The significance of his words wasn't lost on me, and the grass was making him unusually talkative. I took my chance and pressed on.

"Then why are you reading the Qur'an?" I asked gently.

He shrugged.

"Because I wanted to believe what she believed. I wanted to know what she knew. She was so sure of herself, at the end. She always said Islam was a religion of peace. I couldn't see how, and I wanted answers."

"Did you get any?"

He shook his head slowly.

"No, not really. I don't think there are any. Not the ones I'm looking for."

He stared up, his gaze drilling into me. The intensity of those icy eyes was so unnerving, especially after the many, many times that he'd avoided so much as even glancing at me.

"You should go back to your room now, Bel," he said, his voice rough, a warning.

"Maybe I don't want to," I said, meeting his gaze directly. "Maybe I get lonely, too."

I leaned forward, one hand on his chest, one hand on the pillow next to his head, and I lowered my head, resting my mouth on his lips, those soft, pliable, sweet lips. I kissed him gently, peppering light kisses from one corner of his mouth to the other, smiling as his eyelids fluttered and closed.

"Thank you for looking out for me today. I didn't tell you earlier."

He didn't answer and didn't move as I trailed my hand down his chest, feeling his pulse jump beneath my fingers, but as my hand slid down to the growing erection I could see in his sweatpants, he clamped his hand on top of mine and pushed me away roughly.

"Go back to your room, Bel."

"I don't want to," I said again, sounding bolder than I felt and feeling stubborn.

He swore under his breath and stood up suddenly, grabbing my arm as if he was going to throw me out of his room.

But he didn't.

Instead, he shoved me up against the wall, pinning me there with his hips as he rained down hungry kisses on my cheeks, neck and chest.

I anchored my hands on the waistband of his sweatpants and hung on.

But then he shook me free, and without speaking he tugged my sweater and t-shirt over my head, ripped my bra from my breasts, moaning slightly as his head dropped to kiss and bite my nipples.

Startled and slightly stoned, I breathed heavily, then slowly raised my hands to brush over his head, the almost non-existent hair feeling like fur.

His hands were locked on my hips, his fingers digging into the flesh and it felt good. I felt wanted and needed. For a few seconds, I felt as if I was the centre of his world, and I loved that feeling, I craved it.

Ignored and irrelevant for so long, I finally felt like he'd noticed me.

His strong, rough hands swept up my bare back, stroking and kneading the flesh, skating over my spine, then sweeping over my skin to cup my breasts, lowering his head to them again as if he couldn't taste them enough.

Dazed but feeling brave, I reached out to touch the warm silky skin of his shoulders, surprised to see a large tattoo covering the top half of his back.

I tried to read what was inked there, but he grabbed the front of my jeans, roughly unzipping and yanking them down my legs with my panties.

I gasped and let my head thud back against the wall as his fingers probed inside me, stroking the wetness over the lips and targeting my clitoris over and over again, quickly bringing me to orgasm.

Lonely and alone for so long, over-emotional from the intensity of the day, I came hard.

As I crested, his fingers left me and he fumbled with his jeans, releasing his hard cock, purple and gleaming in the lamplight.

He hitched my leg over his hip and thrust inside, roughly stroking against the sensitive nerve endings, over and over until I was a puddle of intense sensation, barely able to stand.

He swore again, his legs stiffening as he pulled out hurriedly, and long streams of cum erupted over my stomach.

For a second, we stood there, chests heaving, the heat between us cooling quickly.

Then, without a word, he tucked himself back into his sweatpants, grabbed his t-shirt from the chair and wiped the sticky mess from my stomach. Roughly, he pulled my clothes into some semblance of order.

"You should go, Bel," he said without looking at me.

Off balance from his touch, from my orgasm, from the grass, I pushed away from the wall with shaky legs—embarrassed and humiliated—and staggered back to my tiny room, falling face down on my cot-bed and slipping into a deep, uneasy sleep as tears stained my pillow.

It was only later that I realized he'd called me 'Bel'.

CHAPTER 14

James

"Shit, for real, Clay?"

He frowned, nodding slowly.

"Yeah, the Chief of Police specially requested your presence at the meeting."

I understood the words, they just weren't making any sense. Maybe the weed had been stronger than I realized. Or maybe something else was throwing me off.

"But why? You're the Supervisor. I'm just the oily rag. Why the change since yesterday?"

"Don't know, man."

"Is this a shakedown?"

Clay's mouth twisted as he sucked on one of his damn lollipops.

"It's possible, but why ask for you to be there? That just creates another witness."

"Have you reported it back to HQ?"

"Yep. They want us to play nice until we know what's going on. For all I know, it could just be that he has additional information about mined areas."

"But that intel was requested and received months ago."

"Maybe something new has come up."

My gut was telling me that this wasn't right, but the only way to figure it out was to go along to the meeting. It was just a shame that Yad would have to be the interpreter. Turul had received an urgent phone call from his wife and had to return home. Although, now I thought about it, that phone call had interesting timing. I would have preferred Turul, but we were stuck with Yad—the Police Chief's cousin.

"We'll leave at ten-hundred-hours."

"Okay."

I started to stand, but Clay wasn't finished.

"Uh, James? I saw Harry coming out of your room late last night."

Irritated with myself, with him, with her, I waited for Clay to continue. He sighed when he saw I wasn't going to make this easy.

"Look, I'm not saying that you can't … shit, I don't know what I'm saying." He stared at me. "She's a real nice girl, James."

I stared back, folding my arms across my chest as guilt bubbled like acid inside me.

She'd offered and I'd accepted, but using her like that then throwing her out … she hadn't deserved it.

But that was all I had to offer.

Clay rubbed his forehead, staring at me.

"Let the light in, brother."

"What the fuck is that supposed to mean?"

"A sealed door makes a dark room. Open the door—you'll see more clearly in the light."

"Are you going to get to the point any time soon?" I goaded him.

He sighed.

"You gotta stop running away."

I raised my eyebrows.

"I'm not running away." I smirked at him. "I'm removing myself from an undesirable situation."

"Yeah, running away. That's what I said—except you used more syllables." His voice hardened. "Leave Harry alone."

I was pissed off for real now.

"Who I fuck is none of your fucking business. *Brother*."

His eyes darkened and anger radiated from him.

"Like I said: she's a nice girl. You're my best friend, James, but if you hurt her, I'll have to fuck you up."

"Tell *her* that," I said bitterly. "I've never met a woman I didn't hurt."

Bel's unexpected arrival in Nagorno had tossed a ticking time bomb into my crappy life. I just didn't know when it would explode.

I left his office with a snarl in my heart, something ugly inside that turned my vision blood red.

I hadn't done anything, hadn't encouraged her. One fucking hit of grass and she was all over me like yesterday's news. I'd stopped her, I'd told her to leave. But the confusion of my body wanting to fuck her warred with my brain that had reeled in shock.

I'd fucked her to feel something. And I'd fucked her to numb any feeling, to stop the throb of voices in my head. I just wanted it all to stop.

But Clay was right—Bel was a good person, and I'd treated her like shit.

I wanted to hit something, hurt something, destroy something the way I'd been destroyed.

It was too many emotions when I'd refused to feel for so long. My brain ached, and I didn't know if I was angry, frustrated or just too fucked in the head to know which way was up.

Fighting with Clay was shit. We didn't fight.

Resentment against Arabella grew disproportionately, to the point that when I saw her crossing the compound, I had to back the fuck away.

"James!" she called. "James!"

"I'm busy," I snapped from between clenched teeth.

"I'll leave you alone, I promise," she said, stepping toward me. "I just wanted to let you know that three Gauss metal detectors will be delivered by the end of the day."

I gaped at her.

"Dad's contacts," she said with a shrug as if getting hold of three £2,000 devices and having them delivered to the armpit of the world in two days was no big deal. The Trust had been promising them to us for months.

Her expression turned cool.

"And I want to apologize for yesterday. I was wrong to come on to you. You'd be within your rights to report me for harassment—if it had been the other way around, well…" She bit her lip. "It was crass and I hope that you'll accept my apology so we can continue to work together in a professional manner."

She didn't even blush while she made her little speech. The Ice Princess was cool, the gaze of her dark blue eyes clear and direct.

My anger cooled little by little as guilt took its place again. I had to acknowledge that I'd been in the wrong, too. If I hadn't been working my way towards being stoned, I'd have slung her out sooner. She wouldn't have been allowed to come within ten feet of my mouth, or to touch my chest, or…

FUCK! This woman was driving me insane.

"Apology accepted," I muttered.

"Thank you," she called after me as I strode away.

Jesus. She was thanking me for treating her like shit! What was wrong with the woman?

An hour later, I walked up to the minibus, surprised to find that Yad had already arrived. He was never on time, always the last to appear, usually unwashed, stinking of the previous night's beer.

Today, there was a malevolent leer on his face, an expression that said he knew something to his advantage and he wasn't going to share.

"James-*syr*," he said, his lips curling around my name.

I nodded, but didn't speak.

Clay arrived looking uncharacteristically on edge, but whether that was because of me or Yad, I couldn't say.

Poor bastard—I wouldn't want to be in his shoes, um, shoe.

Clay reversed the minibus out of the compound and followed Yad's instructions to the police station, positioned at the other side of the small town.

As Clay parked the minibus outside, my gut said that we were being set up.

The feeling intensified when Yad walked up to one of the guards outside and slapped him on the back in a way that established they knew each other.

In that moment, all my annoyance with Clay's earlier comments faded.

"I don't like this," I told him. "Things are about to go tits up."

He nodded.

"Getting those vibes, too, brother."

I loosened my pistol in its holster. Clay did the same, and we both went into threat triage mode. I checked the roofline of the police station and surrounding shops for snipers. Maybe unlikely, but better to know than be surprised with your thumb up your arse.

Clay had parked the minibus with the nose pointing out so we could effect a quick getaway, although how quick we'd be in that piece of junk was another issue.

"I think I should go back to the compound," I said out of the corner of my mouth. "We've left the women unprotected."

Clay shook his head.

"Not quite. Maral has her rifle, and Harry is armed, too."

I glanced at him in surprise.

"She is?"

He gave me a small smile.

"She says she's been using a shotgun since she was eight. She convinced me that she knows enough not to shoot herself in the foot."

I shook my head. Would that woman ever stop surprising me?

Clay looked at me seriously.

"I told her that if we're not back by eleven-hundred hours, to call Halo HQ in the UK, take the truck and leave with Zada and the rest of the team. Head for Baku."

"That's more than 500 miles through the mountains!"

"Yep, but it's their best bet," he breathed out through his nose.

"Yerevan's closer."

"They can't cross into Armenia—Zada and Harry are the only ones with passports. Baku is pretty much their only chance."

"Shit, I don't like this," I muttered, staring through the windscreen at Yad who was gesturing us forwards impatiently.

Clay's face was impassive.

"Let's go play nice with the police officers," he said.

"And if they want us to hand over our side arms?"

"You wearing your SIG, too?" he asked quietly.

"Yep."

I had a SIG Sauer P232, a semi-automatic, in an ankle strap holster: slim, easily-concealed, relatively light weight. Only James Bond wannabes preferred the similarly sized Walther PPK.

He nodded and glanced down at his prosthetic. I happened to know that it hid a matching pair of utility-knife bayonets with seven inch blades.

It wasn't much if we had to fight our way out, but better than nothing.

Expect the worst, hope for the best.

Yeah, well, me and hope weren't what you'd call close friends.

Reluctantly, I followed Clay into the police station.

We were led through the utilitarian building and into the Chief's private office which was only slightly less worn out than the rest of the rooms we passed.

I wasn't happy that we saw three police officers armed with PP-2000 Russian submachine guns en route.

We weren't asked to check our sidearms either, and I wasn't sure if that was a good thing or not. If we were armed—and I guessed that had been caught on CCTV—if we later turned up dead, it would be easier to say we'd pulled a weapon first.

My defences were on full alert when the Chief greeted Yad like a long lost brother, hugging him and kissing him on both cheeks.

Definitely not a good start.

Yad shot an evil grin over his shoulder.

"Police Chief Elnur Kurdov, my cousin."

We were so fucked.

There were three seats in front of the Chief's desk. Clay sat nearest the door and Yad sat one seat over leaving an empty chair in the middle for me. Where I'd be pinned in. Yeah, but no.

Yad gestured impatiently to the empty space, but instead, I went to stand with my back to the wall, so I could see the window, the door, and all the occupants of the room at the same time.

Clay caught on fast.

"Don't mind him," he said with a wide smile. "It's his PTSD—he gets crazy in small rooms with people he doesn't know. He's not dangerous … unless he gets upset."

Yad frowned, throwing worried glances at me, his eyes faltering at the pistol by my side. On the Chief's prompt, he translated what Clay had said, which meant I had two of them throwing angry, anxious glances at me.

I was wearing my mirrored aviator sunglasses so they couldn't see my eyes. Something else to unnerve them. And right now, we needed every advantage we could squeeze out.

Yad and the Chief had a long, unhurried discussion where nothing was translated but they gestured between me and Clay several times.

Then the Chief leaned back and pulled out a cigar. I could tell that Yad was annoyed that he wasn't the one who got to blow smoke in our faces.

"My cousin … apologies … I mean Chief Kurdov," he began. "He is very grateful that you have come to his town to get rid of the landmines. The government," and he spat on the floor, "say they have no money to help. So this is a big problem."

So far so bullshit. Bel's dad, Sir Reginald, was footing the bill from Halo Trust, so our work wasn't costing the area anything. In fact, we were bringing money in because of the wages paid to the teams and money spent on provisions.

The longer he talked, the more it felt like a shakedown.

Yad glanced at the Chief who waved at him to continue.

"We are a very poor country," he said, trying to smile ingratiatingly, but failing by a country mile.

I blamed his dentist.

"And there is much crime. Our valiant police," and he gestured at his cousin, "need to be able to protect the people." He leaned forward. "We need guns and ammunition. Or we need the explosives that you are blowing up. You can see why I was unhappy. It was a great waste." And he shook his head sadly. "It would be much better if you handed over your finds to us, where everything can be…" he searched for the word then smiled triumphantly: "recycled!"

So that was it. They wanted the mines to sell on the Black Market.

Clay nodded thoughtfully as if seriously considering the request.

"It's a difficult situation," he agreed, stroking his beard.

Yad looked relieved as he translated.

"Very difficult, but you see here's the problem, my friend: these mines have been in the ground for years—some as long as two decades—so they're unstable. The same goes for any ammo found—it deteriorates if it's not stored properly." He shook his head sadly, going for his Oscar. "I couldn't sleep nights if I thought the valiant Nagorno police staff were handling unstable explosives, or trying to defend the streets with defective ammunition. I couldn't live with myself," and he let out a long sigh.

Yad's frown as he concentrated on the words turned into a scowl, and the Chief didn't seem happy either, spitting out a stream of words that made Yad cringe.

"Chief Kurdov says we will take responsibility. It is not your problem."

Clay nodded sympathetically.

"That's mighty generous of the Chief, but it's against Trust policy. I'd lose my job, which means all the teams would be laid off, which means there'd be no more de-mining in Nagorno. You see the problem, Chief Kurdov," and he stared across the table.

The Chief stared back, then shot some more words at Yad.

"We will share half the profits, like gentlemen," said Yad, licking his lips.

Clay smiled thinly.

"No can do. It would affect my pension back in the US."

Yad wasn't sure how to interpret that, but the word 'no' had been clear enough for the Chief.

He stood up, pointing his finger at Clay, jabbing it toward me while Yad translated hurriedly.

"He says you are guests in our country and it is better to do as we say. You must hand over anything you find. I mean, *everything* you find. You will have a police escort on every Task from this day."

Clay wasn't rattled even as I inched my hand toward the pistol on my hip.

"I'll relay your request to the Trust, but I'll be advising that they close down the entire operation, and I'm 100% sure that they'll follow my advice." He leaned forward to make the point clear as his voice turned sub-zero. "Which means no more de-mining, which means no investment from coal companies, which means *your* government is going to be very damn pissed at *you*."

Inwardly, I was applauding Clay. Outwardly, I was ready to reinforce his words with bullets.

The Chief and Clay stared at each other while Yad twitched nervously in his seat.

Then without another word, the Chief stood up and marched out of the room. Yad blinked rapidly, then followed him like a well-trained puppy, turning at the door.

"You wait!" he said, then shut the door behind him.

Clay turned to me with an ironic smile.

"That went well."

"Yeah, I think they just crossed us off their Christmas card list."

Clay laughed.

"They're Muslims, James."

"So? That just makes me right."

He gave me a wide smile then stood up.

"I'm thinking we should get the flock out of here, brother."

"Yeah. I'm liking the idea of climbing out the window, sneaking around to the front, and driving like hell."

"Great plan," said Clay, already opening the blind fully.

There were bars on the window.

Clay glanced back at me.

"How quickly can you pick that lock?"

"Two minutes, maybe less."

Clay nodded.

"Interesting education you had, James. Make it less."

The lock was old and uncomplicated, but hard to open because getting the angle was tricky.

All I needed was a couple of paperclips, my utility knife, and something to use as a torque wrench. I scanned the contents of the Chief's desk and found a metal letter opener that was perfect for the job.

The bars opened in 38 seconds.

"Life skills," I said to Clay who was shaking his head.

"You worry me, James. Now let's get the heck out of here."

We slipped out of the window and strolled around to the minibus. The police officers on duty gave us a bored look, but since no one had told them to stop us from leaving, they just ignored us.

This could be the end of our work in Nagorno, which would suck for the people who lived here and the women whose wages were paid by the Trust, but the Chief had bitten off more than he could chew. The Trust had powerful friends in government—we just had to get a message to them.

"You drive," said Clay. "I need to use the Sat Phone and give them the sitrep."

As he relayed the situation report to HQ, I drove us back to the compound, keeping a careful eye on the rear view.

But I didn't hear any police sirens and we weren't followed.

I smiled to myself when I saw Bel and Maral guarding the entrance, one with an assault rifle, one with an ancient shotgun.

Once again, Bel had surprised me.

When she saw it was us, she threw a sloppy salute, then smiled and waved.

"You know how to shoot that thing?" I asked, pointing at the double-barrelled shotgun.

Bel gave me a wide smile.

"Of course! We had pheasant shoots on the family estate when I was a child."

I wondered if she meant 'peasants'.

"And I have good news," she said, cracking open her borrowed double-barrel shotgun and retrieving the two shells so it was safe, "the Gauss's have arrived."

She pointed over her shoulder, and I nearly had a coronary when two handy-looking men emerged from the back of the school, both armed with semi-automatics.

"That's Desmond and Artur," she smiled. "Their company were delivering the Gauss's and when they heard about our predicament, they volunteered to stay and help guard us for a few days. Oh, and they're ex-special forces from France. *Ooh la la!* Aren't they darlings?"

More like double-hard bastards than darlings, but perspective is everything.

"Good to have you on board," said Clay, shaking their hands. "Team meeting in the Mess."

He quickly explained what had happened, and that HQ had told us that they'd be speaking to their contact in the government immediately. In the meantime, we were to hold tight, but wouldn't go on any Tasks until assurances had been given. Furthermore, from tonight onwards, we'd be patrolling the premises at night—armed. Having ex-special forces on the team was going to be a massive help, and they agreed to take the first watch.

Clay watched them go, smiling like the happy bastard he was: he had three shiny new Gauss detectors for the teams, and the help of some real muscle and fire-power.

"Harry, you are one amazing woman. I don't know how you did it, and maybe I don't want to know how you did it, but you've pulled off a minor miracle. Thank you."

"Entirely my pleasure," she said, then glanced at me quickly. "And in case you were wondering, I didn't even have to sleep with anyone to do it."

CHAPTER 15

Arabella

The knock at my door came late that night and I was immediately on edge.

"Yes?" I called, without taking a step to open it.

"It's James," he said, his voice muffled. "Um, I just wanted to thank you for getting the Gauss's, and…"

I opened the door a crack and found James staring back at me in surprise.

"Uh, so I just wanted to thank you. We've been trying to get hold of them for months but there wasn't enough money…"

His words trailed off.

"You're welcome. But it's my father you need to thank, not me."

I started to shut the door, but he stopped me.

"Bel, I owe you an apology. I was a total arsehole and I'm sorry. You didn't deserve the way I treated you." He paused, forcing the words out painfully.

But that was the problem, wasn't it? Deep down I felt that I *did* deserve to be treated like shit. I'd never known anything different from men—certainly my father or brother, and I'd never had anything that you could classify a relationship. I had hookups, not relationships, never a boyfriend.

I shrugged it off.

"Apology accepted. You're off the hook, James."

He closed his eyes and grimaced as if he was in pain.

"Bel, I mean it. You're beautiful and clever and kind, and I'm stupid and fucked up. You don't deserve to get caught up in my shit."

Anger began to build inside me.

"Well, James, maybe I'm a little tired of people telling me what I do and don't deserve. If I recall correctly, it was me who seduced you, and I got a very nice orgasm out of it, so thank you for that. And as for the Gauss's, they're not just for you—they're for every woman on the team who puts their life on the line each time they go on Task. So please, don't think you need to go charging off on your white horse—I don't need a knight in shining armour—I just wanted a nice hard fuck. Goodnight."

I was panting heavily when James's eyes widened and his cheeks flushed. I'd been about to slam the door on him, but suddenly it was our bodies that were slamming together and I couldn't tell who moved first.

His hands were in my hair, his mouth on my lips, his tongue searching and probing as my hands roved over his back, his arms, his shoulders, his chest, sliding under his sweater, finding warm, silky skin.

I groaned, then tugged him into my room, our bodies still joined. He kicked the door shut as we fell onto my narrow bed, a tangle of arms and legs, clothes flying as we stripped ourselves bare.

"I don't have a condom," he hissed as my hands closed over his thick, hot shaft.

"I don't care," I gasped. "Come on my stomach again. I don't care, just … just do it!"

He thrust inside me with one smooth movement and I cried out, my voice lost as he swallowed my screams with his mouth.

I dug my short nails into the thick globes of his muscled backside, hooking my ankles behind him, trapping him inside as he ground against me.

I clung to him as his body covered mine again and again, his face pressed into my neck, his breathing hoarse in my ears.

Then, the sudden explosive pleasure detonated where our bodies were joined, an electrical charge sparking through me that annihilated my senses. I cried out with blind pleasure. The sheer joy of James, thick inside me.

My spine arched, pulling him deeper inside and he hissed, only just managing to pull out at the last second, grabbing his own dick as it spurted across my chest, working it to pull the last few drops of enjoyment from his own body.

The sight of him like that, gripping his pulsing dick, his eyes closed in painful pleasure, it sent another wave rolling through me like thunder.

With his orgasm coating my stomach, he collapsed next to me, his body pressed against mine on the narrow and uncomfortable cot-bed.

As our panting breaths slowed, I closed my eyes, letting my mind drift, refusing to think—only tasting, only feeling, emotions blunted but raw. Just me and him. I refused to feel ashamed of this sudden intimacy.

I'd never had my world rocked by a lover, not like this, not with the sweat cooling on our bodies. He was a jungle cat, a snarling scrappy street dog, moody and solitary, a dangerous, hostile look in his eyes that made people avoid him.

But not me. I wasn't smart enough to stay away.

This man. This wonderful complex man. Understanding him was like learning origami—each new fold created a new shape, and I had to keep folding and unfolding until the true shape was revealed. I still didn't know what that might be.

I wanted so much for this to be real, to be more than sex. But if it was just mutual release, it was good enough for me to want more of it. Much more.

But moments later, James swung his legs from the bed, dressed quickly and parted in silence with a swift look that I couldn't interpret.

It looked a lot like regret and his silence held so many secrets.

What is it about women that make us want to fix men who are broken?

The next morning at breakfast, we were back to the polite coolness of colleagues who didn't particularly like each other, causing Clay to look at us with concern.

Yad slunk back to the compound shortly afterwards, sullen and morose but obedient, eyeing our two new bodyguards with concern. By the afternoon, the Tasks resumed.

Desmond and Artur offered to stay for another 48 hours—72 maximum—but agreed that the immediate crisis seemed to be over.

Their recommendation, however, was to get the hell out of Dodge. The Trust HQ, however, were involved in intense negotiations and asked us to stay put unless we felt our safety was compromised.

Clay agreed to stay but only after a plan for immediate e-vac was arranged, should we need it.

James avoided me for the rest of the day, but that night, and the night after, and the night after that, he came to my room.

We fucked furiously, conjuring heat and passion in seconds, flaring with a dangerous edge as I recklessly poured fuel on the flames, until we both exploded. Then in silence, he left again. We never spoke.

The sex was hot, scalding, frenzied and unstable. We explored each other's bodies intimately. We fucked in just about every way possible, testing ourselves with our limits for pleasure, until there was no part of my body he hadn't claimed. I loved it and I hated it. I felt glorious, and then he left. Afterwards, I felt empty and used.

Each day, the torture increased a little more, until one evening, I'd had enough. I decided to go to his room to have it out with him. I wanted more. I wanted … well, a conversation would be a nice start.

James was a hero, a decorated soldier with the medals to prove it. He was also grieving but keeping his feelings locked away. Neither of which translated well into a relationship with me.

I was surprised to find the door to his room unlocked. It wasn't like him at all. Usually, he was secretive and paranoid, never careless. It made me nervous.

I stepped inside, knowing that he'd hate me being in here without him.

My mouth dried when I saw a small photograph in a frame by his bed. It hadn't been there before. Or maybe it was but I hadn't noticed it. I definitely noticed it now.

It showed a beautiful young woman with long dark hair and dark eyes. She was smiling at the camera, her eyes crinkling with happiness. A smaller picture tucked into the frame showed the same woman in a colourful *hijab*. When I looked closer, I could see the backdrop of a ruined wasteland city behind her.

The likeness to Zada was so obvious, and my heart sank. The man I allowed to possess my body every night was still in love with her—Amira—this dead woman.

I heard the floor creak and knew that James had entered the room. I could sense him behind me, and I was afraid to turn around and see his anger, to see him comparing me with her and finding me lacking, again.

I held the photograph carefully.

"You never talk about her," I said softly, and even I could hear the empty ache in my voice.

"We never talk at all," he answered, his tone flat.

But he didn't sound angry, so I turned around to look at him. He was watching me carefully.

"She was very beautiful," I said, my throat cracking.

"Yes, she was."

"I'm sorry you lost her. Zada's told me a little about her—she sounds amazing."

His lips pressed together.

"You must have loved her very much."

"I wanted to marry her," he said, his voice harsh.

It hurt to hear the words.

I took a quick breath then moved towards him, pressing my hand over his chest, feeling the muscles and warmth through his t-shirt.

"I think I understand your tattoo now. Her death ripped out your heart."

He didn't answer.

"But it's still there, James," I pleaded. "When I lay my head on your chest, I can hear it beating. When I touch you, I can feel it."

I reached up to stroke my fingers over the sharp angles of his cheekbones, to allow myself the guilty pleasure of touching him because I wanted to.

He closed the door behind him and led me to his bed.

We made love, or had sex, depending on your point of view, and it was amazing. It was always amazing.

Usually, at this point, with the sweat still drying on our bodies, James would leave. But this time I was in his bed, and I made no move to go. If he wanted me gone, he'd have to tell me with words.

I was lying next to a man, glowing from sex, a man I could well be falling in love with, a man who'd just admitted to me that he was still in love with his dead fiancée, a man who was possibly even more broken than I was, a man who defused landmines for a living—life was turning out to be very complicated.

A strange alchemy of empathy and jealousy filled me—how could I compete with a dead woman? I couldn't. I never would. She'd always be young, always beautiful, perfect for ever, frozen in time. And me … I was far from perfect.

Was I accepting second best for the rest of my life? Just because I was used to it from my father didn't mean I liked it. Could I accept it from James?

Amira was so beautiful she glowed. I could see that from the photograph. She looked happy, even with the chaos of a broken city behind her; she looked competent and capable.

Maybe in an alternate universe, I could have been her.

Probably not.

I was incompetent and incapable.

Insecurity arrived like the ghost at the feast.

When James slept, I whispered the words I needed to say.

"Loving me doesn't mean you love Amira any less."

But my own inner voice answered me instead.

He never said he loved you at all.

CHAPTER 16

James

We worked to clear the minefield for three more days, long hours of dirt and danger.

Yad was around, sulky and bad tempered, putting everyone's nerves on edge. Turul returned, but he wasn't happy about it, and appeared worried and anxious, as if he was waiting for something bad to happen. Both Clay and I tried to talk to him, but he just shook his head and walked away.

Artur and Desmond had used up all the leeway they'd been given and had to leave for their next assignment. They strongly advised us to leave, too.

But there was work to do.

We settled into an even rhythm, but then ten days after our stand-off with Chief Kurdov, another mine went missing.

I'd just finished laying the command wire to blow all the anti-tank landmines and PMAs that we'd found in one final fireworks display, before moving on to another mined area ten miles down the road.

"Fuck!" I snarled, counting and recounting the mines.

Yep, definitely one missing.

Yad's expression was too blank, too carefully controlled, and I knew that he'd taken and hidden another MON-100 somewhere. I also knew that beating the shit out of him to get the truth would land me in jail—and not the kind where the British Embassy would be able to get to me before I disappeared or was found dead.

Everyone on the minibus knew that there was a mine missing, and the women studiously ignored Yad, whispering worriedly amongst themselves.

When I got back to the compound, I told Clay what had happened. He sighed and tugged his beard.

"We can't let this happen again. I'm replacing the entire team."

I nodded, knowing it was the right decision, but I felt bad for the teams who'd worked so hard—women who'd put their lives on the line day after day without complaint or question.

Being a suspicious bastard sucked.

"I'll get Harry to pack up the office today and I'll make a call to headquarters to see if they can find us another terp. We can make do with just Turul for a couple of days, but after that, he'll have to go, too."

At that moment, Bel's blonde head peeped around the office door.

"Do you need me to come back later?" she asked, glancing at me briefly then focusing on Clay when she saw us together.

She didn't meet my eyes, which was probably just as well. Ignoring each other in daylight worked for us.

"Nah, you're good, Harry. Come on in. I've got plenty of work for you."

"Oh goody!" she smiled with a roll of her eyes. "Just what I always wanted."

Clay raised an eyebrow then grinned.

"Ya see how it's done, James? You catch more flies with honey."

"Who wants to be fly-blown?" I grumbled. "So, are you going to talk to the team? Do you want me to tell Yad he's off the clock?"

Arabella's eyes widened.

"You're firing Yad? I can't say I'm sorry after what he did and the way he behaved towards me, because I…"

Clay's eyes narrowed, a frown appearing on his face.

"What did Yad do to you?"

She blinked rapidly, her gaze darting between us.

"Oh, well … I just think he's a bit of a creep, all the women do, but we can put up with that. The business with his cousin, well, that's different."

Clay squinted at her thoughtfully, then his gaze drifted to me.

"You know what she's talking about, brother?"

I nodded.

"Bel … Arabella said Yad made her uncomfortable. I told her to stay away from him."

"And this happened when exactly?" Clay questioned. "Why wasn't I informed? Has he done something to you? Said something?"

Bel folded her arms across her chest.

"Look, it's not a big deal. Men see the blonde hair and big boobs and they're always making remarks. If every one of them was fired, there wouldn't be any bankers left in London."

I felt the unusual sensation of wanting to smile, but Clay beat me to it, barking out a laugh.

"Well, Yad won't be a problem for much longer, Harry. We're moving on tomorrow and we'll be changing teams. Only Turul is coming with us."

Bel chewed her lips.

"So, it's because of the missing mines not because of me?"

Clay smiled.

"Let's just say it doesn't change my decision any."

I walked out of the office, muttering about doing an equipment check before we left. The tools were locked up at night, but I wanted to make sure everything was accounted for and nothing walked while we were packing up.

Yad didn't take being fired well.

When I heard his bellows across the compound, I jogged over to give Clay backup.

Clay was one of the most laidback people I'd ever met, always smiling, always upbeat, always chewing on something sugary, and with a nauseating love for the human species, but seeing him nose-to-nose with Yad reminded me that he was also a former US Marine, a tough motherfucker, and no one pissed on his parade.

Seeing me arriving on the scene, Yad swore loudly and strode off, his hands balled into fists.

Clay's body relaxed but he followed Yad with his eyes.

"Looks like he took it well," I said.

"Pissed he's losing his job, but can't blame a man for that even though we know he's a lying bastard." He shook his head. "And keep an eye on Harry."

My shoulders tensed.

"Any specific threat?"

"No, just a hunch."

CHAPTER 17

Arabella

I COULDN'T SAY I HAD A BAD CONSCIENCE about Yad, especially after the business with his cousin. Dickheads like him thought they could get away with anything, but in my case, it really just had been a case of the creeps. The suspicion that he was selling mines on the Black Market just cemented his creepoid factor. I wasn't sorry I wouldn't have to see him anymore.

I did feel bad for the women on the de-mining teams. I'd seen them return with James after a Task, just as tired and dirty and drained as him. They put my life of luxury to shame. We all have our trials: mine was to be damned with a lack of love, whilst suffering excessive wealth. At least I was aware of my flaws.

For now, I divided my life into days filled with hard, rewarding work, and nights of lust and obscene pleasure with a man who may or may not care about me.

I sighed, pushing the thought away, as always, and spent the day loading files into boxes, taking down the maps, and putting the coloured tacks back in their container. By the time the sun began to sink behind the distant mountains, I felt grimy and tired, my shoulder muscles aching from stooping and carrying boxes.

I was heading for my room, when Maral sidled up to me. I gave her a cautious smile. We'd become more friendly since Clay had put us in charge of protecting the compound together the day he and James had gone to the police station, but because we lacked a means of communication, we hadn't become really close.

"Paddy," she said, smiling at me then pointing toward the Mess hall.

"Um, sorry?"

"Paddy," she said again, then mimed drinking and eating.

My mouth dropped open when she broke out some moves from *Saturday Night Fever*.

"Paddy!" she said again, pointing insistently at the Mess.

Then I got it.

"Oh, *party!* You're having a party?"

She nodded excitedly, evidently relieved that I wasn't as thick as I looked.

"Well, um, that sounds … fabulous! Okay … I'll see you later."

I nodded and smiled and pointed at the old school hall where we usually ate our meals.

She said something else in her own language and left.

A warm glow of something that might have been happiness spread through me. I'd been invited to the teams' farewell party—not because I was rich, or popular, or because someone thought I'd be a good shag, but for myself, for me.

I gazed around at the muddy compound of ugly buildings, ringed by austere, utilitarian apartment blocks, and felt a tingle of regret.

I'd been so lost, so untethered, but coming to a place so few cared about, I'd found something precious.

And with that thought, I headed to my room to dig out a pair of jeans to party, Azerbaijan-style.

I made a little extra effort with my outfit and wore makeup for the first time in six weeks. I even put on a pair of high-heeled boots to go with my jeans, and a bright pink, long-sleeved t-shirt and lippy to match.

It was the kind of thing I'd wear back in the UK to do grocery shopping in Waitrose, but I thought less would probably be more out here.

Of course, when I walked into the Mess hall, I realized that I'd got it horribly wrong. An explosion of colour filled the room. Women that I'd only seen in drab green and mud brown were wearing bright embroidered ethnic blouses, sparkles, spangles, sequins, and had gone to town on their makeup with false eyelashes fluttering madly and glossed red lips.

I was woefully underdressed by comparison, but for once, I didn't mind not getting it right.

Maral spotted me through the group of women drinking and dancing, ducking around Turul who was attempting some sort of Cossack moves and landing with a thud on his well-padded backside.

She grabbed my arm and pulled me toward the centre of the group, pushing a bottle of beer into my hand, then yelled something at the DJ, a woman who was in charge of the CD player, and the international anthem of women everywhere started pouring from the speakers: *It's Raining Men*.

It didn't matter that we didn't speak the same language, that we didn't follow the same religion, that I had blonde hair and blue eyes, and she had black hair and brown eyes; it didn't matter that I was rich and she was poor. Nothing mattered but here and now, this moment of shared joy. We danced because we could, because we felt silly and happy, and in our tiny world of forgotten people, there was nowhere else we wanted to be.

Zada joined us, surprising me with a quick hug, and we worked our way through an entire eighties catalogue and then juddered into the twenty-first century with some awful Euro-pop, possibly Russian, and I decided to take a break.

Tipsy from my third bottle of local beer, I needed to pee urgently, but when I turned, I bumped into a wall that was surprisingly warm and smelled like laundry soap.

"James!" I giggled, as my new-found friends whistled and cat-called at us, gyrating their hips lecherously.

I turned and waved as they made kissy faces and called his name, urging James to come and dance with them.

I didn't think they knew that we spent our nights together, but then again, the walls were thin and privacy was a luxury.

"Having fun?" he asked, raising an eyebrow.

"Surprisingly, yes. I didn't think they liked me, but we bonded over *I Will Survive* and vintage Kylie."

A small frown appeared.

"Why did you think they didn't like you?"

Eh, not what I'd wanted him to ask.

"Most women don't," I shrugged. "Are you going to dance?"

I was teasing but he reacted like I'd jabbed him with a cattle prod.

"No!" he snorted and turned away.

I watched him, standing with the others, but still alone.

Zada slipped her arm through mine as she laughed at his retreating back.

"You're good for him," she stated simply. "I sometimes think we're too … careful around him, me and Clay. But you don't do that. You're normal with him, you tease him. He needs that. And he likes you."

I blinked rapidly. Did he like me? It was hard to tell since we barely spoke. But Zada knew him better than I did. I smiled at her and forced myself to keep the tone light.

"Really? That's him liking me? I can't imagine what he'd be like if he didn't like someone."

She shook her head slowly, giving me a knowing look.

"I don't think you want to find out, but it's not something you need to worry about either. I know that you're sleeping with him. That's not what bothers me. Look, Harry, the thing you need to understand about James is…"

"Ladies!" interrupted Clay with a happy shout. "Why so serious? We're here to par-ty!" and he grabbed his wife's hand. "I'm a demon on the dancefloor."

He twirled her around and dipped her into a Hollywood hold, dropping the lightest of kisses on her lips.

Envy tugged at my heart, and I despised myself for it. Zada and Clay deserved their happiness. They'd suffered through so much already.

Disgusted by the green haze of jealousy that clouded my vision, I stomped off to the women's lavatory, cursing the beer I'd drunk.

I unzipped my jeans and squatted, careful not to allow any part of me to touch the freezing seat. Without warning, the door flew inwards, knocking me backwards so I hit the toilet pan hard.

I gasped, but a large, dark form grabbed me by my throat, lifting me up and cutting off the air, cutting off the terrified scream that tried to escape. I clawed desperately at his fingers that were squeezing painfully, tightly, but he punched me in the face with his free hand.

As pain exploded through my cheek, I flew backwards, my head thudding against the wall, and I slid to the filthy concrete floor.

But before I had a chance to move, to scream, to fight back, a fist closed in my hair, yanking me up again and twisting my flailing hands away from him.

I couldn't breathe, couldn't scream, couldn't move. It was every nightmare I'd ever had.

Out of shock and fear, my bladder released and urine flowed down my legs.

He cursed and slapped my bare bottom roughly as his foul breath blew in my face before dragging me around by my hair and bending me face down over the toilet. He forced my jeans further down my legs, and I heard the jangle of a belt and the rasp of a zip.

I moaned, trying to form the word 'no', but he crushed my face against the toilet seat.

I tried to fight, I did. I tried to buck him off me, but he was too strong, too heavy, and I was sick and dizzy. I wanted to pass out. I didn't want to know or remember what he was going to do to me.

As if from a long way away, I heard shouting, and suddenly the pressure on my body was gone.

A loud crack sounded so close to my head that my ears rang, followed by a high-pitched scream. More shouting, and then a long, whimpering cry. I was terrified, confused, afraid to move, my body paralyzed with shock.

And then his voice. I'll never forget the sound of his voice. James's voice.

"Bel, it's me! It's James! You're okay. You're safe now. He won't hurt you again. Are you alright?"

Gentle hands brushed my hair from my face, and he held me as I sagged against him, both of us sinking to the cold, dirty floor.

"I … I wet myself," I cried hoarsely, my throat on fire. "I was so scared … I couldn't help it. I'm covered in pee."

I started to cry, soft, humiliated sobs.

His arms tightened around me.

"Shh, it doesn't matter. It's okay. You're okay now. It's going to be alright."

I heard more shouting outside and I shuddered with cold fear.

James held my pain-wracked body, stroking my hair and holding me tightly against him.

Somewhere, I heard Zada's voice.

"James, how is she?"

"Not sure," he said softly as I continued to cry.

"Do you want me to ask her if he…?"

"No. I'll do it."

What did he want to ask me? It felt like it must be important, serious. Poor James, he was always so serious.

"Bel, can you hear me?"

I nodded against his chest, my tear-stained face pressed against him.

"Did he hurt you?"

I nodded again.

"Where, Bel? Where did he hurt you?"

I swallowed several times before I could get the words out, and when I did, they sounded harsh and gravelly.

"He … he grabbed my throat and punched me in the face. I hit my head."

There was a pause as he absorbed my words.

"Anything else?"

His voice was gentle, hardly more than a whisper.

"Bel, did he rape you?"

I shook my head, shuddering at the ugly word.

"Are you sure?"

I nodded.

"He was going to. I felt *it* against my bottom, but he stopped. Why did he stop?"

James's voice was grim.

"Because I shot him."

And that's when my brain stopped working.

Darkness.

"Wake up, Bel. Wake up!"

"I'm so tired."

"You have to stay awake."

I tried to swim towards his voice, but I couldn't. The darkness was pulling me under again.

Darkness.

"Don't fall asleep, Bel."

"So tired."
"Stay awake, Bel. Stay with me."
"You never stay with *me*, James."
"I will tonight."
"I want to close my eyes and forget for a while."
"No, Bel. You have to stay awake."
"So tired…"
Darkness.

The boat was rocking. Why were we in a boat?
Not a boat.
A car? A truck?
"Wake up, Bel. Listen to the sound of my voice. Try not to sleep, luv."
Love. That sounded nice.
"Don't fall asleep, Bel."
"Why? I don't understand."
His body twitched, as if he was uncomfortable, but the strong circle of his arms didn't falter.
"You're less likely to develop PTSD if you stay awake after … an incident." He paused. "And you might be concussed."
I started to cry again.
"Don't leave me, James! Promise you won't leave me tonight!"
"I won't leave you, Bel."
"Promise me!" I gasped, desperate not to be alone.
"I promise. Just stay awake for me, okay?"

CHAPTER 18

James

I sat on the front seat of the truck, jammed against the door with Bel in my arms, as Clay drove westwards toward Armenia, as fast as he dared, Zada navigating as we stayed off the main roads.

I was determined to be what Bel needed. I'd woken up in hospitals enough times, but never to find anyone waiting for me.

I held her more tightly.

When Turul came to find me at the party, saying that he was worried Yad had gone after Bel, my vision sharpened to a narrow focus where the only thing that mattered was saving her. I grabbed my Smith & Wesson and ran after her.

Not again.

I can't let this happen again.

I'd found them both in the women's toilet block, and I'll never forget the sight as Yad pinned Bel to the toilet bowl, his trousers around his ankles and Bel's bare flesh pale in the moonlight.

I dragged him off her and shot him in his calf when he pulled a knife. It was only a flesh wound but he'd squealed like the pig he was.

One of the women patched him up but by then Yad was screaming that he'd have us all killed. Turul and the women were terrified, and Clay decided that we'd all get the hell out of there immediately. Yad was left tied up loosely, giving us about a two-hour head start

Once we were out of reach, we'd inform Halo Trust HQ and our local liaison. We weren't going to stay around to be arrested and killed, or for Yad to finish what he'd started with Bel.

Her face was a mess, but I didn't think her nose was broken. Her left eye had swollen purple then turned black, and her bottom lip was split. All the nails on her left hand were broken, as if she'd been scrabbling on the floor, and I'd seen bruises blooming over her legs and backside as Zada had helped to dress her. Her throat was dark with finger-shaped bruises and she stank of piss, as well. I probably did too, by now, since I'd been holding her on my lap for the last four hours.

Zada was asleep, her head rolling against my shoulder as Clay pushed the whining truck faster.

"You okay over there, brother?" he asked, his voice unusually grim.

"Yeah, she'll be okay. Physically, at least."

"Fuck," Clay said quietly. "I wish you'd killed the bastard. Hell of a mess to clear up for the Trust."

Right now, I didn't give a damn about the Trust.

"Do you think Yad will do time for this?"

Clay shook his head.

"Probably not. You were the only one who could see what he was doing, and one of the women stole his knife. He probably promised to pay her." His lips thinned. "It would be your word against his. James, it's you I'm worried about. I thought you were going to kill him."

"I would have. If he'd hurt Bel, if he'd raped her, I'd have cut his balls off then shot him in the face."

I was stating a fact. Scum like that didn't deserve to live.

Clay hesitated, then I saw a small smile form.

"You might want to leave that part out when you file the official report."

"I'm suicidal not stupid," I replied.

I'd meant it as a joke but Clay didn't seem to think it was funny. I wondered if marriage affected your sense of humour.

I shifted Bel slightly in my arms, trying to stop my legs from going to sleep. She was no feather-weight, that was for sure.

It was hard to tell if she was awake, her head on my shoulder, her eyes closed, but when I whispered her name, her eyes opened instantly, then drooped again. But as I looked down, I could see tears glistening on her cheeks and eyelashes. She cried in complete silence, which was unnerving and somehow worse.

As the road gleamed blackly in front of us, Clay glanced impatiently at his phone clipped to the dashboard, waiting for the signal bars to pop up.

As soon as they did, he tossed me the phone and I woke up some poor bugger at Halo's Scottish HQ, giving him an abbreviated version of the sitrep.

Then it was pedal to the metal all the way to Armenia, another four hours west, where the long arm of Yad's police chief cousin couldn't reach us.

We hoped.

CHAPTER 19

Arabella

I CRIED THE WHOLE NIGHT AS WE drove through the monotone landscape, the snow far behind us.

James held me the entire time, speaking occasionally, his voice low and intimate.

I had time to think, not just about what had happened—or nearly happened—with Yad, but everything, my whole life. It was as if the assault had triggered some seismic change inside me and the old Arabella was gone for good. She died in that moment of panic and fear, that moment when James's pistol shattered the night.

In truth, I think she'd started to fade the moment I set foot in Nagorno Karabakh, but now there was a line beneath my old life. I didn't know what the new Arabella would be like—maybe, for the first time, I could choose for myself. I could be myself.

It was with a feeling of shock that I realized that I'd been a victim my whole life. My mother had died before I was a year old, and although my father tolerated me, educated, fed and clothed me, he had never loved me. My older brother was hardly in my life and I only saw him a couple of times a year, unless we could avoid it. My so-called friends had abandoned me the moment I left London and had stopped being useful to them or paying for our shallow lifestyle—none had stayed in touch when my father had taken me out of the country.

But a lot of that was down to me. I'd *allowed* my father to dictate my life; I'd *allowed* him to belittle and bully me; and I'd *allowed* my friends to use me.

All I'd wanted was someone to say that I was worth liking, maybe even loving.

But it was in this forlorn and war-torn country that I'd found friendship and loyalty. I'd been afraid that people would take advantage of me without my father's power and money to protect me, but instead I'd received nothing but kindness from people who already had so little.

The women de-miners of Nagorno Karabakh had given me their friendship—freely given without expectation of anything in return. Clay had trained me, supported me, given his time and made me laugh. Zada had shown me that there was another way to live and be useful to others, and that marriage wasn't the ball and chain I'd seen amongst many of my friends. Former friends.

And then there was James—enigmatic, charismatic, grouchy—the man who'd saved me from an appalling act of violence, maybe even saved my life. James, broken and sad, he had risked himself; he had been my saviour. And not for the first time.

I'd heard the story from Zada: James had saved Clay's life in a moment of heroism that could have cost his own when he neutralized the bomb in Times Square. I'd been shocked when I found out that was James, my James. That man was a hero, but he'd never been identified—until now. I'd seen that film footage on the news and on YouTube. Everyone said he was a hero. He was famous!

But he'd chosen anonymity, maybe for his own safety, but I suspected more because he didn't care about fame and publicity. So different from the people I'd known my whole life.

And Clay had saved James from drinking himself to death. That knowledge should have been disturbing, but somehow it wasn't. Because I could see that he was different now. Nagorno Karabakh had changed us both.

As my tears washed away my old life, that was the moment I decided not to be a victim anymore. I wasn't sure how, but somehow I'd *choose* not to be that person again.

I sat up straighter and Zada's eyelids fluttered open.

"How are you?"

Those were her first words on waking, her first thoughts. I didn't deserve her concern, but I was willing to earn it.

"I'm okay," I said honestly, aware that James was watching me carefully and Clay was stealing glances at me as he drove.

Clay nodded and smiled.

"Good to hear that, sister."

My eyebrows shot up and then fresh tears formed in my eyes.

"Blast!" I said, wiping my hand across my nose. "You're making me cry again, Clay, and I'd promised myself no more tears."

Zada squeezed my hand then smiled at her husband.

"Okay, team," said Clay, "this is the plan. HQ have reserved rooms for us at a hotel in Yerevan and they're sending someone to do damage control."

"Isn't Yerevan in Armenia or am I still concussed?" I asked, feeling the egg-sized lump on the back of my head."

"Yeah, we crossed the border during the night."

"Oh, the checkpoint—I remember. Sort of."

"So we'll find out how much influence Yadigar's cousin has. We'll only return to Nagorno if the Trust can get iron-clad guarantees that we won't be harmed or harassed." His expression was grim. "The company sponsoring this op will be pushing hard to get us back on track," and he cut a glance at me.

"Oh! You mean my father? Yes, you're right—he'll be furious that access to the coal seams will be delayed, even by a week. He's not a very patient man."

That was an understatement, and I couldn't help shivering at the prospect of seeing him again.

"Maybe you should go home."

I swung my head around to stare at James in dismay, his quiet words cutting me.

"Why? Why should I go home? I haven't done anything wrong!"

"Because you'll be safer," he said flatly.

That deflated me a little, but I glared at him all the same.

"What about Zada? I don't hear you suggesting that she goes home, too!"

"Your father is rich and influential—that makes you a target. We don't know what influence Yad will have if we go back to Nagorno—and that makes you a target, as well."

"You're the one who shot him," I snapped. "Maybe *you* should go home!"

We stared at each other furiously indignant for several seconds before Clay intervened.

"We'll do whatever the Trust advises to keep us *all* safe," he said calmly.

After that heated exchange, we travelled in silence until we reached the hotel, shortly after lunchtime.

James's words had hurt me, leaving me feeling even more abandoned. He wanted to get rid of me. I couldn't blame him—I'd brought him and the Trust nothing but trouble.

Tears formed in my eyes as we checked in to the hotel, the staff staring at us curiously, my battered and bruised face causing hushed comments.

Zada and Clay were kind, ensuring I had everything that I needed and taking me to my room.

"We'll get a doctor to come and check you out," said Clay, his dark eyes filled with concern.

"Honestly, I just want to shower and rest."

"Yeah, but head injuries are tricky. I'd feel better if a medic had seen you."

I gave in, too tired and depressed to argue with him.

The hotel called a doctor who arrived a couple of hours later and luckily spoke enough English for us to manage. Unfortunately, he insisted that I wasn't left alone for the next 24 hours.

"I'll stay with her," Zada offered immediately.

I was grateful, more than grateful. But it was still James's arms that I yearned to have around me. Even after what he'd said, I still wanted him.

As twilight dimmed the room, Zada sat in a chair reading the *Qu'ran*. I was afraid to sleep, so I lay on the bed, stiff and afraid, my one good eye wide open, afraid of what I'd see in my nightmares.

A soft knock on the door startled me.

Zada gave me a reassuring look, but checked through the spyhole first.

"It's James," she said. "Do you want to talk to him?"

I nodded silently.

He walked into the room tentatively, as if he wouldn't be welcome, but I felt safer already.

"Will you stay with me?" I blurted out. "Please!"

He cast a look at Zada who shrugged her shoulders, then nodded.

I mouthed 'thank you' at Zada as she collected her book.

"Are you sure?" she whispered. "I don't mind staying with you."

I gave her a watery smile as I shook my head, and she squeezed my hand before quietly closing the door behind her.

James went to sit in the chair, but I wanted him nearer than that, and I wasn't beyond begging,

"Please," I said, gesturing at the empty space on the bed next to me. "Please, I can't sleep alone. I don't think I can sleep at all. When I close my eyes, it feels like it's happening all over again."

But when I looked up at James, he wore an expression of unease, and my heart sank.

"You want me to sleep in the bed?"

"Yes, God, yes."

He was still hesitating, his worried glances flicking between me and the chair.

"I thought … won't it be worse … having a man in the room, in the bed?"

I met his gaze as my lips trembled.

"I feel safe with you."

Some indiscernible emotion fled across his face and was gone.

We took turns in the bathroom and I slid under the sheets as I heard the shower running. When he returned, his skin had the ruddy glow of heat, and he was wearing only boxer briefs.

"Is this okay?" he asked, concern in his eyes.

"I've seen you in less," I said drily.

He gave a quick smile, shuffled awkwardly until he was lying on the edge of the bed, as far from me as possible, then turned off the light.

It did feel awkward. We'd never done this before, only the frenzied fucking of need and lust.

"Could you … will you hold me?" I asked, already preparing myself for rejection.

There was a short pause, then the sheets rustled and he pulled me against his warm, solid chest.

I sighed with relief. I hadn't lied. I did feel safer in his arms.

"Thank you," I said against his heart. "Thank you for saving me."

His chest stilled as he seemed to hold his breath, then he began to speak, his voice low and soft.

"When I saw him with you, I wanted to kill him. I wish I had."

His admission was shocking. *He'd kill for me?*

"I'm glad you didn't," I said quietly.

"Why?"

"Too much paperwork."

He gave a surprised choke of laughter.

"If you'd killed him," I said more seriously, "you'd have been arrested and God knows what after that. Even the Trust couldn't stop you from be extradited."

"I would have killed him," James said truthfully. "But I couldn't get the angle without risking injury to you."

His voice was hushed.

"I wish I'd killed him. I wanted to. People say they 'saw red' but I really did. I wanted him dead. I wanted to see his blood on the ground. I wanted him to suffer. I couldn't let it happen again."

He stopped suddenly, as if he'd said too much.

I looked up, watching the outline of his face in the darkening room, his sharp profile, and reached up to touch his cheek.

"Again? What do you mean? I haven't ever … oh … someone else? Amira?"

I felt the lurch in his chest under my fingers, and a bolt of pain shot through my heart. He still loved her so much, just saying her name caused him pain.

My own heart shrivelled at the knowledge.

"Yeah," he finally breathed out. "Amira."

He let out a long, shuddering breath.

"Will you … can you tell me what happened?"

He shifted in the bed, and at first I thought he wasn't going to answer. But then he began to talk again, his voice bleeding with pain.

"When she … when Amira and Clay went undercover, there was a mole in the department. Smith, our CIA handler, had done everything he could to keep the op secret, but someone knew. They were compromised from the start. Instead of them infiltrating a terror cell, the terrorists planned to use them both as suicide bombers. But they didn't know about our backup, a guy called Larson who was keeping tabs on everything. He rescued Clay, but was killed trying to save Amira. She saw him being shot and she saw him die."

He breathed deeply, trying to control his emotions.

"The terrorists raped her repeatedly—she had internal injuries. It was … bad." He paused, his voice rough. "I wasn't there for her. I wasn't there. And I promised myself that I'd never let anything happen to her again." He gave a hoarse, bitter laugh. "Failed in that, as well."

I was shocked. Saddened by what had been done to Amira, upset that he thought it was his fault, his failure in some way.

"I didn't know," I said softly.

"No one knew, except the doctors and Smith," he said. "It wasn't made public and she never told her family. They knew she'd been beaten—but they never knew the full story. Zada doesn't know. I think Clay suspects, but I'm not sure. He had his own shit going on at the time."

His hand closed convulsively over mine.

"I'm sorry you got hurt, Bel."

I nestled against him, my mind whirling, but I felt safe, protected. Maybe even loved?

CHAPTER 20

James

I HELD BEL IN MY ARMS, FIGHTING BACK the emotions that I'd kept locked away for so long. One eye had swollen shut and her lower lip was twice its usual size. Fingermarks showed up clearly on the pale skin of her neck, and her whole body was covered in purple bruises.

I wanted to murder the man who'd done that to her. I still would, given the chance.

In the weeks that we'd been fucking, I'd found ways to reduce any emotional component as much as possible. Then I wouldn't have to feel guilty for cheating on Amira. I knew that made zero sense, but that's how it felt.

I'd made up rules that I thought would help: we didn't talk; I never stayed in Bel's room after; we never planned the next time. Although, I knew better than most people that tomorrow didn't always come.

But despite all of that, the way she felt when I was inside her, the way she clung to me, the way she gave herself to me, it was all seeping under my skin.

If I was honest with myself, which I rarely was, I'd started to care.

And now she was scared and vulnerable, and she needed me.

I didn't want to be needed by anyone. I always let them down. People I cared about died.

She shifted in my arms, inching closer, her warm breath fanning out across my skin. I sensed that she was looking at me.

"I'm not good at this, Bel," I admitted, struggling to explain how hard this was for me.

"It feels nice right now," she said.

She wasn't asking for much. *God, I was a selfish bastard.*

She shifted again, a long sigh that sounded defeated.

"I don't think I can sleep," she murmured. "I slept too much in the truck."

"Do you want to watch TV?"

"Subtitled re-runs of *Friends* and *Dallas*? No, I'll give that a miss, thanks."

"What do you want to do?"

She chewed her lip before answering.

"Maybe we can talk?"

Her tone was so tentative, so cautious, so wary of me—I knew I'd treated her badly and it showed in every word she said. I'd been a complete and utter prick.

"What do you want to talk about?"

"Nothing. Anything. Something. I don't mind." She paused. "Why do you still wear dog tags when you're not in the Army anymore?"

I touched the cord around my neck that held the two metal tags with my name, number, blood type and religion, such as it was. I was a sceptic. I didn't know where to put my faith or even if I had any.

"I took them off the day I was discharged from the Army, stuck them in a box and forgot about them. But when Clay asked me to come out to Nagorno, I dug them out and put them on again."

"But why?"

I shrugged, wondering how much honesty she could take.

"They're useful for identifying the body."

She gasped and sat up.

"Are you joking?"

"No."

"Oh my God, James!"

"It's not a big deal, Bel. It's just practical."

She lay down on the bed again, wrapping her body around me. I didn't want to enjoy the way that felt.

"You have the strangest life, James Spears."

I had to smile at that.

"It's normal for me."

"Did you always want to be a soldier? Was the Army in your family?"

"No. I don't really have family anyway."

"What do you mean?" she asked softly.

"I never knew my dad, and my mum was crap—an addict, they told me. I was taken into care when I was six, so I don't really remember her. I was close to my granddad for a while, but he died while I was serving overseas."

"That's it?" she asked, sounding sad. "No brothers or sisters?"

It was a story of poverty and tragedy that I couldn't escape as a kid. How could a woman like Bel ever understand? I'd needed the Army, needed the order and stability, the escape from chaos.

"I don't really know. Maybe my mother had other little bastards. I'd feel sorry for them if she did, but it's possible."

"So the Army was your family?"

"Yeah, I guess."

"Then why did you leave?"

I grunted in amusement, in irritation.

"I didn't leave, I was kicked out. The technical term is 'administrative discharge.'"

She blinked at me, confusion in her beautiful eyes.

"But I don't understand. Why would they do that? Your bomb disposal training took years and, well, you're a hero!"

"I don't know about that…"

"James, you are! Zada told me that you're the hero of Times Square! You're famous! Sort of! I mean, what you did is famous!"

I sighed. *Thanks, Zada.*

"Why do you hide it?"

I frowned.

"Because it was a shit day. Because Amira was…" I took a calming breath. "Because Clay lost his leg. I wasn't fast enough. I didn't *do* enough."

"Surely, you don't think that? I know Clay doesn't, or Zada. The world thinks you're a hero."

"Then the world's a sick and fucked up place."

She was silent, then reached out to touch my arm.

"I'm sorry."

I shrugged it off, but the truth hurt like a motherfucker.

"But I still don't understand," she said, "why the Army, um, kicked you out?"

"I went absent without leave. They don't like people who do that."

"Oh. So, why did you?"

I grimaced, wishing she'd drop the subject.

"I got a call from Amira's parents. They were worried about her. They'd heard that the hospital she worked in had been bombed and she wasn't answering her phone. They asked me to go and find her. In Syria."

"Oh my God, I had no idea! But couldn't you have asked for a few days off? A family crisis?"

I smiled at her naivety.

"I don't have any family, remember? Besides, there's no legal way to travel to Syria unless you have the correct visa; and it takes time and connections to organize that shit, and I needed to leave immediately. A

… friend got me entry into the country, but it was all under the radar. The fewer people who knew, the better."

"Zada told me that her sister was working in Raqqa," she breathed, her voice a whisper. "Even I've heard about all the terrible things that were happening there. I didn't know that you'd gone AWOL."

"Yeah, I did, but by then it was too late anyway. She was already dying from her injuries."

"James…"

We were silent for several minutes.

"The Army kicked you out for that?"

And they couldn't do it fast enough.

"Like I said, it was called administrative discharge. I was fucked up in the head and no one wanted to work with me. I did three months in Colchester Military Corrective Training Centre—military prison."

"I can't believe they treated you like that!" she said, her voice angry. "That's appalling! You were probably suffering from PTSD."

No 'probably' about it.

"After all your years of service! All the amazing things you've done, and they couldn't be bothered to help you when you needed it most. It's just so wrong! Ooh, it makes me want to write to the Ministry of Defence. No! To the Prime Minister! If she knew the circumstances…"

"No, Bel."

"But you can't just leave it like that!"

"It's done. Forget about it."

"I'll never forget!"

"Stop trying to save me, Bel," I said, my voice low with warning.

She grumbled quietly and it made me smile. But I was telling her the truth—she couldn't save me.

You can only save yourself.

If you want to.

"What about friends?" she asked cautiously. "Don't you have any friends? Maybe Army friends?"

I shook my head.

"I cut myself off from everyone after I got out of Colchester. I didn't even return Clay's messages."

"But he's still your friend now?"

I smiled, thinking of Clay's refusal to let me disappear.

"Yeah, but he was there when it all went down. He knew Amira. And by then he was with Zada, so…" I shook my head. "I just wanted to forget everything. I was planning to drink myself to death, if I didn't have the balls to do it quicker."

"I'm glad you didn't," she said, gently stroking her fingers along my cheekbone.

I needed to change the subject.

"What about you, Lady Arabella? What's your story?"

She gave a sad laugh.

"Oh, nothing special. Poor little rich girl who didn't get enough attention, so became more and more outrageous hoping someone would notice her," she said bitterly. "God, that sounds pathetic! It wasn't all bad."

But as I began to understand her a little better, I wondered if maybe she could understand me, too? We all have scars: some we can see, some we can't.

"My life is frivolous and pointless. I know that," she continued. "Nothing is wanted from me, nothing expected … except to marry well. I envy you in some ways. I mean not … what happened to you, obviously. God, I'm saying this all wrong, but you get to travel, you get to make a difference."

Don't envy me. It's lonely.

But I didn't say that. Instead, I asked something completely different. I wanted to see her smile.

"What were the good parts, good memories from your childhood? There must have been some." *I hoped.*

"Good memories?" She sounded surprised. "Yes, I suppose so. I mean, growing up in a castle wasn't bad. It was lonely, but I had a good imagination and 124 rooms to play in, as well as orchards and stables. Some of the staff were kind to me. One of the grooms used to let me help him with the horses, but then Daddy sold them."

"Christ, 124 rooms! I was brought up in a one-bedroom Council flat, and then shared a room with three other kids in care until I joined the Army."

"Yeah," she chuckled sadly, flattening the joy in her eyes. "Like I said—poor little rich girl. Thoreau wrote that most men lead lives of quiet desperation."

I'd never heard of this Thoreau bloke but he could be on to something … although he sounded like a miserable bastard.

"What happened to your mum?"

Bel sighed.

"She died ten months after I was born. I like to think that it would have been better if she'd lived, but I really don't know. She couldn't have been all that wonderful if she'd agreed to marry Dad."

"He sounds like a bit of a bastard."

"Oh, he definitely is! But he's also brilliant in business, completely ruthless, of course. I've been quite useful being his escort to balls and events in the last eight or nine years. He says it keeps the gold-diggers away."

"Nice," I said, my voice dripping with sarcasm.

"Hardly," she laughed.

"Why did he bring you to Nagorno?"

"Oh," she grimaced. "That's rather embarrassing. It was either go with him or go back to rehab. Well, sending me to Nagorno was definitely cheaper than rehab, and I'd been twice anyway and it hadn't taken." She shrugged. "Why be sober when life is so shit?" She paused. "I probably shouldn't say that to you."

"You're not saying anything I haven't said to myself a thousand times."

"Yes, well, you had good reason. You lost your fiancée."

I stilled.

"Amira wasn't my fiancée."

Bel turned her head to look at me.

"But I thought … you told me that you'd asked her to marry you?"

"I did ask her, but she said no. She chose to go to Syria to work as an ER nurse instead, at the hospital where her brother died. She wanted to do good, that's what she said. Instead, she died there."

"James! Oh my God!"

I heard her soft sobs and felt like an utter shit.

"Don't cry for me, Bel. It's the way it is."

And if Amira had lived, we might have had a chance, but there was no guarantee.

That was the truth that I hid from myself. I'd loved Amira with everything in me, and I think she cared about me, too. But whether we could have created a life together?

I'd never know.

"I'm so sorry," whispered Bel, wiping her eyes.

There was nothing else to say, so we lay in silence for several minutes, but I didn't think either of us had any chance of sleeping.

I wasn't sure why I'd trusted Bel to tell her that. Zada and Clay had always assumed that there'd been something more between me and Amira, and I'd been too messed up to say anything different. By the time I was in Nagorno, it was too late and there was no point.

As a rule, I didn't trust people. They all left sooner or later: family, friends, lovers. They all left.

Amira. I'd carried the weight of her loss for so long, I didn't know I'd been staggering from the burden. *Maybe I've been holding on too tight?*

The moment I thought that, I felt a looseness, a lightness, a breath of possibilities.

Finally, Bel spoke again.

"Thank you for trusting me enough to tell me. I won't say anything, I wouldn't dream of it. But I do appreciate you telling me." She took a deep breath. "You don't need anyone's permission to smile again, James."

And she placed a soft kiss on my lips before lying back on her pillow, her words spinning around inside my brain.

"Clay and Zada are great, aren't they?" she said, longing in her voice. "What they have together—I get so jealous. But I hope they get their baby. They'd be great parents, don't you think?"

You can't miss what you've never had. Yeah, and I was calling bullshit on that one. Because when I looked at Bel, I felt the pull of an intense longing that scared the fuck out of me.

"I wouldn't know what great parents look like."

"Me neither, but I think they'd be great."

"Yeah, I guess."

And it occurred to me that if Clay was half as good a father as he was a friend, their kid would be alright.

He was the one person who hadn't left me, even when I'd tried to shake him off. Him and Smith.

Bel squirmed about a bit, brushing her peachy arse against my crotch.

I was hard in seconds, but even I knew that sex wasn't what she needed right now. I did have some morals. Well, maybe one.

"Why did you let your old man bring you to Nagorno?" I asked, genuinely curious and needing a distraction. "You could have said no."

"Yikes! No one says no to my father," she said, shuddering.

"Did you try?"

"Eh, not really. He took all my credit cards, cut off my allowance, and said I'd shamed the family. Besides, he won't let me work and I'm not good at anything…"

My eyebrows shot up.

"He won't *let* you work?"

"I know, it's all so Victorian. He's just waiting to marry me off to someone who can advance his business affairs. A marriage of convenience."

"You're kidding, right?"

"Only half joking. But he keeps me totally reliant on him, so sometimes I feel like I have no choice. You haven't met my father—he's not someone you stand up to."

"Jesus, Bel! He doesn't *own* you! And what do you mean you're not good at anything? Clay has been singing your praises since the day you arrived."

"Aw, really? Well, Clay's a sweetie."

"Clay's a former Marine—he doesn't put up with time-wasters or tossers."

"Oh, well," she paused. "Thank you."

A deep dislike of the over-privileged twat who called himself Bel's father began to build inside me. She was bright and beautiful and kind, and her self-esteem was in the toilet.

"You're worth a lot more than you give yourself credit for," I said gruffly with certainty in my voice.

I felt her smile against my chest.

"This is nice, us talking. I mean, I really enjoyed the sex, too—I know every part of your body, your tattoos, that cute little mole on your neck, your beautiful dick, even your scars, but this—talking—it's almost more intimate. Does that make sense?"

"I can't believe you just called my junk beautiful! Magnificent, enormous, yeah, but beautiful?"

She laughed happily, and that sound—*that* was beautiful.

"Well, you *are* magnificent and enormous, but also beautiful. And not just your dick. It's ridiculous how long your eyelashes are, and you have such pretty blue eyes. Your body should be on the cover of *Men's Fitness* and your face—my God! You could be an Armani model!" She laughed lightly. "You're totally yummy—I'm sure all the girls tell you that."

"Nah, there aren't any."

She seemed surprised.

"None? No one at all?"

I scratched my chin, a little uncomfortable.

"There was one hookup when I was drunk. I probably didn't even manage to get it up. Some tart who picked me up at the pub."

I didn't tell her I'd ended up with crabs from that brief encounter. And I was taking that truth to the grave.

She chewed her lip again.

"So, you've only … once … since, since you left the Army?"

"Yep. Until you."

"Oh!"

Her voice was surprised, shocked even, but then she cuddled up against me.

"That's sweet," she said. "I think you must have been making up for lost time! Anyway, tell me about your first girlfriend, your first time—when you lost your virginity."

"What? Why?"

"Go on, please! I'm interested."

Bloody hell! The things this woman asked!

"Fine, I was 15, her name was Rose Hogg and she was 16½…."

"Ah, the experienced older woman."

"Yeah, something like that. It lasted about 20 seconds and she never spoke to me again."

"Ooh, harsh."

"Can't blame her—totally shit for her. What about you? There must have been a load of blokes drooling over you."

She gave a lazy smile.

"Yes, lots of 'blokes'. But none were memorable—until now."

We talked the rest of the night about everything and nothing. I told her about life as a kid in care, the loneliness, the fear, the camaraderie with the other kids, the bullies; the nice carers, the shitty carers, and the carers that you avoided being left alone with. I told her about joining the Army, and the struggle and years of studying to become an ATO. I told her about some of the missions I'd been on, and when I told her about the friends who'd died, the on-going nightmares that my hands had been blown off, she held me and kissed my fingers one by one.

In turn, she told me about the emptiness of her life growing up, despite the money and houses, the skiing holidays to Klosters and Davos, the summer trips to the Seychelles, places I hadn't heard of when I was a kid.

She came from money and I came from the gutter, but that emptiness we'd both experienced, it meant we had a lot in common.

We talked about everything except Yad's attack.

If talking was a distraction from her nightmares, then I'd talk until my tongue fell out.

I couldn't fool myself any longer. I cared about Bel. And that was a major fucking problem.

Finally, as the darkness began to fade and the first grey light of dawn appeared in the east, we fell into a light sleep.

Which was why I wasn't sure if I'd imagined it or not when she said,

"I love you."

Shit.

CHAPTER 21

Arabella

I WOKE SUDDENLY, AN UGLY DREAM tugging at my consciousness.
"Bel, are you okay?"

James's voice was drugged and slurred with sleep, but also warm with concern, and I felt the smallest of smiles lift my lips upwards. I turned to look at him, his features brushed with the softness of sleep but already hardening into the emotional armour he wore each day.

"I will be. Thank you for staying with me."

His eyes were wary, but he smiled back.

"Didn't have anywhere else to be."

Not an undying declaration of love, but almost as good, coming from a man who spoke less than most people, but who meant more when he did.

"You don't smile much. I like it when you do."

"What? I do. Don't I?"

"No."

"Oh."

And then he kissed me, gently at first, testing the waters, so to speak. But finding me ready and wanting, he took it further.

His strong hands tracked down my body and within seconds those clever, work-roughened fingers brought me to orgasm. And when he made love to me, he took his time, showing a gentleness and care that I had hardly known he was capable of.

We still didn't have any condoms, but we'd become used to that by now.

And afterwards, we lay entwined, limbs tangled, and I felt loved.

It was a dangerous sensation, loving a man who was as untamed and wild as the wind. At any second, I could turn my head and he'd be gone, invisible, leaving only the memory behind.

But he was here for now.

I'd long ago learned to accept less than I wanted; to do without. To brutally deaden any hopes for the future.

We showered together, enjoying the extraordinary, excessive, luxurious pleasure of standing for twenty minutes in plentiful, hot water, soapy hands sliding over heated skin.

He'd shaved again. He knew that I loved the feel of his smooth skin over his strong jaw when we kissed. He hadn't shaved his head yet, although I guessed he would soon, but I l enjoyed touching the soft, fine pelt of hair covering his head.

I brushed my fingers over his lips.

His rare smile still had the power to knock the breath from my lungs, but I was slowly becoming used to it.

We'd missed breakfast by several hours, but walked down to an early lunch, hand in hand, finding Clay and Zada sitting in the hotel's bar drinking mint tea.

Zada's eyes widened when she saw us holding hands but tactfully said nothing. Clay, on the other hand…

"Dude! You've finally pulled your head out of your ass! Nice one, bro! Harry, you could do better, but he's a work in progress. There might even be potential…"

To all of which James replied:

"Fuck off."

Clay laughed and Zada hid a smile.

"How are you feeling?" she asked me.

I sat down, surprised to find that James had pulled out my chair for me. Surprised, but very pleased.

I thought about Zada's question before I answered.

"Better," I said eventually. "Still freaked by everything that's happened, but it seems more like a really scary nightmare now. To be honest, I'm trying not to think about it too much. Have you heard anything?"

Clay shook his head.

"HQ is trying to find out what happened after we left, but it seems as though the women have scattered and gone, which is for the best, I think. There's no news on Yad. They're keeping a watching brief and our instructions are to stay here. So think of it as a paid vacation."

I gave a hollow laugh.

"Right. Well, in that case, I'm going to see if I can find a hairdresser and someone to fix my nails, which are a complete disaster. Then I want a massage. A gentle one."

"I can do that for you," said James slyly. "I also have hairdressing skills to offer."

My cheeks turned pink. He'd gone from fucking me in privacy and silence, to sexy smiles and innuendo in a single night. A girl could be forgiven for being confused.

I did my best to roll with the emotional punches and embrace this fun side of him that I'd never seen before.

James was relaxed, almost playful. It was new, and fragile hope exploded inside me.

"Yes to the massage, but a giant no to the hairdressing. Once was enough, thank you all the same."

Clay's eyes widened.

"Bro, don't tell me that *you* cut Harry's hair? What the heck?"

James shrugged.

"What can I say? She begged me."

My mouth dropped open and I poked him in the arm.

"Not quite how I remember it!"

He grinned at me, a wide, genuine smile.

It made me want to kiss him, wrap him up and take him home, then fuck him senseless.

THOSE DAYS SPENT in a two-star hotel in Yerevan remain some of the happiest memories of my whole life.

The air of Autumn was crisp and clean, and for the first time in several years, I had no drugs or alcohol in my body. I could think clearly and feel every emotion with painful clarity.

I covered my bruises with makeup and pretended that we were an ordinary couple like everyone else, taking a city break together.

I'd always preferred fairytales to real life.

We visited thousand year-old fortresses and thousand year-old churches, walked the ancient Silk Road and the modern Republic Square. We ate together, explored together, woke up together and made love together.

Every day James revealed a little more of himself to me, and I cherished every moment.

I was surprised and confused when I saw him kneel down to pray in the mornings, facing East.

I'd learned from Zada that Muslims did this five times a day as one of the Pillars of Islam, but James just did it once, every morning. Perhaps, in his own way, he was honouring Amira. I didn't feel it was my place to ask. Just because I shared his bed, it didn't mean I shared his thoughts.

But he held my hand at every opportunity and it felt like he loved me. He just never said the words.

We were sitting outside a small café, only just warm enough in the chilly air, drinking hot, spicy coffee.

"The first time I saw you," he said, "I thought you were Helen of Troy."

Surprised and pleased, I raised my eyebrows.

"Why on earth would you think that?"

He gave me a warm smile and slung his arm around my shoulder.

"Because you're the kind of woman men go to war over."

"I don't want anyone fighting over me," I said quietly. "Once was enough," and I shuddered at the memory of Yad.

His cool blue eyes softened as he stared at me, brushing his warm lips over my cheek.

"That's not what I mean—even then, that first day, I knew that you were something special. I was pissed off because I thought, I *knew* that you'd never be interested in a man like me."

"You thought wrong," I smiled, snuggling into his side. "You're exactly the man for me."

He sighed, and I knew the words that I'd hoped to hear weren't what was coming next.

"Bel, I'm not a good prospect. I have a small Army pension that pays the mortgage on a boring two-bed flat outside Reading. That's it. I have no savings and I do a job that could send me pretty much anywhere in the world but nowhere anyone would want to go."

"Well," I said carefully. "I'm not looking for 'a good prospect'. My father can find me plenty of those and I'm not interested. You, on the other hand, interest me a lot. Besides, a person can only live in one room at a time—who needs fifty bedrooms anyway?" I sat up straighter. "Look, James, let's not put a label on this. We're having fun, more than fun, but you're right, everything is up in the air. I've been thinking about us and how we can hold on to what we've got…"

I held my breath waiting for him to say that there was no 'us' and that this whole relationship was in my head.

But he didn't.

I let out a hopeful breath and continued, daring to put my dreams into words.

"I've thought about applying for a job with Halo Trust for real. I know an awful lot about the work on the ground now. I'm hoping that they'd consider sending me as a sort of assistant to Clay. What do you think?"

Myriad emotions flew across his face.

"I think you're amazing, Bel. But it scares the crap out of me to think that you'd make a career out of going to some of the shitholes that I'd be working in."

I gave a small smile as I reached up to kiss him, the sound of his dog tags chinking together eliciting a Pavlovian response of lust and need.

"Then you know exactly how I feel, and how I've felt every day since I went on Task with you and saw what you do."

He kissed me softly, then after a few moments he pulled away and kissed the top of my head, an unmistakable age-old need in his eyes.

"Shall we go back to the hotel?"

And because I wasn't a stupid woman anymore, I said yes.

We'd also found a shop that sold condoms.

While we stayed at Yerevan, the Trust were intervening in Nagorno.

Finally, word came that Yadigar Aghayev had been arrested and taken to a police station beyond his cousin's influence, and we all breathed easier.

We expected that we'd be sent back to finish our work in the valley. But after more delays, the news came that we weren't going back to Nagorno at all. Another team was being sent to finish our work—the Trust were taking precautions, no doubt thinking it too dangerous to send us back in case there were reprisals. I hoped that they'd find a job for Maral. She was good at her work and very brave. They needed people like her.

As for us, well, there was plenty of work for us on the Armenia side of the border. Another team was schedule to arrive from the UK, but James and Clay were going to set up the taskforce of locals and get the training started. It looked like we'd be staying Yerevan for at least another six weeks. Secretly, I was delighted.

But after that, Zada and Clay were being sent back to the US for a month's leave, and then transferring to another heavily mined country, Angola, a west-coast country of south-central Africa. James would be going, too.

As for me…?

James asked me to go with him. But it wasn't the conversation that I'd hoped for.

"Bel, I'm not sure it's a good idea for you to work for Halo Trust."

I turned on my side in the bed, staring at him in surprise.

"But you said … you said that it *was* a good idea. You said I was amazing!"

"I know, and I haven't changed my mind—you *are* amazing. But I need you to be safe more than I need you to have a job. If you go *with* me, I can look after you. But if you go wherever they send you and it's not with me … I don't think I could cope with that."

I was shocked by his honesty, then annoyed.

"Wait, you're saying that working in one of the Trust's offices is more dangerous than what *you* do?"

He frowned.

"No, of course not, but…"

"No, hold on. You'd be too worried about me working in one of their offices, but I'd have to watch you go out on Task every day neutralizing bombs? Double standards much?"

"You're twisting my words!" he snapped. "I'm just saying that you're safe with me. If you take a job with the Trust, we can't control where you'll be sent. Just come with me as my … as my girlfriend."

I knew that this was a huge leap for him, but he'd changed me, and now he had to accept the consequences. And I had to remind myself that it wasn't the same as my father refusing to allow me to work.

"James," I said gently, reaching out to touch him. "I've learned so much by coming out to Nagorno. You've taught me so much, too. I'm learning to stand on my own two feet for the first time in my life, but I'm not quite there yet. If I come with you as just a hanger-on, I'll never be anything else, do you see?"

His anger flared quickly, the storm brewing in his eyes.

"A 'hanger-on'? I say 'girlfriend' and you say 'hanger-on'? Nice, Bel. Classy."

"Don't be miffed," I said, trying to keep my patience. "Perhaps I chose my words poorly…"

"Yeah, you think?"

"…but what I meant is that being there as your *girlfriend* without any official role makes me utterly dependent on you. I can guarantee that my father will cut me off. I'll *need* to work, I'll need the income."

"I'll be earning," he said, a mulish expression on his face. "We can live on that."

"I can't live on *you*!" I said, my voice rising with his. "Amira worked as a nurse…"

As soon as I said her name I knew that I was opening freshly-healed wounds.

"And look where it got her!" he yelled, leaping out of bed gloriously naked, and pacing the room, his hands on his head. "It got her killed! I asked her to wait, I told her I'd go with her and she fucking died! Yad nearly raped you—he'd probably have killed you!"

"There's no reason that would happen again," I shouted back, frustrated that I wasn't getting through to him, upset that he'd mentioned Yad again. "I'll be doing paperwork and…"

"At least Amira was doing something important, not working in a fucking office!" he yelled in my face.

Why do we hurt the people we love the most?

"Saint Amira!" I shouted back. "How can I ever live up to the pedestal she's on?"

"Shut up! Just shut your mouth! You don't get to say her name! Not *ever!*"

How could I have been basking in his passion just minutes ago, the sweat from our love-making still drying on our naked bodies, but now we were screaming hateful and hurtful things at each other, piling up the rubble of those walls we'd spent the last few days pulling down.

We'd both said too much and I burst into tears, disappearing to cry in the bathroom.

I was still sobbing on the floor when I heard Clay's voice in the bedroom. I couldn't hear what he was saying but it sounded urgent.

I grabbed a towel and opened the door a crack.

"What's going on?"

James wouldn't look at me when he spoke.

"Work," he said coldly.

Clay looked puzzled by James's curt response and turned a worried face to me.

"The police have received warning that there's a car bomb outside the city hospital. They're clearing the area now, but they can't get their own EOD team here for nearly an hour." He rubbed a hand over his face. "They've asked for our help."

"What does that mean?" I gasped, stepping out of the bathroom, not caring that I was flashing Clay a lot of flesh.

He looked away respectfully as he answered.

"James is going to assess the situation."

My heart galloped then stopped.

"That doesn't make any sense! They have their own army, their own experts. I've seen armed police everywhere. Why do they want James? How do they even know about him?"

"I've wondered the same," he said quietly. "But it's an urgent situation. They can't evacuate the whole hospital because there's an operation going on in the wing next to the bomb. They need our help. They need James's help."

I gasped.

"You mean they're going to send him to neutralize the device… he's going to wear the bomb suit!"

Clay nodded.

"Oh my God!" I whispered, my legs shaking. "No!"

"It's what I do, Bel," James said between gritted teeth. "Deal with it."

CHAPTER 22

James

"WHY DO THEY WANT JAMES? *How do they even know about him?*"

Bel's words echoed in my head as I automatically started prepping the equipment in the truck.

Clay was acting as my Number Two—what the British Army called the assistant to the ATO. He wasn't trained to do it, but he knew enough to be useful.

Bel was right—this set up was all wrong. *How* did they know about me? *How* did they know I had all the equipment I needed with me? *How* did they know where to find me?

Despite those thoughts thundering through, the call-out was real: an abandoned car next to the hospital had been found by police, packed with accelerant or some sort of incendiary device. Wires were seen, and at that point, the police had called the local Bomb Squad. As it turned out, they were already dealing with a landmine incident sixty minutes out of the city. Interesting timing. It sounded like a decoy to me.

Someone wanted me at the scene.

Even as I had these thoughts, my emotions were shutting down one by one.

I wasn't a shrink, but I'd come across enough of them in my time to understand what was happening. Emotions were there for a purpose, but to me they were an expendable resource.

When you'd had trauma after trauma, self-preservation eventually kicked in and your emotions ran dry. Some people spiralled down into despair and become non-functioning—that's what had happened to me after Amira died.

Just recently, I'd begun to wonder if there was a way back—perhaps my emotional resources would refill and emotions would return. Like in relationships: you meet someone, you trust them and you get hurt … how many times before you're involved with someone but never allow them close enough to hurt you again?

My mind and body had conditioned itself to the environment, protecting itself by reducing the emotional risk. But I had begun to hope that with time, with Bel, a positive relationship might heal some of the damage and allow a return to normal functioning. Whatever that was.

But during those minutes, as Clay drove the truck with our police escort to the cordon area, I knew that there was no normal for me. Perhaps I could still display something resembling emotion. If I picked the right subject and pushed hard enough—like when Bel had been assaulted. But was it an act? A memory of how I used to be? Because I still had the ability to switch off emotions at will. The problem was, would they ever switch back on?

Oh well, it had its uses.

A steady drizzle had settled in, and I watched, hypnotized, as the wipers ticked across the windscreen like hands on a clock, counting down: *tick tock, tick tock, tick tock.*

I'd been here before, so many times, too many times.

I remembered the rain of an Afghan winter, that miserable feeling of waking up in a dry sleeping bag to find the pitter-patter of rain on the tent. I knew that I was going to get wet, but what was the alternative? Say no to the Troop sergeant?

So I'd crawl out of my sleeping bag, bitching about the fact that the bottom of the bag was soaked, check out the sitrep in the Ops room, then outside the Incident Control Point, I'd pull my rig on—the bomb suit.

It's heavy, hard to kneel, hard to lie flat. Peripheral vision is reduced to almost nothing, but even so, I'd be on the alert, watching, searching the skyline, the buildings, the gutter. Nothing moves, nothing to see except the drips rolling down the front of my helmet and the car bomb that I'm walking towards. My only option was to plod on.

How was it different to now? I smiled grimly to myself—I'd chosen to be here. I'd dared to think that I could have a life beyond all the crap, all the pain, all the desperate humiliation, but I'd been wrong.

I had a strong premonition that I was going to die.

And I didn't care.

Memories shivered through me, relentless and stinging.

In Afghanistan, it was freezing cold in the winter and baking hot in the summer.

Regardless of the misery, a soldier accepted the weather and had more important things to worry about. I'd only consider the conditions if they could affect my work: numb fingers as I tried to manipulate the pliers or the screwdriver or my knife, and even then all I'd do is adjust, adapt, accommodate.

But the summer heat out there was blistering, you simply can't understand it—even the blast of heat from opening an oven door only mimics it for a second. It was the kind of heat that tested tempers, drained energy, and put you on a slow, irritable boil, sometimes resulting in explosion. Everything smelled burnt or the stifling scent of ball sweat.

I remembered it all.

While I was out there, I'd attended six suicide bombings—which means I'd be called out after some bastard had blown himself up along with anyone who happened to be walking past.

Was that what I'd find by the hospital?

I tried to remember that it was a car bomb, not a suicide bomber—no one had died yet. But in my mind, other memories filtered through.

I remembered the smell, that sticky metallic smell of blood that hits you when you first get on scene. But then it was the smell of burning. Pieces of burnt flesh would be stuck to every surface: up the walls, on the vehicles, and all those burned bodies meant to me was that they helped me to determine the direction of the blast. The humanity, the loss, I couldn't think about that. I focussed on the work: where did the bomb originate? How much force did it have? What evidence could I find?

The human tragedy meant nothing. See? No emotions. What use were emotions to me then? What use now?

In a war zone, a dull thump in the distance would be followed by an almost imperceptible ground shake. Somewhere another atrocity had occurred.

I'd already be prepping the team before the call came in. I'd grab my kit and head to the Ops Room. The Battle Orders were always the same: half the team with gloves and plastic bags to pick up the evidence from the scene—and the body parts to identify the DNA of the bomb maker; the other half of the Quick Reaction Force would be watching for a potential second suicide bomber who wanted to take me out. It was personal.

And I thought about the lies our politicians told us: 'Go to Afghanistan, fight terrorism, destroy the drug trade, hunt the Taliban. It's better to fight the enemy overseas to prevent them bringing the fight to our shores…'

Lies. All lies.

As we drove on, closer to the hospital now, I began to scan the few vehicles approaching, checking the verges of the road, eyeing every pedestrian we passed.

"James? Are you doing okay over there, brother?"

Clay's words broke through my bubble, and I rubbed my face.

"Yeah."

He gave me a worried look, pulling up as the police cars slowed behind a hastily erected barrier.

"We need to move the cordon back 50 metres," I said immediately. "We're too close."

While Clay spoke via an interpreter and the police started retreating, I peered through the pouring rain and spotted an ancient Russian Lada parked at a skewed angle, half on, half off the pavement.

The bomber wanted the car to be noticed. I wondered if he was watching. Did that mean it was a remote controlled mechanism, or maybe on a timer?

Clay had insisted on having electronic countermeasures, a signal jammer, as part of our kit. It definitely wasn't standard issue for Halo Trust teams. But neither of us would work without it. Not after Times Square.

We'd need it now.

Once the cordon was moved back, Clay came to help me suit up—one of the jobs for my Number Two—layering the pieces of body armour into place one at a time—three times the weight of armour that de-miners used.

But the weight was familiar, almost comforting, and the musty smell filled my nostrils as he lowered the helmet over my head.

We checked comms, and when I could hear him loud and clear and he could hear me, I began the lonely walk. All that was between me and the device was my training and 80lb of body armour.

Memories of Amira tried to send sparks of adrenaline through me, but I slammed them back. There was no hostage here, no one I loved on the line, just me and the bomb.

The closer I got to it, the more the anticipation grew. I was consumed in my own little world, my personal battle.

I saw what the first officers on the scene had reported: cans of petrol and wires sticking out from under an old blanket.

Some brave or suicidal police officer had already smashed in the window, so all I had to do was reach in and pull the blanket clear.

Using a hook and line, I attached the hook to the blanket, backed away 20 metres and knelt down, cautiously tugging on the line. The blanket was heavy, sodden from the rain pouring in the broken window. I tugged gently, but it was snagged on something. I tugged harder, almost falling backwards when it came free. I imagined the wet, slapping sound as it fell in a puddle, but all I could hear was the harsh sound of my breathing.

I walked toward to the car and peered inside.

I recognized the device immediately—a MON-100. And I was pretty sure that it was the same mine that went missing on my last Task with Yad.

Jesus. Two kilos of high explosives, plus an incendiary device attached to the car's petrol tank. Outside a hospital.

The sick fucker and his cousin were sending one hell of a message.

I relayed the intel to Clay, then focussed on the job ahead.

I needed to work to take the detonator out of the device. This bomb maker wasn't skilled, and there were no booby-traps that I could see, except on the car door. I was glad that crazy police officer had only smashed the window and not tried to open the door.

There were other problems, as well: I could see two command wires going into the device and 7.5m of wire. It would be a long, slow job as my fingers slowly went numb and my hands slipped in the rain.

The angle was awkward, too, leaning through the window.

I heard a faint 'pop' beside me, followed by the sound of automatic gunfire from the police.

I hit the deck and started to crawl away from the car, something that was almost impossible in the bomb suit, and I grunted with the effort.

Clay's voice came over the comms.

"Lone shooter. Police have him pinned down. Wait for my command."

I lay face down on the freezing wet road, listening to the sound of rain pelting across my helmet, feeling the water soak into my clothes and trickle down the back of my neck.

It seemed like a lifetime before Clay gave the all-clear.

"Sniper neutralized."

I wondered if they'd caught him alive. Intel was more useful than a dead body.

As I approached the car again, I could see a bullet hole in the car door next to where my head had been. If the bullet had hit my body armour, it wouldn't have done much damage, but I suspected that the shooter had been aiming at the booby-trap in the car door.

It took 45 minutes to neutralize the smaller device attached to the door, and even after it wasn't a problem, I had to borrow a set of 'jaws of life' from the fire team that was standing by because the doors were locked.

I continued to work.

"Clay, there's no RC, but keep the ECM jammer on just in case."

"Wilco."

Finally, the detonator was exposed.

I rubbed my hands together to get some feeling back into them before the next stage, the final stage, the most deadly stage.

The fucking anti-personnel mine was old and had been in the ground for over 15 years when I'd found it. It was badly corroded. My fingers turned orange from the rust as I wrestled with the metal, starting to sweat, despite the icy rain.

It took another 40 minutes of hacking at it with my screwdriver, knife and pliers before it finally came free.

I'm not dead.

A huge feeling of relief filled me, and I signalled the Fire Chief to bring his men to put the devices and explosives somewhere safe.

It was only then that I felt the exhaustion flow through me.

I trudged back to the police cordon, my whole body aching, my mind spinning faster and faster.

"Nice job, brother," said Clay, lifting my helmet and helping me take off the body armour.

"Oh my God, James! You're amazing! Are you alright?" asked Bel, her voice shaking.

She stood next to Zada, and the two women were hugging each other tightly, their faces wet with rain.

I stared at her, not yet able to reconnect to my emotions. I knew that I was supposed to feel something when I looked at her. But it was too soon.

I was still rewinding the events of the past hours. *I could have been killed—what the fuck was I thinking? That device was a gnat's balls away from detonating. What if? What if? What if?*

I nodded at her, seeing her face fall as she continued to stare at me, then I turned away.

Somehow, when you've been a soldier, when you've faced death, that's not where it ends, because I don't think the living ever get to go home. Not really.

CHAPTER 23

Arabella

JAMES TURNED AWAY FROM ME without replying and I felt the first crack in my fragile heart.

"Give him time," said Zada, tugging on my arm. "He gets in a weird place after a Task, you know that—I can't imagine how much more intense this was. Dear Allah, when the sniper started shooting…" she shook her head. "I'm still shaking."

I could feel sporadic tremors running through her, feel her fear. Now, I just felt numb.

"I want to be there for him," I said hesitantly, but it sounded like I was begging.

"You can't be," she said firmly. "I saw the same thing with Amira after a bad incident in the ER. I'm the same when I've been working in NICU and we lose one of the babies. It's just the worst, and if you're not part of it and haven't been there…" She blew out a long breath. "He needs time to process it all in his own way."

Her words slashed at me: I *was* part of it; I *had* been there. Not in the way she meant, but I'd gone through it just the same.

She shrugged sadly.

"That's why so many doctors and nurses end up with alcohol problems or other addictions. It's the pressure." She sighed. "At least he's not drinking…"

She wasn't being particularly reassuring, although I knew she meant to be. Maybe her certainty came from the knowledge that Clay loved her. I had no such certainties to comfort me.

While Clay and James were answering questions from the police and clearing up their equipment, Zada and I went to sit in the back of the police car that had brought us. The officer had left it unattended, so the engine wasn't running and there was no warmth.

For two hours, we huddled together, dozing fitfully, until Clay tapped on the window, making us both jump.

"We're done here, ladies," he said, yawning widely, his eyes red with tiredness and concern. "We're all getting a police escort back to the hotel." He paused. "We'll also have armed police guards outside our rooms."

"What?"

My lungs froze with fear.

"I know," he said. "But we think this car bomb was set up to lure James out."

"Oh my God! How do you know? Are you sure?"

He shook his head.

"I can't say too much now, but it seems as though the Army EOD team were lured out of town deliberately, and there was the sniper on the roof at exactly the right moment, too." His face was tight with anger. "He'll be helping police with their enquiries when he regains consciousness. Took a bullet to his chest. Could be a while. Meanwhile, we don't know who's targeting us."

"It's Yad or his crazy cousin!" I snapped. "It must be!"

"There's a good chance," Clay agreed, "but until we know for sure, that's just speculation." He raised his hands at my furious expression.

"I know. Look, let's just go get some shut-eye and we'll talk more in the morning."

"Fine," I said softly. "Is James going back to the hotel with you?"

Clay looked uncomfortable.

"Yep. We're all going. We need to stick together."

"Then where is he?"

His voice was solemn.

"Harry, you need to give him a lot of space, okay? He's just been through the most intense kind of continuous focus and pressure that's hard for anyone to understand, even me. He needs to decompress. I'm sorry, hon, but I don't think you should be around him right now."

I swallowed and looked down.

"I see."

"I'm sorry."

"It's okay," I said flatly. "It's not your fault. It's not anyone's fault."

He squeezed my hand briefly, then kissed Zada.

"See you back at base soon, babe."

He closed the door and waved the driver on. I watched him disappear from view as we sped into the night.

"He's right," said Zada softly. "Just give James time. And for the record, what I said at the party, I meant it: you're good for him."

I sniffed back some tears and gave her a watery smile.

I felt like a piece of thread that had been stretched and stretched, taut, with my nerves twanging, beginning to fray—I couldn't take anymore or I'd break.

Zada fell asleep on the short drive back, but I was wide awake, terrified that I'd lost James already. I couldn't give up on us yet, but I didn't dare to hope.

Clay and Zada both said I had to give him time. But I couldn't be blind to the fact that I'd fallen in love with him. What a stupid, stupid, careless thing to do.

And if what he needed was time, I'd give him every second of my life.

As Clay had promised, at the hotel, armed guards escorted us to our bedrooms, searching them thoroughly before we were allowed in.

It certainly brought home to me how real the threat was.

With a police officer outside, I stood in the middle of the room that I'd been sharing with James, tiredness pulling at my body while my brain buzzed in dizzying circles.

Will he come? Or will he stay away? Will he come? Or will he stay away?

In the end, I decided to have a shower. Few things were as soothing and comforting as steam and hot water against your skin.

But when I turned off the water, I realized that I was no longer alone.

"James?"

He was standing in the centre of the room, staring into space.

I took three steps towards him before I came to a halt, almost feeling the force-field around him, the isolation that made an impenetrable perimeter.

"James, are you … okay?"

He nodded.

"I need a shower."

"Oh, okay … I … okay."

He left the room abruptly, shutting the bathroom door firmly behind him.

I climbed into bed, not naked as usual, but wearing one of James's t-shirts. It was old and faded in Army green, but the badge was still clear to read: '321 EOD & Search Sqn'.

I needed more defences than bare flesh to face him again.

But when he came out of the bathroom, he was naked, magnificent, beautiful, but utterly distant and closed-off.

He slid into bed without a word and turned off the light, rolling onto his side away from me.

I was used to silence being used as a weapon—my father did it all the time. And I was used to silence from James being used as a shield, keeping everyone away from him. But this silence was … absence. He was here physically, but his mind was far away, somewhere I couldn't reach him.

I lay in the bed where we'd made love so many times feeling as if it had become our own personal minefield: any movement could cause an incendiary explosion; the wrong word, the wrong touch.

Tears leaked from my eyes as we lay side by side and a million miles apart. It felt like someone was scorching the earth around me. Would I burn with it? Or would I be frozen by the coldness of the man I loved.

I had so many things that I wanted to say, but bit them all back.

An hour passed, then two, but I sensed that James wasn't asleep either. In the end, the need to speak became unbearable.

"You were amazing out there, incredibly brave. I'm so proud of you."

The words were quiet but heartfelt. They hung in the air until they slipped away without a sound.

He didn't reply.

THE NEXT MORNING, the silence continued, growing heavier and more oppressive with each second. He didn't ignore me, but he wasn't with me either.

Clay and Zada cast worried looks over the breakfast table as they tried to keep a light conversation going; not easy when armed guards loomed over us, following our every move.

The hotel management weren't thrilled about our new best friends either, and I heard them asking Clay how long they'd be here.

His reply was short: *As long as they're needed.*

It was at times like this when I saw the former Marine within him. James carried his service like a weight on his shoulders; Clay wore his like a badge of honour that he only showed to a few people when it was needed.

The morning was spent with the police, being interviewed through an interpreter, which made everything very slow and tedious.

I couldn't understand why they seemed more interested in Yad's assault on me than on what had happened last night. It was horrible going over and over the story, seeing the suspicion in their eyes.

By then, Clay had told me that the device in the car had been a MON-100, identical to the mines that had gone missing back in Nagorno. So why were the police focussing on what happened with Yad? Surely his cousin's influence couldn't extend as far as Armenia?

Apprehension flickered through me, and I could see that mirrored in Clay and Zada's eyes. James remained aloof and distant.

But when the police tried to question me for a fourth time about the assault, he finally engaged.

"She's answered your questions three times now. Her story hasn't changed. It's enough. So how about we ask why a MON-100 that I *know* I lifted from the ground in Nagorno ended up in Yerevan? Has the sniper talked yet?"

The police were defensive, then aggressive—almost implying that James and Clay were involved in arms dealing—then passive and respectful when a senior Armenian Army General interrupted, and took the time to thank James and Clay personally.

After that, the police backed down, but none of us were happy to stay here any longer, and Clay immediately began to make plans for us to leave the next day.

I'd been so grateful when James had intervened with the police for me and hoped it might mean that he'd start talking to me, at last, but he didn't.

We weren't alone again until late that night, three hours after I'd gone to bed by myself, and by then, I was close to falling apart. I needed *something* from him—the silence was punishing.

"Where have you been?" I asked him as once again he slid silently beneath the sheets.

He threw me a surprised look.

"You're awake? I thought you'd be asleep by now."

"No. I've been waiting for you."

The expression on his face didn't change.

Where are you, James?

Gently, I cupped his face with my hands, kissing his lips lightly.

"Where have you been?" I asked, softly tapping the side of his head. "In here? In your mind?"

He let out a long breath.

"I don't think it's a good idea for…"

"Stop right there! Stop freezing me out! I don't deserve that. Please! Just *talk* to me."

"There's nothing to say."

I wanted to show how frustrated that made me; I wanted to hit something, but I knew that wouldn't help.

"Then *I'll* talk."

He stared at me warily.

"What you did last night was beyond heroic. Was that really just another day at work for you?"

I knew that my voice was shaking but I couldn't stop it.

James just looked at me and nodded.

It was as if he'd shut off his emotions as easily as turning off a tap. There was no hint of the passion which I *knew* he was capable of. It was eerie and it scared me.

"Well, it was amazing. *You're* amazing. And I get, sort of, why you need to think it through on your own," my lips trembled. "But you're not alone. I'm with you."

He looked at me for the longest time, searching for something in my face. I didn't think he'd found whatever he wanted, whatever he was looking for, but at least he spoke.

"All the time in Nagorno, you were counting the days until you could go home. But why, Bel? What have you got to go back to?"

I swallowed, blinking hard. I'd changed so much since I'd left the UK. It was hard to remember the emotions I'd felt when my father had dumped me there. Even so, his question wrong-footed me. Why had he brought that up now?

But at least he was talking again.

I tried to explain.

"At first, I just felt lost. But after I was in Nagorno for a while, I began to … fit. I was useful. I told you that I'd never had a job before, so it felt good to be able to contribute to something important."

"Yeah, I get that, so why go home to that old bastard?"

"It probably doesn't make much sense to you—or to anyone else—but I need to go home to face up to who I am. I have to face up to my father, to stand up to him, or I'll never be able to be strong. Do you understand?"

Oh, sure, I had a plan. Go home, tell my father that I didn't need him, then prove it by living my own life. But all of that meant leaving James until I'd got my life sorted out. I just wasn't sure my heart would survive it.

I could see from his expression that he didn't understand what I was so badly trying to explain to him.

"I asked you to come with me, but I won't beg. Not again. The door's open, but you're the one who's got to walk through it."

"I…"

"What do you want, Bel?"

You.

"I want an everyday love. I don't want a shooting star, I want a love that lasts."

He didn't even blink.

"Don't you get it? Guys like me don't do relationships *because we can't*. You think you can fix me, but you can't. What if we did the whole marriage and kids thing…"

I was stunned, but he didn't notice.

"…and five years from now something sets me off? I'm a ticking time-bomb, and you do not want to be around me when I explode."

I held my breath as the pain in my chest grew worse.

"You'll want me to give this up. You'll want me to do a 'normal' job," and he pulled a face. "I can't, and you know why? A shrink told me once why danger is addictive. The bigger the event, the bigger the hit of dopamine, but then it loses its novelty so you keep on needing bigger hits. So, no. I can't give you that. All I have is this, me."

He was giving out mixed signals. Possessive, but ready to bolt at the first sign of affection; demanding, yet aloof.

I was so in love with James, I couldn't remember how my life had been before him.

And he was wrong, so wrong, but he couldn't see it. I knew the real James was in there, screaming to be let out, but I couldn't reach him, couldn't touch him, and if I didn't find a way to unlock his prison, he might be trapped there for the rest of his life.

Maybe he would understand in time.

We were leaving in the morning with a flight booked to Paris. We'd be there for five days to be debriefed by the Halo Trust team. Part of this would involve meeting with their shrink, which was standard practise after a long deployment or an incident, apparently. Then there'd be a couple of days to decompress and enjoy the city. After that, Clay and Zada were going home on leave, before prepping for Angola in five weeks.

Clay and Zada seemed to assume that I was going back to the UK with James, but I wasn't certain of any such thing. I wasn't certain of anything at all.

I lay there, chilled and panicked. Finally, I screwed up every tiny piece of courage I had and turned to James.

"Make love to me?"

He hesitated long enough to stop my heart.

"Are you sure?"

"Don't be with me because it's easy, James, because I'm here, because I'm convenient, because I won't say no to you." I took a deep breath, studying the closed expression on his face. "I want you to choose me. Do you understand? Choose the living, not the memory. You have to make a choice. You have to decide. You have to *choose me*." I paused and looked down. "I'll understand if you don't."

He ran his rough fingers down my cheek, his mouth finding mine. A tentative kiss turned to a heated one and our bodies shared the emotions that our lips would never speak.

For a few hours, we were together again.

When I woke in the morning, uncertainty still hovering over me, I felt James's hand on my stomach. I breathed in deeply, the essence of our bodies and lovemaking in the air around us.

But his hand slipped away, and I heard the rustle of the sheets as he stood up.

A second later, he dropped a soft kiss onto my shoulder, and I smiled.

"So I was thinking," he said, "after we've done our debrief in Paris, I'm not really interested in going back to the UK. Clay says we can tag along with him and Zada. I wouldn't mind seeing California. What do you think?"

It sounded wonderful, but my heart sank. Hadn't he heard *anything* that I'd said to him yesterday?

He didn't give me a chance to answer, relaxed as he turned on the hot water in the shower.

I joined him quickly, because I wanted to remember forever the way he felt now, his warm silky skin under my fingers. He looked surprised, but he didn't send me away.

Then I had to hurry to dress and finish packing before meeting Clay and Zada for breakfast.

James hadn't pressed for an answer to his suggestion, and I wasn't sure if that was deliberate or not. Anxiety was a great appetite suppressant, and I picked at the *Pamidorov Dzvadzekh*, a sort of tomato dish with scrambled eggs added in. It was certainly more appealing than the other traditional item on the menu: *Hash*, a dish of simmered cow's hooves.

We all heard the *whop-whop* of the helicopter's rotor blades at the same time. Clay frowned as he stared out of the window.

"It's private, not military or police. I'd say for a diplomat, but they probably wouldn't stay in a two-star hotel."

They all turned to look at me, and my stomach fell as the helicopter noise increased.

We watched as it landed in the ornamental garden in front of the hotel, crushing the rhododendrons.

There was only one person who'd act with such arrogance.

"Better be up front and centre," murmured Clay, standing up and heading outside.

We all did the same, and I squared my shoulders, knowing that I'd see my father soon.

He was the first to step out of the helicopter, his steel-grey hair and overcoat as familiar to me as breathing. I knew that he'd be wearing one of his power suits, probably with a red tie.

Clay looked at me, a question in his eyes. I shook my head and stared at my shoes.

"Williams," barked my father, extending his hand.

He shook hands with Clay but ignored James and Zada who were standing at one side, then fixed his gaze on me.

"Well, Arabella. Trouble follows you, even here."

My jaw dropped open.

I should have known he'd blame me for everything that had happened, I just hadn't expected to hear the verdict given so brutally or so publically. I should have known better. I really should have. But

I'd honestly thought there'd be a shred of concern for what we'd been through—for what *I'd* been through. I was wrong.

"Your daughter survived a serious assault, sir," said James, striding forward his arms folded across his chest, his eyes glacial. "I'm sure you're concerned for her well-being."

My father used silence like a sword. His contempt for me showed in every breath, every blink of his eyes.

Dad simply turned away from James without replying and focussed on Clay.

"I trust this won't hold up work for too long. I've told your superiors at Halo that I expect the Nagorno project to be completed on time regardless."

Clay's eyes flashed with anger. It took a lot to make him lose his cool, but my father had a way of getting under everyone's skin.

"The Trust will undertake a risk assessment to ensure the safety of any replacement team," Clay said clearly. "That will be their first priority. And it will take time."

"More delays," my father spat out. "Fucking ridiculous. What sort of show are you people running? I was told you were professionals."

"We are," said Clay. "Which is why the safety of the personnel comes first. I hope I've made that clear, Mr. Forsythe."

I saw my father bristle. If there was one thing he hated, it was not having his title used. He glared at Clay, and some silent message passed between them. Then my father turned to me again.

"Your presence has endangered the team and my company's investment," he said to me. "Get in the helicopter, Arabella. I'm sending you home."

My humiliation was now complete. I didn't have the strength to fight him, not here, not now, not while I was still so raw inside. I needed to go home and pick my battleground. I hoped that James would understand. It was a very tiny hope.

I turned to Clay and Zada.

"Thank you so much for everything," I said. "You guys have been amazing and I've learned so much."

Clay wrapped his arms around me, bending his height to hug me back.

"Look after yourself, Harry. Don't be a stranger."

But Zada's gaze threw daggers, her anger palpable.

I stepped back, shocked.

Then James grabbed my hand and turned me to face him.

"Bel, don't go. You don't have to go with him."

His voice was low and gruff.

I stared up at him, tears threatening as I forced them back.

"James, I have to go. Please! Remember what I told you."

My father glanced at his watch impatiently.

"Very touching, now get in the fucking helicopter."

James walked away without another word. I began to go after him, but my father caught my arm and gave me a warning look.

Clay started forward, but I shook my head.

"It's okay…"

It really wasn't.

Zada's lips curled, and she gave me a hard, thorough, dismissive look.

"You're not worthy of taking her place. You haven't even tried to fight for him."

I nodded once, as if confirming what I'd feared, and I walked away, my head held high. I pretended that I understood, I pretended that I wasn't crushed, and I pretended that I still had a sliver of pride.

I didn't. I had none, nothing. And now I had no one.

As I boarded the helicopter and Yerevan began to fall away, growing smaller with each second, I let the first tear fall.

For all that I had lost. For all that I had found.

CHAPTER 24

SIX MONTHS LATER...

Arabella

Mist drifted over the moat making Roecaster Castle eerie and mysterious, a modern-day Brigadoon. The rural rhythm had been shattered by hundreds of guests, and the gravel driveway was lined with Bentleys, Rollers, and a ridiculous display of high-performance sports cars. I spotted Alastair's new Ferrari parked at a jaunty angle across the croquet lawn.

I stared out of the small, leaded window, pressing my face to the cold glass. Down below, the grounds sparkled with a thousand miniature lanterns and I could hear the party-goers shouting with laughter.

Once, I would have been down there with them—the loudest of them all, the drunkest, the wildest.

I miss him. I miss him. I miss him.

Even surrounded by crowds of party-goers, I'd never felt so lonely. I didn't know missing someone could be so physically painful, as if half my body had been hacked away.

I loved James Spears with my heart and soul, and every breath.

Something that only happens once in a lifetime … if you're lucky

And he was missing someone, too, but it wasn't me. It would never be me. Not in the same way, never. And how could I compete with the idea of a woman like Amira? Someone who was perfect—beautiful, committed, a martyr to humanity. Killed saving lives.

I was just a waste of everything—space, life, the air I breathed.

If I understood the intense pain I felt, maybe I could make friends with it?

But without love, what's the point of any of it?

If only that could have been our happy ending—all that hope, all that optimism. But life isn't like that.

We were going to defy the odds, defy everyone. I thought I understood how hard it would be, but I was wrong. So wrong.

James knew. James who'd left school at 16, James who hadn't passed his GCSEs, he knew. My expensive private education, my three years at university, the Swiss finishing school amounted to nothing compared to his knowledge, his understanding of the brutal realities and complexities of life.

The last six months had been hard. Such a small word for everything that I'd felt, everything I'd endured.

I'd come back to London with my father, but couldn't stand being in the same house as him; so complacent, so overbearing now he'd brought me to heel.

The only thing that kept me going was the belief that I wasn't worthless—and I needed to make things right for James. For the first time ever, my life had a direction and purpose. I had the *why*; I just needed to work on the *how*.

Licking my wounds and sick to my stomach of London and my feckless and false friends, I headed for my childhood home, Roecaster Castle.

There, in the empty rooms and empty nights, I'd begun to formulate a plan that could achieve my goals. At first, it was tentative and weak, but each day my vision became clearer, my idea stronger. And I began to believe that I could pull this off. I just needed a little help and a speck of luck.

Well, I wasn't my father's daughter for nothing. All those endless business dinners that he'd dragged me to, all those tedious events, all those bores that I'd had to entertain and charm for him—I knew people, I had connections. And I planned to exploit them as ruthlessly as my father ever had. But not with threats and bullying; with persuasion and smiles, with charm … and with justice on my side.

I was doing it for James and all the men and women who risked their lives, like him. I was doing it for myself, too.

And if there was one thing I knew, it was how to throw one hell of a party.

I took a deep breath and pulled the ice-blue satin dress over my head, feeling the soft rush of material against my bare skin. Then I turned to stare in the mirror. I'd chosen this dress because the colour reminded me of James's eyes. Even thousands of miles away, he was always with me.

I let that thought settle into my heart with a pained smile.

Always with me, but forever apart.

And I was finding my way to live with that. I'd found my cause, my reason for living. I'd be okay on my own, I knew that now. It was James's final gift to me.

I straightened my spine and swept from the room, gliding along the thickly carpeted hallway until I reached the top of the stairs.

I gazed down the wide double staircase that framed the entrance hall of Roecaster Castle, the Forsythes' ancestral home, taking in the glowing crystal chandeliers, the vibrant bouquets of gardenias, their intoxicating fragrance drifting upwards.

And beyond, I saw the scarlet tailcoats of the Hunt members, the women pale jewels in the ballroom beyond. It was a scene that had been reenacted for hundreds of years in this very place, only the beeswax candles making way for electricity, the women's dresses a little racier, the décolletage a little deeper, the gowns clinging to subtly tanned bodies, whitened teeth, and carefully dyed hair.

The clink of glasses and the sound of laughter filled the vast rooms. It looked perfect, if you ignored my father's simmering resentment, the shallowness of the friendships, the desperate, forced enjoyment. Ah yes, looks were everything, and I was an expert at faking it.

I paused at the top of the staircase, allowing the crowd to run their greedy little eyes up and down me, smiling coolly as a ripple of applause began as I descended, step by step.

"I say, Harry, you look absolutely delish," cooed Alastair, abandoning Lady Marchman's daughter, Cordelia, to take my elbow and escort me into the ballroom.

"You are a darling," I smiled, shedding his arm with ease as I snagged a glass of champagne from a waiter. "Do give my regards to your mother when you see her."

He gaped at me open-mouthed as I sailed past.

Sinclair, our ancient butler, bowed when he saw me.

"Everything is ready for the slide show, Lady Arabella."

"Thank you, Sinclair."

"And if I may be so bold, Lady Arabella, I'm very proud of you."

Tears sprang to my eyes. I'd known Sinclair my whole life, grown up with his silent glares of disapproval as he prowled the many rooms of the castle. He saw everything, knew everything, and sealed it all behind thin lips and an impassive exterior.

I blinked rapidly.

"Thank you," I said, my voice hoarse. "Thank you."

He gave a tiny smile, bowed, and continued with his duties.

Collecting myself, I walked to the head of the room, graciously greeting and smiling at these people that I'd known my whole life, and I felt a cool, calm detachment settle inside me. For once, I was in control; for once, they would listen to me; for once, I had something worth saying.

I gave the band leader a small sign, allowing the music to die away, then I picked up a silver spoon and tapped it against my glass, drawing all attention to me.

"Good evening," I said. "It's so lovely of you all to come and support our annual Hunt Ball. Especially this year, because in a break with tradition, the proceeds of the silent auction from your *extremely* generous gifts, won't be going to the Dorsetshire Hunt. Our wonderful Master of Hunt, Teddy Throsgrove, has agreed to support a charity that has become very close to my heart."

My smile dimmed and I spoke with a clarity and vehemence that surprised even me.

"Earlier this year, my dear father, Sir Reginald Forsythe, began his support of the landmine charity Halo Trust. I was fortunate enough to visit one of their operations in a remote area on the border between Armenia and Azerbaijan. I'd never heard of Nagorno Karabakh before I went and I couldn't find it on a map a month after I'd been there…" *laughter*, "but … whilst there, I witnessed daily acts of bravery by women who earn an annual salary of less than a year's membership to a club in Mayfair."

At my nod, Sinclair began the slideshow behind my head: a photograph of our mountain compound, a sign warning of a minefield, the women in their body armour with tiredness etched on their faces, a set of mines encrusted in dirt ready to be destroyed, and then a live demolition that I'd shakily filmed with my smartphone—even here, the sound loud enough to make people jump, watching as the picture blurred with soil raining down in front of the camera.

"The operation in Nagorno was run by an extraordinary man, a former American Marine, Alan Clayton Williams. Although you won't know his name, you will know him as the man who risked his life and lost a leg in the infamous Times Square Bombing, two years ago."

A murmur of recognition rose into a swell around the room.

"I came to know Clay and his wife Zada very well, as I worked with them. The conditions were harsh, cold, and difficult. And those of you who've seen me sinking Singapore Slings at Annabel's wouldn't have recognized me sloshing around through six inches of mud to a concrete shower block…" a peel of laughter rang out. "But I did it. There may have been a few grumbles at first," I took a deep breath, "but these small inconveniences were nothing compared to the heroism of my co-workers, the sheer dogged determination to make a better country for their children." I paused. "It was humbling."

I stared out at the sea of faces turned to me, and the annoyed glare of my father.

"And it's for that reason that I've been honoured and delighted to share this special moment with you."

I turned to the Master of Hunt, a short, round man, whose flushed face matched his scarlet coat. He beamed at me.

"Teddy, be a darling and tell all the lovely people how much our little Hunt Ball has raised."

He stood next to me, sweating and avuncular, and cleared his throat.

"Thank you, Lady Arabella," he said, bowing low and casting a quick glance at my cleavage. "It is my absolute honour and delight to announce…" and he rustled through three pockets before he found a scrawled piece of paper, "that this year's Hunt Ball has raised £642,073 and 25 pence for the Halo Trust. I'm so glad my 25p could make a difference."

Everyone laughed, then cheered as he reached for my right hand and placed a damp kiss on the back of it, and the invited reporters lit up the room with their camera flashes.

As the cheers died down, I held my glass up, catching the crowd's attention.

"There was a second man on the Nagorno team—the bomb disposal officer, a man who trained the locals to neutralize explosive devices such as anti-tank mines and anti-personnel mines. Even though I have seen him at work, it is still impossible to comprehend the level of skill, bravery and coolness of action that is necessary. A man who daily put his life on the line, both as a member of the British Army and," I took a deep breath, "as the man who neutralized the Times Square Bomb."

Murmurs of surprise fell to shocked silence as I raised both hands.

"Yes, that information surprised me, too, when I found out. Here he was, famous around the world for an incomprehensible act of extraordinary heroism, and instead of doing speaking tours and making appearances on chat shows, he has continued his daily job of doing what none of us could do. He is a man who walks towards a bomb that he knows will kill him if he has a second's lapse in concentration, a single moment of inattention. Every day, in harsh conditions, he takes on the trickiest challenges, the hard to access devices, the booby-traps deliberately designed to maim and kill the Ammunition Technical Officer, or ATO in the British Army."

I took a breath as every eye was fixed on me.

"Yet he has remained anonymous until this moment—although people all around the world have wished to thank him for his heroism that day. This man deserves a medal, don't you think?"

A roar of agreement and applause sprang up, echoing from the ancient stone walls.

"Well," I said, as the roar died, "he didn't get a medal. Instead, a great wrong has been done to this man. Whilst suffering from PTSD after over a decade of honourable service to our country, he was hounded from the British Army and given what is called an 'administrative discharge'—to all intents and purposes as a way of brushing the problem under the carpet, gone and forgotten. It was a shameful way to treat a hero. It shames us all. A mean, shabby way to treat a hero—and I'm not the only one who thinks so." I gave a soft sigh and placed my hand on my heart. "My own dear father, Sir Reginald, is making it his personal mission to ensure that this unconscionable wrong is righted, and this man, this incredible man, receives the acknowledgement of his bravery and sacrifice."

The crowd ate it up as dozens of guests pulled out their mobile phones to record this touching moment, and I stared at my father's granite face, knowing that fury bubbled under the surface. I also knew that I'd checkmated him in public. There was no way he could back out of this now. I raised my glass and blew him a kiss. "I love you, Daddy. And it's time to let the world know of all your tireless, behind-the-scenes work to right this terrible wrong."

I held out to my hand to my father as he came towards me, perfectly playing the part of grandee who hadn't wanted a jot of publicity.

Yeah, right.

I turned to the front again, holding on to my father's hand to force him into the limelight.

"Disgraced, discharged from the Army, unrecognized, unrewarded—is this how Britannia treats her heroes? I say no! No! A thousand times no!"

A great roar of 'noes' filled the room, and I knew that I'd got them.

"My dear friends, I know in your hearts that you agree with us and wish to make amends on behalf of our country. We *can* make a difference, and we *will* make a difference. It starts here, today, right now. My dear father and I are starting a petition that we will take to the government—we will *force* them to see the error of their ways. I'm so proud that the first name on that petition will be my father's."

I forced myself to ignore the thought that James was going to want to kill me when he found out.

I handed my father a fountain pen and a sheet of paper, and more camera flashes caught the moment as thunderous applause and cheers echoed through the vaulted ceilings.

Keeping the smile pinned to his face must have been painful for him, and I enjoyed every millisecond of his discomfort.

The second name was mine, and soon the petition was being passed around the room, which was full of a complement of peers of the realm. The petition would be hard to ignore after this.

But I hadn't finished yet. I was intent on outing James for the hero I knew him to be.

"So, Honourable friends, ladies and gentlemen, please raise your glasses in a toast to the bravest man I have ever had the honour to meet…"

And at my nod, Sinclair pressed the mouse to advance the slide to the last photograph.

In it, with a backdrop of the silent mountains behind him, was James, his beautiful face in sharp relief, a smudge of dirt across one cheekbone as he stood with an anti-tank mine in his hands.

It was stark and beautiful and the sense of his loneliness and isolation bled from the picture.

I turned to the audience.

"Staff Sergeant James Spears."

More thunderous applause and the camera flashes went berserk.

My father walked towards me, a warm smile on his cold face as he embraced me.

"Well played, Arabella," he whispered into my ear as he kissed my cheek. "I'll see you in my study later."

He squeezed the tops of my arms, almost hard enough to be painful.

"I look forward to it," I smiled back, ice in my eyes.

Had I seen a gleam of approval in his expression? No, probably just the light of combat.

He backed away as a stream of reporters surrounded me, a hundred questions bubbling as they thrust phones in my face to record my pearls of wisdom.

I told them everything that I knew about James: everything that I'd seen for myself and everything that Clay and Zada had told me. James, the man himself had said the least of all, but I was prepared to fill in the blanks for his sake. But not just for his sake—for the silent, unacknowledged heroism of all the men and women who worked in mud and blood to neutralize bombs and make the world a safer place.

Resolve hardened inside me, but I had a small twinge of concern that James might not want his life turned upside down again or plagued by my conscience, but I'd convinced myself that it was the right thing to do—and there was no backing down now.

Talking about Amira was harder, but again I told the journalists what a hero she'd been, how much in love they'd been, and how tragic the outcome of that love. I talked about how touched my father had been and how important he thought it was to right the wrong done to James. They couldn't get enough of it, crowding him with questions that he answered solemnly and with heartfelt sincerity, the old fraud.

Several of the reporters phoned in copy to their newspapers and online news sites there and then.

By morning, the story would be worldwide. The Halo Trust would be thanking me—but not my father and not, I suspected, James. I'd just have to wait and see.

After the reporters had finished, so many of the guests came to congratulate me, to bask for a few seconds in my reflected glory, that it was hours before I could get to my father's study. For once, I wasn't afraid.

"Well, Arabella," he said as I serenely sat before him, the thick oak desk a welcome barricade between us. "It's been an interesting evening."

"Yes, hasn't it?" I replied cheerfully. "Thank you so much for your support in such a noble cause."

He shed the relaxed pose as easily as a snake sheds its skin.

"You think you can fuck me over and get away with it?"

I smiled grimly. *I'd learned from the best.* Once I knew how to fight, it was something to look forward to.

"I don't know what you're talking about, Daddy. Those people out there think you're a hero. I've done more for your public image in one night than an entire team of PR specialists could ever do. You should be thanking me."

His cheeks darkened with anger.

"Get out!"

I stood up slowly, relishing the moment when I'd finally beaten my father.

"Gladly," I smiled. "Goodnight, Daddy."

CHAPTER 25

James

THE AIR QUIVERED WITH HEAT, and even though everything was covered in a thin layer of dust, the colours of Africa were vibrant and warm. The vast canyons, steel cities and wide, lush valleys; the wealth, the poverty, and acres and acres of minefields. Three decades of civil war had ended 17 years ago, but its legacy survived in the form of millions of landmines that maimed or killed thousands every year: welcome to twenty-first century Angola.

Other demining teams that I'd been briefed by had unanimously described my current deployment as 'the armpit of the world' or 'least-wanted assignment'.

But this complex, damaged and beautiful country spoke to me. Here, I could slowly begin to heal; here, I could start again. If I was honest with myself—a new habit that I wasn't yet fully on board with—my reawakening had started 4,000 miles away on a remote mountainside encased in snow and ice, but it was continuing here.

The first two months after Bel left with her bastard father had been brutal. Every day, I'd been tempted to take a drink or three, something to blot out the seeds of hope that she'd given me during those few days in Yerevan.

Clay and Zada had stuck with me, taking me back to the US with them when they were on leave because they didn't trust me go back to London alone. They were probably right about that.

Instead, I'd gone to California with them and met Amira's family again. They'd taken me into their home and shown me her year books and all the family photographs from childhood upwards, and finally, I'd made my peace with her death.

I think a lot of that had to do with the quiet dignity of her parents. They'd shown me that there are other ways to grieve, other ways to respect the dead that wasn't through anger and self-destruction. Amira had known that. Of course she had. She'd told me from the start—she wanted to *do good*. That's how she planned to cope with her own grieving for the loss of her brother.

It was fucked up in so many ways that it had led to her death in Syria.

And now we were in Angola on the west coast of Africa, a long way south of the Equator, living in a dangerous land where the people were still trying to come to terms with a civil war that had torn the country apart. Even 17 years later, old wounds were hard to heal.

Today had been a long, tough day. My team of de-miners were exhausted but motivated by the fact that more land had been cleared, more lives saved.

Arriving back, I signed them off and headed to the back of the truck to check that all the equipment was in good working order for tomorrow—a job that I didn't entrust to anyone else.

My clothes were sweat-stained and white salt marks ringed my baseball cap.

I was still checking the inventory when our local Mr. Fix-it, whose parents named Yamba Asha after a famous Angolan footballer, came limping up to me.

He'd lost his left leg in a landmine incident when he was a kid. He said that he'd never got along with his prosthetic and preferred crutches. He'd been a lucky find for us, knowing exactly how to oil the wheels of cooperation.

"*Senhor* James! Boss wants to see you bad!"

"Yeah, okay. I'm on my way over there now. *Obrigado*."

"No worries!" he grinned.

I wondered what had got Clay wound up. He didn't usually send Yamba to hurry me along.

Still, I went at the same careful pace, checking that all the equipment was put away correctly before heading to the command hut.

Clay looked up as soon as I walked in, his expression hard to read.

"Dude, you're back! Thank, fu— I mean, fudge."

My hands were still encrusted with dirt from the day's Task and I was too tired to play games. I stared tiredly at Clay, wondering what planet he was on and whether it was nice this time of year.

"Yep, 27 anti-tank mines, 13 PMAs, no casualties, no issues—destroyed with a nice little firework display. I'll start the report and…"

He waved a hand.

"Do it later. I've had HQ ringing the phone off of the fudging hook all day. They want to talk to you, bro."

"Are they bringing in the Casspir de-miner truck we requested *two months ago*?"

The Casspir was a steel-armoured demining vehicle, with a V-shaped hull to deflect a bomb blast, and could be driven over minefields. Great on wide, flat ground, but it still required trained personnel to check the ground after, in my opinion. But it definitely saved time.

"Because," I continued, "the field next to ours has fucking thousands of anti-tank mines. I'm thinking it was one where the Cubans used a mine-laying machine, so…"

"No, listen!"

"Is it about Yad?"

I knew that the sniper had died from his injuries and that Yad had been arrested, but investigations were still on-going in Nagorno. Neither us expected that any action would be ever be taken against that evil bastard and he'd probably be released any day now.

"Shut the fudge up will you! Nah, man! It's good news!" He rubbed his forehead. "Potentially good news—eh, you'll have to decide for yourself."

What the hell did that mean?

He swivelled his laptop screen around to face me, and a two-inch high headline stood out.

TIMES SQUARE BOMB HERO NAMED

My eyes widened, the tiredness vanishing in an instant.

I bent down to read the rest of the story as my heart hammered, filled with the kind of adrenaline that flows when it's time for fight or flight.

It was all there in black and white: my name, Clay's, Amira's, even Zada's.

All of it, for the world to see.

And it ended with a call to action for people to sign a petition to reverse my 'dishonourable discharge' as they wrongly called it, and even asked for me to be awarded a medal.

I started to ask how the hell the Press had got ahold of the story after so long. But as I scanned to the end of the story, I answered my own question.

"Arabella."

Clay nodded gravely.

"It says her old man is behind it, but I guess we both know better. They're doing cartwheels over at Halo Trust HQ; they say their fundraising page has been blowing up with donations—over a quarter of a million spondoolies since the story broke this morning which is amazing and…" he paused. "How do you feel about it?"

"Pissed off," I said, turning on my heel and heading to my room.

I couldn't believe that Bel had betrayed me like this. *I decided who to tell, not her!* I *knew* I shouldn't have trusted her. I'd been so fucking lonely, so fucking weak.

And I'd spent six months forcing myself to forget her—to forget how she'd felt beneath me, surrounding me; to forget how her eyes shone when we were together, how her voice sounded sinfully husky when she woke up in the mornings. I'd forced myself to forget; trained myself to go a whole minute without thinking of her, then five minutes, then a whole hour.

But now the memories all came rushing back in technicolour.

My blaze of anger dissipated quickly.

The truth was I didn't know what to feel. I was a professional at keeping my emotions turned to zero, and I'd spent the last two years closed off to human interaction. But Bel had crept under my skin. I'd told myself that getting involved with her was a bad idea, that she'd never stand up to her father. But here she was, proving me wrong. Again.

A strange feeling floated inside me, a bubble of lightness, a feeling that might have been hope.

Damn her.

CHAPTER 26

Arabella

Since I'd hijacked the Hunt Ball and earned my father's subsequent anger, I'd been staying at the London townhouse. A strategic withdrawal, also known as, abject cowardice.

I'd taken the offensive on my plan to regain my own life, starting with a quiet word here and there that had culminated with the Master of the Hunt agreeing that the fundraising could, for once and against all tradition, be diverted to the Halo Trust.

I'd dropped ten pounds in the weeks before the Ball, terrified that someone would reveal my plans to Dad, which would mean that he'd stop them dead in the water. But, thankfully, that hadn't been the case, and I'd been able to start on my second project: to clear James's name, to have the 'administrative discharge' struck from his record, and for his heroism to be acknowledged.

What I hadn't expected was a call from the Halo Trust's HQ to ask to meet with me.

The very next day, I'd flown up to their offices in Dumfries, 80 miles south of Edinburgh in the Scottish Borders, excited and nervous. I desperately wanted this part of my fresh start.

In the charity's small reception, I was met by the Director of Operations, a lean, weather-beaten man with steel-grey hair and intense brown eyes. Obviously ex-Army. After spending so much time with James and Clay, I could spot the signs a mile away.

"Lady Arabella, very good to meet you at last."

"And you, Sir Graham, but my friends call me Harry," *and the man I love calls me 'Bel'.*

I banished the thought immediately.

"And I'm Gray. Tea? Coffee?"

"Tea would be lovely, thank you."

He barked an order at a female member of staff who rolled her eyes at him, then smiled at me.

"Please, come through to my office. Forgive the clutter—we're dealing with a situation … a serious problem with a team in Syria at the moment," and he frowned, the heavy lines of his forehead as deep as a ploughed field.

"I understand," I said quietly.

And I did. I really did. I'd been there, I'd lived it.

His eyes narrowed and his hard face became even grimmer.

"I would like you to know that what happened to you…"

I held up my hand to stop him.

"I don't hold the Trust responsible, Gray. One bad day doesn't negate the value of my experience in Nagorno Karabakh or your work. Not for me. Yadigar Aghayev was arrested—I know that he has connections and the outcome isn't clear…"

Gray gave a thin smile.

"One of the reasons that I wanted to see you was to tell you in person that the bast— person in question has been formally charged and could well see a number of years behind bars."

My eyebrows shot up.

"Really? I thought his connection with his police cousin made him untouchable."

"That was his second mistake," said Gray. "His first was laying one miserable finger on you." He tapped the desk with his pen. "Let's just say that the regional government values the capital potential that clearing the land of mines will bring, more than the value of a corrupt official or his relatives."

I gave a weak smile of relief.

"So he can't hurt anyone else? What can I say? Thank you."

Gray shook his head.

"It should never had happened. And I wouldn't have blamed Spears for killing the bastard."

I paled at the sound of James's name, and Gray backtracked quickly, but for the wrong reasons.

"My apologies, Harry. I won't mention it again. Just know that it's been dealt with."

"Thank you," I said weakly.

"Now," he said, moving on rapidly. "Damn fine job you did with that Hunt Ball. We appreciated that cheque. And three Gauss's for Clay Williams' team. Excellent!"

"You are very welcome."

"And the publicity for us has been incredible. We've had donations that have doubled the money you raised."

"Oh my goodness! That's wonderful!" I said, stunned and delighted.

"Yes, it is. So, I'll get to the point. Firstly, we're fully behind your father's petition on behalf of Spears, and we've got our PR team working on it now. He's been a hard man to contact, comms being what they are in Luanda, but by now he's been made aware of the situation."

I winced inwardly. I could only imagine how angry James would be now that I'd outed him to the world's media. I'd stripped him of his right to privacy. And even now, with the additional money raised for the Trust, I wondered if I'd done the right thing.

Gray drew my attention back to him by slapping a document onto his desk in front of me.

"We'd like to offer you a full-time paid position as our Director of Events Fundraising. It's a self-starting position, so you could work from home, with occasional visits to HQ, on a need by need basis. What do you say, Harry? You're just the man, um, woman for the job."

I was very nearly speechless, but all those ghastly months at Finishing School were useful for something.

"It would be my honour," I said, my voice shaking.

"Excellent!" he grunted, pushing the papers towards me. "Read the contract and sign it when you're ready." He leaned forward. "Frankly, we want to capitalize on all the publicity that you've sent our way. We need you, Harry."

I felt tears spring to my eyes. No one had ever needed me before. It felt wonderful.

It was several minutes before the blurriness cleared from my eyes and I was able to read the contract.

Gray was tactful enough to bustle about while I sipped my tea and read the papers, signing with a flourish at the end.

I pushed the signed contract back across the desk to Gray.

"I'm ready to start."

We both stood up to shake hands.

"Excellent," he said. "Come and meet the rest of the team."

The next few days flew by. If my father thought that he'd be able to wriggle out of helping James, he was wrong.

I'd long ago learned his email login, so I was able to check his calendar, which meant I could direct journalists to doorstep him wherever he went.

It worked beautifully, and with every interview and comment, he dug himself in deeper. Even he wasn't stupid enough to realize that backing out now would do him permanent damage.

Playing him at his own game was enormously empowering.

Which wasn't to say that I wasn't ready to shit a brick when Mrs. Danvers informed me with an evil smile that my father had arrived at the townhouse and wished to see me.

"Immediately, Lady Arabella."

I smiled at her as she walked away.

"And may warts grow on your vagina."

"I beg your pardon?" she gasped.

"I said I do hope that you've recovered from your angina."

"I don't have angina," she snapped.

"Oh, my mistake. I'm so glad."

When I continued to smile at her, she turned away with a puzzled look.

I knew that it was petty to bait a member of staff, but the old cow had lorded it over me my whole life. I really did hope she got warts. Lots of them. Everywhere.

I took a deep breath, and began the feared walk to my father's study, when a shocking thought occurred to me: *I don't have to do what he says anymore.*

Liberated by that thought, I turned around and headed to my room. I had work to do for the Trust. People were relying on me.

It felt scary, but wonderful.

Twenty minutes later, Mrs. Danvers was back.

"Lady Arabella, your father is *still* waiting for you!" she hissed.

"I'll be down shortly," I said distractedly, scrolling through a cascade of emails on my laptop.

"Now!" she snapped.

I turned around slowly, surveying her from head to foot, then spoke with the quiet, authoritative tone that I'd learned from James. I just wished I could infuse it with the same sense of danger, an unspoken threat. Maybe one day.

"As you can see, Brown," I said clearly, remembering her real name just in time, "I'm rather busy with something that actually matters. You may tell my father that I'll be available when I've finished in approximately 45 minutes. And," I continued, my tone hardening even further, "I don't appreciate being spoken to in that peremptory manner. Please close the door behind you on your way out."

She gasped, her face going stiff, and left the room shutting the door with a firm click.

Three minutes later, my father barged in without knocking, all but frothing at the mouth.

"I've had enough of your fucking games, Arabella."

I stared at the stranger who called himself my father.

"Why's that, Daddy? You've been playing games for years: mind games are your favourite past time—after making money, of course."

His face started to redden.

I was honestly scared and my heart was hammering as if I'd been sprinting, but I refused to show it. After all, I'd survived Yad's attack, and I'd survived watching the man I loved walk up to neutralize a booby-trapped car bomb, so I knew I was strong. My father had made me resilient, too—I just hadn't known it until this moment. He could stamp and snarl and shout all he liked; he could even hit me, and I wouldn't change a single thing.

"You stupid cunt!" he shouted. "What do you think you're doing? I've had to waste hours on fucking journalists. Hours! It's going to stop! NOW!"

I gave him a wintry smile.

"It's not, Daddy. It's really not going to stop. It's going to go on and on and on, until this terrible wrong has been righted. Don't you want to look like a hero, Daddy?" I taunted him. "Because we both know that good publicity is just the other side of the coin from bad publicity. If you back out now, everyone will see you for the cold-hearted bastard that you really are."

For a long moment, I really thought that he was going to hit me, but then an ugly smile formed on his face, and he crossed his arms, leaning against the doorframe.

"Oh, so that's what it's about. You fucked him, didn't you?"

And he gave a loud, vicious laugh.

"Jesus Christ, Arabella! You really are a stupid cunt, falling for a fucking failure like Spears."

"He's not a failure," I said hotly, beginning to lose my careful control. "He's a hero."

"He's a one-minute wonder, and a penniless one at that. You're really pathetic. Couldn't you at least have chosen an officer? Someone of your own class, for fuck's sake! God, you have the standards of a guttersnipe."

"And you have the morals of an alley cat, so I think that makes us even," I said, lifting my chin, even though I was ashamed to sink to his level of name-calling.

An icy silence descended.

"Say that again and you'll regret it," he said coldly.

"I will say this: I love James and I want the best for him."

I certainly wasn't going to tell the old bastard that my relationship with James had already irretrievably broken down. That wasn't the point. Not for any of this. It never had been.

He lunged forwards and grabbed my shoulders, pushing his face into mine so I could see the tiny blood vessels in his eyes.

"You really think this is what you want, Arabella?" he asked, shaking me roughly so my brain sloshed around inside my skull. "A grubby little life with a shabby little man?"

"How dare you!"

My father's expression was that of a tank about to drive over everything I cared about.

He shook me again then dropped me like a piece of rubbish, but he'd changed his bullying tone to one of amused reasonability.

"Arabella, are you willing to leave behind your class, your clothes, your £150,000 a year allowance? You know that without me, without the family name, you'd be lost." He smiled thoughtfully. "We've all had our little *affaires* with the servant classes. They can be very diverting. I remember a stable lass we had when I was fifteen. Great way to get broken in, but I can promise you this," and his voice became threatening again. "Once the sex becomes a bore, monotonous, or he tires of you, whichever comes first, you'll be back here, begging me…"

"I won't! I don't want anything from you."

He slammed his hand against the wall by my head.

"You have no skills! You'd never survive. You're an infant with a woman's body, but no brain! You'd never survive in the real world. You can't even boil a kettle."

A year ago, I'd have agreed with him, but not anymore. My body was trembling, but I wasn't giving in without a fight, a tiny gesture of disagreement.

"I disagree, and besides, what I don't know, I can always learn."

He laughed, giving me a fatherly smile that chilled my blood.

"Four boarding schools and a finishing school in Geneva would beg to differ," he said drily. "You're nice to look at, Arabella, but you're rather dim. But that doesn't matter—many men prefer a stupid wife."

His expression darkened again. It was the quixotic temper that he used on his business enemies, wrong-footing them constantly with his changeability.

"But *that* man! He's a squaddie with no family and no prospects. Oh yes," he smiled as I couldn't help a surprised intake of breath. "I've had PIs looking into every aspect of his life: I know everything, and a hell of a lot more than you, you poor little cow. My God! He doesn't even care about you—he loves the ghost of a coloured woman—a Muslim, for Christ's sake. It's degrading to even think about."

And with that, he'd finally managed to wound me, but he didn't stop.

"Are you really willing to throw it all away for this man?"

His tone was disdainful and disbelieving, thinking that he'd won already.

I stared back, my eyes traveling across his pressed shirt and three-piece suit, the Windsor knot in his silk necktie. He never had understood me.

I cocked my head to one side.

"What is it that you think I'm throwing away, Daddy?"

He raised his arms wide, gesturing at the hand-painted wallpaper, the Georgian credenza that I used to store my underwear, the silk coverlet that had been imported from Xian in China for a mere £15,000.

"You think you'll be happy living with him in an ex-council flat because that's all you can afford?" he sneered. "In fucking Reading of all places! Jesus, what a flea-infested ghetto. Is that the best you can do?"

"Fine by me. Anything else I'm throwing away?"

His expression was nonplussed.

"Your name, your rank and position in life. Your family."

I counted to five. I didn't have the patience to go any higher.

"I have a new family now." I meant the Trust, but he didn't need to know that. "Nothing else matters."

He laughed. He actually laughed at me.

"He's hardly suitable, Arabella.

"Of course I understand that James isn't 'suitable,'" I said bitterly. "James is non-U … Not One of Us. You didn't think he mattered when you left me alone in Nagorno; he wasn't someone you'd have to worry about. I could have a discreet little affair with him. Is that what you thought? After all, I'm too shallow, too selfish to care about anyone other than myself. Isn't that right, daddy dearest?"

He looked away, already bored.

"See if you feel the same after you've given up all those lovely credit cards that I pay for. I'll give it a week."

My cheeks reddened, but I held my head up high.

"Done."

I reached into my purse and pulled them out, slapping them down onto the credenza.

For a moment, he didn't know what to do. Then he snatched them up, bent them in half and stuffed them in his pocket.

I picked up my phone and pressed the button that I'd had ready to order myself a taxi. I'd always known that this moment was coming, one way or another.

James didn't think I'd ever stand up to my father, but now I was doing it. I was really doing it. James had given me the tools that I'd needed, but now I was using them all by myself. Well, almost by myself.

I picked up my handbag, coat and laptop bag. My suitcases were already packed and in the hallway closet.

"I'm leaving now, Daddy."

He didn't even look at me as I brushed past him.

Silence was his favourite weapon and he employed it ruthlessly. But it couldn't hurt me anymore.

"And the difference is," I said slowly and clearly, "James loved me when I had nothing, he loved me when it mattered, and he loved me just as I am."

"Get out," said my father.

CHAPTER 27

Arabella

My black cab dropped me at Alastair's house overlooking Hyde Park. I'd been there many times before and I knew that he wouldn't turn me away.

His lovely old housekeeper, Mrs. Evans, opened the door. So different from Danvers—because she actually liked me.

"Lady Arabella! What a lovely surprise. Mr. Russell-Hyde didn't tell me you were visiting. Let me help you with your bags, dear."

"Good heavens, no!" I smiled, hauling the two large suitcases into the entrance hall with me. "Alastair can do that. I'm not having you put your back out again, Mrs. E. Is he up yet?"

"My dear, it's six o'clock in the evening!"

"And we both know that doesn't necessarily mean that Alastair is awake, don't we?"

She gave me a conspiratorial smile, but didn't answer.

"Ally!" I bellowed up the stairs. "Get your skinny arse down here and help me with my luggage!"

Alastair appeared at the top of the stairs in a striped dressing gown, his hair stuck to his head on one side, obviously only just awake.

"Harry, what are you doing here scaring me half to death?" he grumbled. "I thought the bloody place was on fire."

"I'm staying for a few weeks and I need you to carry my bags upstairs. I'm *not* getting in that deathtrap you call a lift."

"Oh, right," he sighed, making his way downstairs. "Hang on, why are you staying with me? What's wrong with your place?"

"My dad's there," I said flatly.

He snickered like a horse.

"Not too happy about the Hunt Ball, eh? I thought you were bloody marvellous."

"You are a dear," I said, kissing him on the cheek. "I just need a place to stay for a while, and you owe me."

"Alrighty," He said good-naturedly. "Don't s'pose you're up for a little poke for old times' sake?"

"It only ever was a little poke, Alastair," I said, marching up the stairs while he wheezed behind me with my suitcases.

"God, I'd forgotten what a bitch you are!"

"Don't whine, Ally. Am I in the blue room?"

"Yes, fine," he sighed again. "Whichever you like. Anyway, the yellow room is being redecorated." He paused. "Or it might be the Chinese room. I can't remember. Blue's fine, I think."

The blue room was my favourite when I'd stayed there before. The pretty four-poster bed was swathed in duck-egg blue drapes at each post which could be pulled together if wanted; the wallpaper was handmade in imitation of the original Georgian style that had once covered the walls; and the ceiling was painted to look like dawn on a summer's day, with the dark blue of night fading to palest blue.

I collapsed backwards onto the four-poster and stared up at the ceiling. I loved lying in bed here like this. It felt so peaceful.

"Up for a quickie?" Alastair asked again with a hopeful expression.

"Don't be silly. Now fetch me a glass of bubbly and put some clothes on. Wait, put some clothes on and *then* fetch me a glass of bubbly. We have work to do."

"I don't like the sound of that," he said glumly.

"Ally, you've never worked a day in your whole life, but *this* you're going to enjoy, I promise. We're going to make a list of all our acquaintances and think of ways to put the squeeze on them all."

"Oh, that sounds more like it," he said cheerfully. "Bubbly on the way. Oh, and how about a bit of Bolivian marching powder to see us through?"

I shook my head, not even a little bit tempted.

He started to leave, then poked his head back around the door.

"Um, Harry?"

"What?"

"Your solider friend, the scary good-looking fellow … he's not going to come charging over to beat me up 'cause you're living here, is he?"

"Probably not," I smiled awkwardly.

"Right-o," he said.

My high spirits evaporated. No, James wouldn't be charging over to rescue me—not this time.

Determination settled over me, driving back the tears. No more white knights in my life, but maybe I could do something for him.

No. No maybe about it. I was going to make this happen.

Alastair returned with a bottle of vintage Moët & Chandon, and we started work, making a list of promising people whom we could plead with, persuade or pressure into helping us. Since Alastair's father was a Peer in the House of Lords, he knew a lot of MPs on both sides of the House, as well as in the Commons.

"You know, Harry," he said thoughtfully, "if you want to get noticed, you have to make waves. You've made a good start at the Hunt Ball, impressive PR and all that, but you've got to keep up the pressure: keep the hits coming so that they can't cool off or back down."

"Makes sense," I agreed, flipping through our list.

"But what people really want to see is the man of the hour himself. Get your soldier to come to London and meet all the great and the good—they'll be falling over themselves to be associated with a hero."

I sighed.

"He won't come," I said glumly. "He hates all the razzmatazz and publicity. He wouldn't do it."

Alastair's eyes widened.

"Then why are we breaking our balls to help him out?"

Anger flared inside me.

"Because what they did to him was *wrong*," I said sharply. "He's saved so many lives and they treated him like rubbish."

"Oh, you really meant what you said at the Ball?"

My eyebrows shot up.

"Of course I meant what I said! Wait, what did you *think* I meant?"

He shrugged uncomfortably.

"Well, we just sort of assumed that you wanted to give him a leg up after a leg over, so to speak."

My mouth dropped open.

"You really thought that? And who's 'we', by the way?"

He cringed.

"Well, come on, Harry! Don't forget we know you, all your old chums, even if you've forgotten us. It was a fair assumption. Look, I'm really sorry, old thing, but let's face it—the Harry we know and love would think it was a laugh to pull off a stunt like that."

My anger deflated.

It was true, everything he said was true. I felt ashamed. I gathered a few shreds of pride and turned back to my laptop.

"That's the old Harry. I've changed since then."

Alastair patted my shoulder awkwardly.

"I can see that. Sorry, darling."

"You're forgiven," I sighed.

We began work on our second list: influential party-goers.

I'd been to enough fundraisers to know that the best ones had the perfect blend of the great, the good and the infamous: ideally, blue bloods from the UK with some European royalty added in, wanker-bankers who actually had money to throw around and other well-heeled but otherwise dull individuals, then sprinkle a little Hollywood stardust with some A-listers plus a couple of badly-behaved B-listers—shaken not stirred—and that equalled maximum cash and maximum press coverage.

"You know," said Alastair after we'd been sitting in comfortable silence for half an hour, your soldier friend…"

"His name is James."

"Yes, well, your soldier friend *James* is best known for what he did in New York, correct?"

"Yeah, so?"

"So why not get in touch with the Ambassador at the US Embassy? He's an awfully nice chap, pretty decent wine cellar, too."

I looked up from my laptop, my eyes widening.

"Oh my God, Alastair!"

"Sorry, stupid idea," he mumbled.

"No!" I said, springing to my feet and pacing up and down the room. "It's bloody brilliant! Why didn't I think of that?"

Alastair's eyes brightened.

"Did I just have another good idea?"

"Darling, Ally! You absolutely did!"

"Marvellous!" he grinned. "Any chance of a shag, then?"

"None whatsoever, but I love you anyway."

I gave him a quick hug then went back to work.

Alastair was the perfect accomplice, and we plotted late into the night.

As Christmas loomed, the campaign grew and grew, questions were even asked in Parliament about the way veterans were treated, and a whole section of Prime Minister's Question Time was devoted to the subject.

The Press ate it up, with many column inches, particularly about anything to do with the men and women working in bomb disposal.

And the hastily put together parties I threw were a great success, raising lots of lovely cash and maximum publicity for the Halo Trust. They were delighted with my work and talked about sending me abroad as an ambassador for them.

It was all wonderful and energizing, but the one person I never heard from was James. Clay emailed me from time to time, and even Zada returned the single message that I'd sent her. But from James, there was only silence.

Clay's emails were full of fascinating details about the Tasks in Angola which I carefully worked into Press Releases, but he generally avoided mentioning James. I knew he was working with Clay, but that was about all. It hurt. I longed for his forgiveness, but I still had so much to prove.

Gray's voice sounded subdued when I answered his phone call, two days before Christmas.

"I'm sorry, Harry, but Spears doesn't want anything to do with the campaign. I've tried talking to him several times, but he's determined: he won't come back to the UK to be your, um, our show pony."

"Did he actually say that?" I asked, my voice sharper than I would have liked.

Gray cleared his throat.

"Words to that effect. I even tried to get Clay Williams to persuade him, since he's Spears' Head of Operations, but he's not had any luck either." He paused. "I think you might have to let this one go, Harry."

My chin went up.

"No, absolutely not. Fine, well, if he won't come to the UK, send a camera crew out to Angola to film him at work."

Gray was silent for several seconds.

"Yes! That's a great idea, Harry. And now we've got some extra funds, we can afford to do it." He hesitated. "Do you want to be part of the team that goes?"

I shivered with longing, my heart at war with my head. Then I sighed.

"No, it'll go better if I'm not there."

"Okay," said Gray quietly. "Your decision."

I lay awake that night, full of regrets for what could have been.

But a week later, just in time to ring in the New Year, I received a message that changed everything.

CHAPTER 28

James

"A FUCKING FILM CREW? Are you shitting me?"

Clay grinned.

"No, sir! I shit you not. Meet your new best friends, Jay and Danny. They'll be following you from the moment you open your eyes in the morning to the second your ugly mug hits the pillow at night."

"After a couple of days, you won't even notice that we're here," said Jay, or maybe it was Danny.

"Great," I snarled. "I'm going to the shitter. Want to follow me there?"

I stomped off, leaving Clay to do what he did best and make apologies for the fact that he worked with a miserable bastard.

I knew I was acting like a dickhead, and I knew that the publicity was great for the Trust, which meant more staff, better equipment—things that made life that little bit safer for everyone. It was the fact that *she* was behind it, her fucking ladyship.

I'd spent a lot of energy *not* thinking about her, because when I did, I'd get this hollow feeling inside my chest. I was pretty certain that if I ever keeled over on the job, a surgeon would open me up and find that a miracle had happened—I'd been walking around without a heart.

Jesus, what a crappy start to the day. Taking a dump was the highlight.

But over the next few days, Jay proved to be right: I did forget the film crew were there for large chunks of time. They were careful not to get in my way or impede the work in any way. It turned out that they were both ex-Army so knew enough about which orders had to be followed, and which you could be more creative with.

Clay liked having them around, and he was good at explaining the work and the processes. They filmed life in the compound, and Yamba had them grinning like idiots as he told his jokes and tall stories. I may have smiled, as well, but only once.

We'd only been at this location a couple of weeks, so they had a lot of footage of the training sessions, starting in the classroom but quickly moving to the training fields. That's when shit got serious and the jokes were dark ones.

Zada set up a kids' clinic at the compound, too. I wasn't very happy about that, not because what she was doing wasn't important, but because minefields and children weren't a good mix, but at least Yamba and me could do some improvised lessons on mine risk education.

It wasn't enough, it was never enough.

Maybe the pressure was beginning to get to me—I could feel it building inside me, a rising rage and fury that everything took so long to do: every piece of equipment had to be begged for, a case made, a proposition written, even now with the extra income the charity was benefitting from.

Then one day, I lost it.

The crew had been filming me all day, keeping their distance as I became surlier by the second.

All the searchers in the demining team had put in long hours in the relentless heat, flagging up a massive minefield and we were still only halfway through. It would take weeks to neutralize everything we'd found so far.

Sweat glued the dust to our bodies, making everything raw as if we were wearing sandpaper, but it was my nerves that were being worn down.

Zada was standing outside her makeshift clinic, cradling a smiling girl with red ribbons in her hair.

"This is Nzingha. She's named for a warrior princess. Hey, baby, say hello to Uncle James."

Her voice was soft and happy, and the little girl waved back, giggling.

I stopped and stared, my eyes transfixed on her small hand waving at me, then the gap where her other arm should be.

My eyes travelled down to her legs but she didn't have any.

I met Zada's eyes, pulled down with sadness.

"She was playing in the fields outside her home. Her mother had told her not to go there, but she saw a butterfly with pretty colours and she was following it. James, I know…"

I turned furiously, my fists clenched, my throat choking with fury, and I strode towards to Jay and Danny who'd been following me as usual.

"Why are you filming me?" I raged. "She's the story right there! This little girl! These fucking landmines were laid over 35 years ago, but the war here has been over since 2002. What the fuck have people been doing since then? Nothing! That's what! While children are being killed or getting their arms and legs blown off. Why aren't more people out here helping? Why is it left to charities to sort out the shit that armies leave behind? When the fuck will we learn?"

My voice had risen to an incoherent scream and I realized that my face was wet. I swiped at my skin in disbelief as tears streamed down my face.

I was crying? I was actually crying.

I turned away in disgust, knowing that I'd just given them great footage. I didn't blame Jay and Danny—they were decent blokes and family men themselves; they'd been just as affected by what they'd seen.

I strode away, leaving them standing, needing to be alone.

Crouched in the shadows on the floor of my hut, my head fell to my hands. All the grief and all the loss had finally caught up with me, and there was nothing I could do to control it anymore. I couldn't hold it back.

All the darkness poured out of me in a continuing stream; all the hopelessness, the helplessness, and I couldn't stop it.

My body shook uncontrollably, all the emotions slamming into me, again and again and again.

I didn't know how long I'd been crouched in the dark, but I wasn't surprised when my door opened and Clay entered. Dirt on the floor and heat in the air, he sat with me in silence, just being there.

I cried for everything I'd lost, gained and lost again; for all the injustices that left a playful, inquisitive child with three limbs torn away; for a world where we spent more on weapons that we did on aid; where wars that had ended decades ago could still inflict terrible injuries. And I cried because I was needed here and I had to go on, I just didn't know how anymore.

Finally, spent and ashamed, I ran out of tears. The emotional well was empty again.

I'd almost forgotten that Clay was there, but then he began to speak.

"With every mine that you neutralize, you're saving another child like that little girl from a lifetime of struggle; you're saving a woman like her mother from a lifetime of worry that she'll die before a daughter who needs her; you're saving a man like me from blisters and calluses because prosthetics aren't as good as the real thing. With every mine that's taken out of the equation, you're saving families from loss and trauma. With every mine that's cleared, that's a win for the good guys. That's you, James. One of the good guys. Never forget that."

He stood up awkwardly, his tall silhouette framed in the doorway.

"You're not the only one who has dark nights, bad dreams, and darker days. You wouldn't be human if you didn't. I'm proud to know you, brother."

I sat alone in my hut, listening to the world beyond the thin, plywood door. I heard Clay and Zada's voices, talking to people who'd visited the clinic that day and to the teams who'd been on Task with me. I heard Jay and Danny talk about the footage that they'd got and how they were ready to go home and start editing it, that they'd caught some incredible moments to show the world. I wondered bleakly if I was one of those 'golden moments' that filmmakers talked about.

I was too tired to care anymore, because they were right. If my rant made someone else sit up and take notice, or put their hands in the pockets to make a donation, then it was job done, right?

My head pounded with a dull ache, but I couldn't be bothered to get up, didn't want to face the others, couldn't care enough to eat or drink or move.

I thought about Amira, her strength, her fears, her sadness, her smiles. I finally understood the choice she'd made to go back to Syria; I finally understood why she couldn't, wouldn't wait for me to go with her. She couldn't because there was so much need, so much to do. I could spend three lifetimes clearing minefields around the world and the work would never be done, never be finished, never be over.

How did anyone cope with that?

I wasn't a hero, I knew that, but I could make a difference. Sometimes it felt like there was too much weighted against the work we did, but it all mattered.

I sat alone, lost in my thoughts.

Night fell suddenly, like the turning off of a switch, and the evening sounds filled the cooling air, the crickets singing and a dog barking nearby.

I thought about life and I thought about death. Was this the reason that I hadn't killed myself? Because there was still work to be done? Because I had a purpose? Because despite everything, there was still a place for me in this fucked up world?

And I thought about Bel. I understood, at last, why she'd gone back to London with her father. Because she knew, because she understood, because she'd already worked out that she had to fix herself first. And from what I'd learned via Clay's occasional mentions of her name, she'd taken a fundraising job with Halo Trust and was bringing in the big bucks, as well as getting the charity some great publicity. I was happy for her, I really was. I surprised myself when I realized that all the bitterness had finally leached away.

And I knew that I'd been an idiot. But what else was new?

Stiffly, I pulled myself up from the dirt floor, muscles cramped and sore, then went to find Clay and Zada.

Because despite what I'd been telling myself for years, I didn't want to be alone and I did need my friends.

CHAPTER 29

Arabella

"IS THIS REALLY HAPPENING?"

Gray raised his eyebrows and gave me a fatherly smile.

Over the months that I'd worked for him, I'd learned more about the positive role of a parent than I ever had in my entire life.

Gray had A-R-M-Y stamped through the centre of his body, a career officer, but at the age of 56, he'd finally met his match in Heidi, a feisty Scottish woman who'd turned him from a Colonel into a father.

Eight years on, they had a son of five and a daughter of seven, and I'd never seen children more loved. I finally understood what I'd been missing all these years. But it didn't make me sad—well, maybe a little—instead, it gave me hope.

Gray was driving me to the airport in his uncomfortable old Land Rover that rattled alarmingly over potholes, and sounded as loud as a tank.

"Yep," he said, answering me at last. "It's really happening and you, Harry, you made it happen."

Then he glanced across at me and smiled.

"Time to finish the job now."

I nodded even though I wasn't sure I could do that.

"I'll try," I said, at last.

"Nay, lass," he said, copying Heidi's accent and making me laugh. "You'll be wonderful. I'm proud of you, Harry."

"Oh my God, don't say things like that or I'll be a blubbering mess before I even get on the darn plane."

He winked at me, then swerved suddenly into a parking spot in the drop-off zone.

As I tried to prise my fingers from the seat, he wrapped his arms around me in a hug.

"You're stronger than you know, Arabella," he said.

And this time, I couldn't stop a stray tear escaping.

Gray carried my suitcase into the airport, then left me with another swift hug and an order to call him and Heidi later to let them know how I was getting on.

He drove away with a loud roar of diesel fumes as I waved him off.

I was nervous; not because I was a nervous flier, far from it. I loved getting on a plane and being served champagne before nodding off and waking up in a new country ready to shop.

Well, that was the old Arabella. The new one couldn't afford to travel First Class as she worked for herself and earned her own money, and she definitely wasn't the kind of person who'd expect a charity to fork out for an expensive seat.

But when I went to check-in with my luggage, I found that those lovely Air Miles that I'd accumulated while I had Daddy's allowance were still valid. As I got upgraded to Business Class, I imagined the look on his face.

I'd changed, and a thousand times for the better. I'd taken responsibility for myself and my life, and I was spending my days doing something worthwhile that would benefit others. The 'poor little rich girl' was in the past. Now, I was just an ordinary working woman, doing my best, not always getting it right, but trying hard.

I settled into my seat with a sigh, kicking off my pretty-but-uncomfortable shoes and wriggling my toes.

"Business or pleasure?"

I opened my eyes to see the handsome man in the Armani suit who was sitting next to me.

"Definitely business," I said with a cool smile.

He got the message and left me alone.

Eight hours later, I opened my eyes again to bright sunshine.

My luggage had arrived with me at Dulles airport—always a bonus—and I felt a rush of enthusiasm, a hunger for this day to start.

Washington D.C. in the Autumn was beautiful. The roads were lined with trees blazing with colour, their leaves in shades of vivid orange, red and gold—a sign that we were coming towards the end of another year. The grand, stone buildings and wide pavements reminded me of London as my taxi moved at a stately pace through the morning traffic. I caught a glimpse of the White House, smaller than I'd expected, but gleaming in the sunshine.

Tourists were strolling in shorts, heading for the Lincoln Memorial, and diplomats in suits took a moment to enjoy the parks and fresh air, with the Washington Monument pointing upwards like a beacon in the distance.

I took a deep breath, trying to calm my racing pulse. If everything went right tomorrow, it would be the culmination of months of work, a testament to the last year of my life.

Or it could mean a complete cockup and utter humiliation.

I closed my eyes tightly.

Please make this right.

And I couldn't tell you who I hoped was listening.

CHAPTER 30

James

"ARE THERE USUALLY THIS MANY tourists outside the White House?" I asked, glancing through the tinted windows of the limo. "And news crews?"

Clay threw me a look of amused disbelief.

"Have you been hiding under a rock, James my man? You're big news. Huge. The Press were cheated of their hero last time—they're not letting you get away again."

An unpleasant awareness trickled down my spine.

When I'd received a letter from the White House Chief Staff, an invitation of sorts, I hadn't thought much about the publicity side of things. I should have. I really should.

I'd honestly thought that all the nonsense that Bel stirred up had died away. Okay, so yeah, there'd been that film crew shadowing our work for a few weeks, but it wasn't just me that they'd interviewed: they'd talked to Clay, Zada, the de-miners and Yamba. They'd even interviewed that little girl's mother.

Nzingha, that was her name, the little girl—named for a warrior princess. I got a familiar lump in my throat when I thought about her.

I knew that the Trust regularly sent film crews all over the world to record the work because it was good for publicity—essential for the public to see what a difference their donations made. When Jay and Danny had turned up, I'd just assumed it was business as usual.

Or maybe the truth was I didn't want to think about any of that shit; I'd just wanted to be left alone. But that had changed, too.

Nzingha had become a regular visitor to the compound and spoiled rotten when she came. For some reason, she'd taken a shine to me, which seemed bizarre, but she always yelled for me to pick her up. I couldn't say no to her.

"This is going to change your life, bro," Clay said gently. "Everyone will want to know the hero of Times Square."

I shook my head in denial.

"Fifteen minutes of fame, maybe. But once I disappear back to Luanda or Nagorno or somewhere like it, no one will give a damn."

He grimaced, his words at odds with the gesture.

"Maybe, I guess it's possible."

"What about you?" I asked. "You were there, too."

Clay shrugged.

"I already got my Purple Heart while I was in the hospital."

Zada glanced at him impatiently.

"Yes, and I had to clear it out of the trash twice."

I stared at them both. I hadn't known. Clay hadn't shared that last detail.

"I was having a bad day," he said with a small smile as he reached for his wife's hand. "A couple of bad days. But you kicked my butt for me."

"Yes, I did," Zada said, her face softening with love.

I had to look away.

Bel's blue eyes flashed into my mind, but I couldn't afford to think about her now. Or ever.

"Maybe they'll let us leave by the back entrance," I muttered, eyeing the crowds of journalists and general public as we cruised past in our limo, courtesy of the US Government.

Clay laughed loudly.

"Dude, you do know that the Bronze Star with Valor is the fourth highest decoration in the US, right? Only one other Brit has ever received it, and that was in 1946."

I turned my head and gaped at him.

"What?"

He snorted, choking on his own laughter, while Zada rolled her eyes.

"Clay, are you yanking my chain, because I'm about to meet the President and get some more chest cabbage pinned on me, and I don't want to look like the village idiot."

But talking to him wasn't getting me anywhere. Clay was splayed out on the backseat, weak with laughter, tears rolling down his face.

Zada was half amused, half irritated.

"No, my husband, who has just regressed to adolescence, isn't 'yanking your chain', James. The Bronze Star with Valor is a very big deal."

"Bloody hell," I grumbled. "No one told me that."

"I think most people would have Googled it," Zada pointed out, a raised eyebrow underlining my stupidity.

"Is that why you made me buy a new suit?" I asked, light dawning.

"Dear Allah!" she shrieked. "You're about to meet the President of the United States! You couldn't just rock up in jeans!"

I leaned back against the upholstered leather seat. Yeah, I probably should have looked into all this medal crap before now.

"Amira would have been proud of you," she said softly.

As Clay's laughter faded, Zada swallowed and looked down.

Silence filled the limousine and it was several seconds before I could speak.

"Thanks," I said, my voice hoarse.

Would there ever be a time when hearing her name didn't hurt? Why this death and not another? Because Fate is a random bitch? There was never any answer to that.

Amira's parents had chosen to receive her posthumous Meritorious Service Medal in private. Zada had argued with them about that but hadn't been able to change their minds. They preferred to grieve in private. Zada thought that Amira should be celebrated, too. And her parents hadn't factored in that Zada would be standing right next to Clay when he received his Bronze Star, so privacy would be in short supply.

At Zada's insistence, I'd worn all my British Army medals, too. I had mixed feelings about that because of the way they'd kicked me out, but I'd earned those medals with my blood and sweat, and good friends who should have been buying me a beer had paid the ultimate price. My medals honoured them.

As we arrived at the entrance, I could see camera flashes before the limo door opened; it was like stepping out onto the red carpet at a blockbuster film premiere. Cameras flashed in all directions and people were calling my name like I was their best friend.

I kept my head down, refusing to look at the photographers as I helped Zada out of the car, followed by Clay, only slightly awkward on his prosthetic.

Clay lapped it up, waving to the crowd, a huge smile on his face, his other arm draped around Zada. She stood serene and beautiful, wearing her colourful headscarf that was a twin with the scrap of silk I carried with me everywhere.

Clay was making a point by highlighting his relationship with Zada, the message clear. *See, she's a Muslim; her sister's a hero; this is my wife. Deal with it.*

I didn't have any interest in making a political point, but I wouldn't be surprised if Clay went into politics a few years down the line. He'd be one of the decent ones. He could be the second black man to be President.

There was a brief moment of quiet as we entered the White House and shook some hands, names of the men and women who worked there that I instantly forgot.

We were left in a hospitality area for several minutes, and I studiously ignored the alcohol and miniature pastries, preferring to help myself to a cup of extra-strong black coffee. Or have it poured for me by a guy in a penguin suit.

"Thanks," I mumbled, then wandered away to look at the photographs lining the room so I wouldn't have to talk to anyone. Coming here was beginning to feel like a huge mistake. Bloody Clay had talked me into it.

My eyes were drawn to a series of photographs that were tucked away in a quiet corner; something had caught my attention…

I'd noticed a small black-and-white photograph of former President Barack Obama. I peered even closer, a smile settling on my face.

"That bloody bastard," I muttered.

"Excuse me?!" said a horrified voice.

I glanced up to see a woman in an expensive dress gazing at me with disgust.

"Oh, sorry. I didn't mean him…"

But she sniffed and walked away.

"Making friends?" Clay asked with an amused glance at the woman's retreating back as shook his head at me.

"Yeah, you know me. Hey, look at this. Recognize anyone?"

He squinted slightly, then laughed out loud.

We were both looking at the man by Obama's shoulder, sunglasses on, earpiece in place.

"Oh, is that your friend?" asked Zada.

"Yup, that he is," Clay agreed. "Nathaniel John Smith—our favourite spook. I guess when he said he 'knew people', he really did."

It certainly explained how Smith had been able to pull strings and collect favours in so many different places.

My smile dimmed. Smith had got me into Syria to find Amira, but I'd been too late to save her. Too damned late.

"Hey," said Clay, nudging my side. "I've just seen someone else you know."

"Yeah?" I asked, turning around without much interest.

The breath froze in my lungs and my heart stopped dead, then began to gallop to a new beat, a faster rhythm.

Across the room, Bel was smiling at us, her expression schooled into polite pleasure, but I could see the anxiety in her eyes.

She was a bright column of colour that dimmed the rest of the room, her scarlet dress sweeping across her amazing body, her hair a halo of gold. I wasn't even sure she was real.

All the emotions that I'd locked away spilled over, making me dizzy with want and need, lust and hope. And love. I knew what this feeling meant now: I loved Bel. I hated her and I loved her.

"James," Zada said quietly, "give her a chance."

I stared at her, surprised. She'd been one of Bel's biggest critics until Clay had told her to leave it alone.

"You're taking her side after she outed me?" I asked, completely staggered at the turnaround.

"People have their own battles to fight," she said softly. "I, of all people, should have understood that—but my family love me and always have. I didn't understand what she was fighting. I do now. So you should give her a chance to explain."

Clay prodded me in the arm.

"Go to her, you dick."

"I don't know…"

He gave me a little push, making me stumble and nearly take out a wine waiter.

I cursed under my breath as I started to cross the room, shuffling because I was so nervous that I couldn't feel my feet.

Bel blinked rapidly, the tight smile still pinned to her face.

I was within touching distance when a Four-star Army General reached her first, his eyes skimming her body with more than appreciation before he corrected himself.

A dangerous red mist of rage descended and I was by her side in a second.

"Ah, the man of the hour," he said. "Staff Sergeant Spears. Allow me to introduce you to Lady Arabella Forsythe, director of the Halo Trust."

"How kind," said Bel crisply, patting his arm. "But James and I are old friends. Would you be a poppet and excuse us for a moment, General Erikson."

"Of course, Lady Arabella," he said smoothly. "We can talk later." He glanced at me, his grey eyes steely. "A pleasure, Spears."

I nodded absently as he strolled away.

"Hello, James," said Bel, her voice low and rich. "How've you been? I wasn't sure you'd be here today. I'll have to thank Clay. And Zada."

With a loud clang, everything fell into place.

"This is because of you, isn't it?" I accused her. "This medal shit. You were the one who talked them into this!"

She cocked her head to one side, smiling.

"I really couldn't say."

"You're the one who started the petition in the UK to have me reinstated, not your father, right?"

Her eyes flashed.

"My father only cares about himself."

"Then how come he got involved?"

"I persuaded him," she said, her voice dangerously sweet.

A tiny block of ice that had kept my heart frozen began to melt.

"Guess you finally stood up to him."

She smiled happily.

"Guess I did."

We stared at each other like a couple of idiots. I had no clue what to say. Luckily, Bel did.

"James, I owe you an enormous apology. I made such a mess of things and I'm sorry I didn't explain it to you properly. But I had to learn to stand up to my father by myself. If I'd let you do it for me, I could never have looked at myself in the mirror, let alone face you. Please tell me you understand?"

I sighed and looked away.

"Yeah, I do. It took me a while—and Clay was definitely batting for you. I just didn't want to hear it—all I could hear, all I could feel was that you'd gone."

Bel nodded slowly.

"Zada was rather annoyed with me, to say the least. She told me that I didn't deserve you, and she was right. And I know that the way I left, how it looked … you thought I'd left *you*. James, I didn't want to. But … I'll never be as brave as you, but I had to try and be a little bit brave."

I gave her a small grin.

"From what Clay says, you took on the British Army, the British government and the American government."

"You bet your sweet arse I did!" she said, bristling instantly. "How dare the British Army treat you like that? It was an appalling breach of their duty of care. It's not the way to treat a hero. And I will keep on fighting and petitioning for you to be accorded the respect you deserve. If I have to get the Americans onside first, so be it." Her anger evaporated as quickly as it had come. "But your spy friend Smith was a complete darling and expedited the paperwork for me. Such a sweetheart. I must remember to send him a thank-you note. I've never met him, you know. But I'd like to."

A reluctant smile spread across my face.

"I don't even know what to say to that."

"Well," she said carefully. "You could say thank you…"

"Thank you, Bel."

"And you can tell me how adorable I look in red."

I shook my head. She was so much more than adorable. She was brave and clever and beautiful.

"You're breathtaking."

She smiled, her red lips parting to show those perfectly even white teeth.

"Thank you. And I meant every word, James, you're a hero. But more than that, you taught me so much. It was because of you that I was finally able to stand up to my father. So I thank you for that, too."

I looked at her quizzically.

"From what it said in the newspapers, your dad has been very vocal about his support for former members of the armed services."

She gave a catlike smile.

"Dear old Dad. Yes, he has rather made a stand, hasn't he? It's done wonders for his reputation, which, to be honest, was a trifle tattered. He's made you a *cause célèbre* and made himself a lot of new friends in useful places. I may have had to give him a little nudge towards doing the right thing for a change."

I shook my head in amazement.

"You really are incredible."

Her smile dimmed.

"No, I've simply learned to be as devious and manipulative as him, my father." Her smile was wistful. "But I promise to use my newfound powers only for good." She rested her hand on my arm. "You, James. You're incredible. You're brave and loyal, and you save lives. You are a good man, James Spears. I'm honoured to have known you."

My stomach lurched uncomfortably.

"Then why does that sound like goodbye?"

"Oh, you'll see me around as long as we both work for the Halo Trust," she smiled tightly, removing her arm from mine. "But I promised myself not to bother you … in that way … and I won't. I know you'll only ever love Amira. And I do have some pride after all. Who knew?"

She took a step away from me and it was already too far.

Yes, I'd loved Amira with all my heart, but Amira was gone. She wasn't ever coming back. Life goes on, that's what they say. And I found that my broken heart was in two separate pieces. One half loved Amira, and always would. But the other half had found another broken soul. Someone in this life, in this world, who cared about me.

Unlikely as it seemed, the disgraceful Lady and the disgraced soldier had found peace with each other.

"Bel, wait," I said urgently as I spotted the Chief of Staff coming towards me with a determined look on his face. "Bel, don't disappear. Wait for me? Please?"

"What am I waiting for, James?" she asked softly.

"A chance," I answered, ignoring the liaison people who were trying to urge me away from her and toward the President. "Give me a chance, please?"

She blinked rapidly.

"Haven't we said everything to each other already?"

"No!" I said fiercely. "I never said that I love you!"

Silence spilled out around us, and even the President paused with his hand outstretched towards Clay.

"You love Amira," she said carefully.

"Yes, but I love you, as well. Very much. I want to live, and I want my life to be with you. I've been a fucking fool to wait so long to say it."

Her blue eyes swam with tears.

"I'll wait for you, James."

"That's all I need to hear."

I was ushered away, staring over my shoulder as I saw her wipe under eyes.

"Wait for me!" I yelled.

She smiled through her tears and nodded.

I was distracted all through the ceremony, even when the President tied the ribbon for the Bronze Star with Valor around my neck and shook my hand.

"Thank you for your service, Sergeant," he said.

I almost corrected him that I was a Staff Sergeant, then remembered that I'd been kicked out of the British Army and didn't give a shit.

"Thank you, sir," I murmured as he squeezed my shoulder in a fatherly way that would play well with the Press.

Clay received his Bronze Star, smiling and chatting with the Leader of the Free World like they were old buddies. He even pulled up his trouser leg to show his prosthetic, and the photographers went into a frenzy.

I had to smile. The guy was a natural when it came to working the crowd. Clay even broke protocol to introduce Zada to the President.

I could see the Chief of Staff shaking his head, but he was smiling, too. It was hard to be angry with Clay.

But even with all this going on and the Press Conference that followed, my eyes were on the bombshell in the red dress standing at the back of the room. She standing next to Zada and they were both smiling. Then Bel glanced towards me and our eyes met. When I saw her smile at me, I thought that maybe the world wasn't such a shitty place. For once, all the radio chatter in my head was silenced.

After the President made a speech, praising me and Clay for our bravery and service to his country, they showed the film footage of those grim minutes in Times Square. I remembered that it had been technically challenging, but mostly I remembered the fear on Amira's face, even as she begged me and Clay to save ourselves.

I remembered the fear I felt for her, the determination that this wasn't going to be how our story ended—a story that had barely started. And I remembered Clay telling her to pray with him. I remembered every painful second, the *tick tock* in my head as the time counted down.

I looked away when the camera zoomed in on Amira's terrified face. Instead, I fixed my gaze on Bel. Amira was my past and would always have a place in my heart, but Bel was my future. I hoped.

The footage tactfully left out the part where Clay's leg was blown off, but briefly showed the aftermath, where me and Amira had huddled over him as paramedics ran towards us.

There was a short, respectful silence, then the President let the journalists loose with their questions.

A woman in the front row, specially chosen to ask the first question, stood up and looked at me. Her hair was a perfect brunette helmet, her makeup a careful mask.

"Sergeant Spears, when you defused the suicide vest of Amira Soliman, were you scared?"

I stared back, careful and begrudging with my words.

"You don't have time to be scared. You focus on the job. Emotions have no place … emotions will get you killed."

She blinked, surprised and not very pleased with my answer, but I'd already turned away from her to the next questioner.

"James, is it true that you and Amira were more than friends?"

An older woman in a sharp-looking suit had asked the question, her microphone stretched out in front of her as she leaned forward.

I focused on her intently. I had to be very careful. As far as the public were concerned, Amira had been working undercover, but Clay and I were simply caught up in the crisis, accidental bystanders. The official line was that I was on leave in New York, and that Clay also just happened to be passing. Whether people really believed that or not was irrelevant.

"Amira Soliman was one of the bravest women I ever knew," I said, speaking slowly and clearly as the room stilled and silenced. "When it looked like time was running out and that I wouldn't neutralize the device, she begged me and Master Sergeant Williams to leave her to save ourselves. She begged us to go, knowing that she'd die but that we might live. That … connection between all of us that day was special, intense, deeper than friendship. So yes, we were more than friends."

And that was all they were getting from me about Amira.

When someone tried to ask about my so-called 'administrative discharge' from the Army, the White House Press Officer answered with some platitude and led the questions to the work in Nagorno and Angola.

The woman in the sharp suit raised her hand again.

"Is it true that you're in a relationship with Lady Arabella Forsythe from the Halo Trust?"

I gave my first smile of the whole Press Conference.

"A guy would have to be pretty lucky for that to happen, but I guess dreams are free."

Laughter met my non-answer, and shortly after that, Clay was given the stage.

He charmed his audience and had them eating out of his hand. He made an impassioned plea for more to be done to support veterans, and talked about how their military training could contribute and be adapted to the civilian workforce and the economy.

He spoke seriously, eloquently and movingly.

"I only have one leg but that sacrifice was for my country, for a cause I believe in. We all want the world to live in peace. I'd love to see the day when guys like me aren't needed. But until that day, no matter how many legs I have or don't have, I will serve and protect my country. And I'll also use my skills and knowledge to continue the work of the Halo Trust." He paused. "You know, it shouldn't have taken the support of the late Princess Diana to bring the work of demining former war zones to the public's attention." And then he glanced at me. "It shouldn't take the act of heroism of men like James Spears or women like Amira Soliman to bring the work of bomb disposal to the public arena, but I guess it does. With our skills and training, I believe we have a duty to give our help where it is needed, anywhere in the world it's needed." He paused, his expression serious. "All the de-miners who work around the world are heroes. James Spears trained for seven years to become a high threat operator, and was in the British Army for 11 years. He still risks his life every day—he's my idea of a true hero."

Bastard.

I scowled at him as he grinned at me and threw a mock salute. I almost returned him a two-fingered salute, but remembered at the last moment that the White House probably wasn't the place to do that.

"Aw," Clay laughed, grinning at me. "He's shy," and the crowd of journalists laughed with him.

Yep, definitely going to make him regret that.

Finally, the torture was over, and after a shaking a lot of hands of people I didn't know, I was allowed to leave.

Bel walked towards me, a small smile on her face.

"So, do you feel lucky?" she asked, her smile widening.

I answered with more emotion than was safe to feel.

"Bel, I'm probably not a good bet in life. I do a crappy job for crappy wages, I'm a miserable bastard at the best of times, but," and I took a shaky breath, "if you take a chance on me, I promise that I'll spend the rest of my life showing you how lucky I feel right now."

Her lips turned down and tears swam in her blue eyes.

"Don't cry," I whispered. "I'm not worth it."

"You're wrong," she cried softly. "And I don't see it as taking a chance, James. I really don't."

She leaned her head on my shoulder, her arms looping around my neck, lightly stroking the ribbon that held my new medal.

"Then trust me, Bel, I won't let you fall."

My hands rested gently on her waist and we stood there as the people around us ebbed and flowed unseen.

"I'm not sure I can make you happy. But I'm damn sure that no one else will get the chance to try."

"Then let's make it forever, James. Not one day less."

Her words echoed through me. 'Forever' sometimes meant a few shared moments and the long, echoing silence of death. After that truth, I'd believed that the secret to existing was to not want what you couldn't, or shouldn't have.

But now, I believed in more. And I was going to do everything in my power to give Bel the world.

"Forever," I agreed quietly.

CHAPTER 31

Arabella

"ARE YOU SURE YOU WANT ME to come with you?" I asked.

James turned to me, his expression grave.

"Bel, I'll always want you next to me. But is this too much to ask? Because I'll understand if it is."

My heart twisted with love, then cracked open a little wider for this brave, broken man. With each word and gesture, he became more necessary to me, more a part of me.

"I would be honoured to stand next to you," I said, and I meant it. "If it's okay with Zada."

Zada smiled sadly, holding Clay's hand more firmly.

"My sister would have liked you," she said. "You remind me of her in some ways—except for, you know, being white." Her smile wobbled. "You're both a little crazy but you're both brave. And you both love James." I felt him start as she said his name, and it made me sad that he'd never been sure of Amira's love for him. I was certain that she'd loved him—how could she not?

Zada gave me a weak smile, her lips trembling.

"You are worthy, Harry, you are. I'm so sorry that I ever doubted you."

I squeezed her hand quickly, completely unable to reply.

The limousine moved slowly through the rows and rows of white headstones at Arlington Cemetery. I'd never been here before but I knew that James had—with Amira. I was glad I could be with him to support him in this today.

Eventually, the car came to a halt and we all clambered out, our breath misting in the crisp air as leaves swirled by our feet.

It was heart-breaking to see the rows and rows and rows of white grave markers stretching across the rolling hills, a light dusting of frost covering the grass.

We stepped from the path, moving towards our final destination.

Two white headstones lay side by side, together but separate from the others.

Brian Edward Larson
Master Sergeant, US Marines
Iraq, Afghanistan

A small flag, the Stars and Stripes, fluttered beside it, between the two headstones. I turned to read the second as Zada knelt down, sobbing softly as Clay rested his hand on her shoulder.

Amira Soliman
Meritorious Service Medal
For service to a grateful nation.

I felt James's hand slide into mine, his fingers rough, his skin warm despite the chilly temperatures.

"Hello, Larson," he said quietly. "It's been a while. I brought you a couple of beers. I can't drink them myself, 'cause, you know, recovering alcoholic and all that, but I thought you'd like them."

He let go of my hand, popped the ring-pull on two cans and poured them over the grave.

"Thanks for doing what you did," he said. "You were a tough bastard."

Then he turned to the second headstone where Zada still cried quietly and knelt down next to her.

"Hey, it's me."

He spoke to the silent grave, and my heart squeezed painfully.

"Sorry I missed your funeral. I was kind of in prison at the time, a shithole at Colchester Barracks. But I wish I could have been here. I wish I could have … said goodbye." Then he stood up and reached for my hand. "This is Bel. She's special to me. Well, I love her. I wanted you to meet her. That sounds weird, but I know you'll understand."

Tears formed in my eyes as he bowed his head, praying alone, a final goodbye to the woman he'd loved so much, the woman he'd have died for.

I heard someone step up behind me, and turned to see a handsome older man with salt and pepper hair curling at the collar of a beaten-up leather jacket, wearing jeans and aviator sunglasses. I knew who he was immediately, not really surprised to see him here.

James turned abruptly, then gave a small smile.

"Smith, you bastard. Should have known you'd show up. This is Bel, Arabella Forsythe. Bel, this is Smith, our favourite spook."

Smith smiled and took my hand, kissing the back of it while James rolled his eyes.

"It's good to meet you at last, Lady Arabella," said Smith, grinning at me. Then he turned to Clay and Zada. "Good to see you both, as well. Glad to see you're looking after each other." He paused. "Your sister was a brave woman, Zada. Clay says that you're a lot like her."

Zada looked up, her face tear-stained, imprinted with the signs of a long-held grief.

"I'd like to think so," she said, wiping her face with her fingers.

There was a short silence as Smith paid his respects to Amira and his friend, Larson. Then we walked back to the waiting limousine together.

"So, you and Obama?" asked Clay.

A slow smile formed on Smith's face as he grinned.

"Saw the photo, huh? Impressed?"

"Not even a little bit," Clay lied. "So, what's he like?"

"I didn't think you were interested," Smith teased him.

"Okay! Okay, I'm interested," ground out Clay, hands held up in surrender.

Smith looked at him thoughtfully.

"Obama … nice guy. Shitty golfer."

We all waited for more.

"That's it?" queried Zada.

Smith just winked, then changed the subject.

"I'm recruiting if anyone's interested."

Zada grabbed Clay's hand and frowned at Smith.

"Absolutely not!" she snapped. "We already have jobs, Mr. Smith."

Clay grinned down at his wife.

"You heard her. We're already gainfully employed, so thanks but no thanks."

Smith shrugged then turned to me and James.

"Sure I can't tempt the two of you to join me?" he asked, raising one eyebrow. "Lots of danger, not much money, but I have a really cool undercover name for you: Lady and the Tramp."

I jumped when James laughed loudly.

"Nope, not interested," said James. "And neither is she."

"*She* can talk for herself!" I replied. "And *she* concurs. We will have to gratefully decline your gracious offer, Mr. Smith."

"Pity," he smiled. "It's a waste of a good undercover name."

Then he turned around and loped away, hands shoved deep into his pockets.

"I have a feeling that won't be the last we see of the enigmatic, Mr. Smith," I said.

James smiled at me and placed a soft kiss on my cheek.

"I concur," he said teasingly. "The dude keeps turning up like a bad penny."

We took one last look at the graves of two people that I'd never met but whom none of us would ever forget; two people who were there at the start of our story, and were there for the beginning of the next chapter. Because life does go on. Battered and bruised, dented and changed, we go on.

The man at my side had a lot of healing to do, and I hoped that I would play a large part in that process. Knowing him, knowing James, loving James—those things had already changed me for the better. My life's work would be to make his life better, too.

God willing.

Or as James would say, *Inshallah*.

EPILOGUE

NINE MONTHS LATER...

James

THERE ARE NO CERTAINTIES IN LIFE. I'm proof of that. Living proof.

When Amira died, a part of me died with her, but it seems another part of me was saved. I didn't know the reason for the longest time, but now I do.

I have to live the biggest life I can—for her, for me. Arabella, my Bel, she understands that—and it's why she means so much to me. I love her with every part that's left of my heart. A piece was buried with Amira, but life goes on. I go on. With this amazing woman.

She's different from Amira, and yet the same in strength, the same devotion to her cause. And somehow, I've become Bel's cause. And she's mine. Everything else? That's just decoration.

Life can be short, brutal and cruel. It can also be beautiful. Sometimes it takes another person to point out that beauty to you. Or maybe you find it with them.

I'm standing with the brutal African sun burning down on my neck, staring at a dusty minefield in a dusty, forgotten country, with men and women looking to me to help them make their land safe again.

Officially, Bel is the Director of Events Fundraising at the Halo Trust, and she travels the world raising money for the charity. Unofficially, she heads up the Mine Risk Education programme here while Zada runs a clinic. Well, Zada is taking it easy at the moment as she has precious cargo on board.

Yep, Clay finally managed to get her in the family way, and they're expecting the birth of their son in three months. I was right, too, because Zada refused to be sent home, although she has agreed to travel to the best hospital in Angola's capital city, Luanda, to give birth. Other than that, she refuses to leave Clay's side.

I give them two years, maybe three, before they decide to go back to the States to live, and Clay will go on to the next stage of his life.

As for me, I'll go where the job takes me, wherever I can do some good.

Do good.

That's what Amira wanted, and I'd like to think that I honour her name when another mine is neutralized, when another cache of munitions is taken out of the equation.

I've been lucky to have loved two women in my life—that's more luck than an unwashed squaddie like me deserves.

The Right Honourable Lady Arabella Elizabeth Roecaster Forsythe goes by Mrs. Spears these days, unless she's working on some snooty donor who wants her illustrious connections to the British peerage. Her dad taught her more than he knows, but I think he learned from her, too. I know I have. Every day she teaches me to be a better man.

Bomb disposal: I do a dangerous job in a dangerous world, but it's not the sum of who I am. Bel taught me that, as well. She taught me a lot of things. She taught me that I am worth loving—I am worth the effort. If a woman like her can love me, maybe there's something worth saving.

We're living in a mud hut village in a no-name desert, and she still wants me. She doesn't need Paris or Rome and five-star hotels. I am enough. It's humbling.

Because I am loved.

Who the hell expected that? Love takes some getting used to.

Our life won't be easy—we haven't chosen an easy path, but we've chosen it together and that's what counts.

Me and Bel against the world. And you know what? I'm betting on us.

The End

REVIEWS

Reviews are love!

Honestly, they are! But it also helps other people to make an informed decision before buying this book.

So I'd really appreciate if you took a few seconds to do just that.

Thank you!

DON'T FORGET TO CLAIM YOUR FREE BOOK!

My acclaimed novella PLAYING IN THE RAIN was featured in Huffington Post's list of Top Ugly Cry Reads!

You'll receive it for free when you sign up to my newsletter, as well as the opportunity to read ARCs of new stories.

Sign up at www.janeharveyberrick.com

MORE ABOUT JHB

"Love all, trust a few, do wrong to none"—this is one of my favourite sayings. Oh, and 'Be Nice!' That's another. Or maybe, 'Where's the chocolate?'

I get asked where my ideas come from—they come from everywhere. From walks with my dog on the beach, from listening to conversations in pubs and shops, where I lurk unnoticed with my notebook. And of course, ideas come from things I've seen or read, places I've been and people I meet.

If you've seen me at any book signings you'll know that I support the military charities Felix Fund in the UK and EOD Warrior Foundation in the U.S. Both are charities that support the men and women who work in bomb disposal, and their families.

Sales from SEMPER FI go to support these charities.

www.felixfund.org.uk – the UK Bomb Disposal Charity

www.eodwarrriorfoundation.org – the US Bomb Disposal Charity

www.nowzad.com – helping servicemen and women rescue stray and abandoned animals in former and current warzones

ACKNOWLEDGEMENTS

This story is personal to me in many ways. I have friends amongst the EOD community, so it's important to me because of that. I've tried really hard to get the details right, although I have no military background myself. Yes, I did have people I could go to ask for further information. **But any mistakes are mine, and mine alone, as is any creative licence with the story.**

Wanting to write, being a writer, it's a lifelong lesson, and one that I'm still learning. But there are a number of people who have helped guide and sculpt *this* book. So I'll start with these women, all amazing in their own rights, all different, all supportive.

To J and J. Again. To Danny C.

To Krista Webster, for stepping in to help when I needed it, and for sorting out those pesky timeline issues.

To Kirsten Olsen, friend, confidant, editor, whose support never fails me.

To cover model Gergo Jonas, who is so much more than a handsome man, and has become a good friend, too.

To cover model Ellie Ruewell, whose good humour and big smiles made the photoshoot the *best* fun.

To the real Alan Clayton Williams who asked me to give him an awesome death, but became a hero instead.

To the real Rose Hogg, who is standing in for James's 'first time', the lucky lass.

To Tonya 'Maverick' Allen, travel buddy and my own personal cheerleader.

To Sheena Lumsden and Lynda Throsby for many things, including their friendship and wicked organisational skills.

To all the bloggers who give up their time for their passion of reading and reviewing books—thank you for your support.

And to my readers. Not only do you have great taste, but you rock!

Thank you **Jane's Travelers**. You know how much you mean to me and you never let me down. You are my go-to gals, advising, supporting, making me laugh when I need it, reporting pirates, and generally being the best reader group and friendship group I could want. I love all your messages, and thank you so much for being my eyes and ears out in our amazing book world while I hide in my writer's cave.